The Shocking Miss Shaw

The Shocking Miss Shaw

Justine Wittich

Five Star • Waterville, Maine

This novel is a work of fiction. Names, characters, places and incidents are either the product of the author's imagination, or, if real, used fictitiously.

First Edition
First Printing: May 2003

Set in 11 pt. Plantin by Myrna S. Raven.

Printed in the United States on permanent paper.

Library of Congress Cataloging-in-Publication Data

Wittich, Justine.
    The shocking Miss Shaw / Justine Wittich.
        p. cm.—(Five Star first edition expressions series)
     ISBN 0-7862-4767-3 (hc : alk. paper)
     1. Americans—England—Fiction. 2. Extortion—
Fiction. 3. England—Fiction. I. Title. II. Series.
  PS3573.I925 S54 2003
   813'.54—dc21   2002035941

For Mark
You should have stuck around

CHAPTER ONE

Washington, D.C., January, 1885

Geoffrey Trowbridge did only one honorable thing in his life. Even though his body was never found, he was declared legally dead after the paddle-wheeler *Charity* exploded on the Mississippi River.

Now, two years later, Sierra Shaw wasn't surprised to learn he might not have had the decency to truly die.

"Five witnesses saw him at the rail before the boiler blew!" her stepmother wailed, her soft voice plaintive. "He couldn't have survived."

"It wouldn't surprise me if that slick polecat wangled nine lives," Sierra responded, positive that her stepmother's first husband could have worked a deal with the devil to do exactly that.

She pried the crumpled letter from Melanie Shaw's fingers to smooth it against the polished surface of the parquet table beside the sofa. Gaslight refracting through the crystal prisms of the overhead chandelier cast a flickering pattern on the creased parchment.

"Are you sure he wrote this?" Sierra asked.

Melanie closed her eyes helplessly and sighed. "It's been so long since I've seen Geoffrey's handwriting that I . . . I'm not certain," she answered, spreading her arms in despair. "But I had the strangest feeling when I saw the London postmark. A part of me *knew* who it was from."

"Well, whoever wrote it seems to think you'll send him Geoffrey's railroad shares in the next post. Melanie, the man made you live like a squatter! I'd tell him to go to blazes, dead or alive. Ever since the *Charity* exploded, I've pictured him shoveling coal into the everlasting fires. It's my favorite fantasy."

"Those shares are worthless, Sierra. Your father checked for me. Why should I keep them?"

Sierra wanted to shake her stepmother. The naiveté that was one of her father's second wife's most endearing characteristics could also be frustrating.

"Geoffrey left them to you, Melanie. They're yours," she reminded the older woman. "Did it ever occur to you there might be some reason he held on to them?"

Sierra scanned the dashing script once more. "How did whoever wrote this letter know you'd remarried? You only married Daddy two months ago."

"Perhaps there was a story in the newspaper."

"Why would a British paper report on the second marriage of a United States Senator?" Sierra felt protective of her new stepmother. Melanie might be twelve years older than her own twenty-four, but her guilelessness sometimes gave the impression she was years younger. Sierra could only guess at what her life with Geoffrey had been like, but she knew a yellow-bellied crook when she met one, and the deceased had qualified on every point.

The year before his death, Geoffrey had drifted into Paradise Valley selling fake gold and silver claims. Melanie's innocence and her unhappy plight as Geoffrey's wife had been apparent to all, but Sierra's father had not unmasked the Englishman. Instead, the Senator had hired him as a land agent, then sent him off to train with one of his reliable assistants.

Although Geoffrey learned quickly, each quarter when the Englishman received his remittance check he deserted

8

his job to gamble until the money was gone. Which was how he had ended up on the *Charity*'s last voyage.

A blessing, to Sierra's way of thinking. She paced the room so energetically that, to her ears, the rustling of her taffeta petticoats sounded like a bonfire. "Do you understand what the letter says? If you don't send him the only thing he bequeathed you, he threatens to come here for the certificates himself. Melanie, anyone in the world could have written this. He knows you'd be . . . afraid of a scandal."

"But what if Geoffrey's truly alive? That would mean I'm a . . . a bigamist! And your father . . . his career . . ." Melanie crumpled into the corner of the sofa and crushed her handkerchief to her lips. Tears rolled down her pale cheeks. "You know how he carries on . . ."

"For heaven's sake, don't tell him! Daddy's up to his suspender buttons trying to preserve the treaties the government signed with the Paiutes. If he hears about this, he'll drop everything and set off for England, where he'll bluff and bluster until he starts a war." Sierra ceased pacing and parted the lace curtains to stare thoughtfully at the grimy piles of snow edging the sidewalk in front of their Georgetown home.

"I'll take care of it," she said. One more time, just one more time, she would smooth her father's path, as she had been doing ever since she became old enough to realize how much he could accomplish—if he were kept from leaping before he looked. After that, either Melanie could take on the task or her father would have to learn to control his rambunctious temper.

Her stepmother straightened her slender shoulders and squared her quivering jaw. "This is my problem, Sierra. I'll do just as the letter asks."

9

Sierra whirled, crying, "Don't you dare! Alive or dead, do you think the demands will stop with some worthless stock? Blackmail never ends. When he discovers how afraid you are of scandal he'll ask for more, and then more after that. The crook thinks he's struck gold. My father's." She crossed the room to kneel and enfold her stepmother's icy fingers with her own warm, capable hands. "Write back. Try to sound helpless. Tell him you have to be sure he's who he says he is."

"How will that help?"

"It will buy me time to sail to England and find out if it was really Geoffrey who wrote the letter. I'd know that snake from a country mile away." Sierra swallowed compulsively. Being confined in a stateroom on a steamship would be the worst part of the scheme.

Melanie pulled her hands away. "Surely he'll disappear when he discovers you've come after him."

Sierra smiled impishly. "I'm still positive Geoffrey's dead. Whoever this blackmailer is, he'll never suspect an empty-headed, social-climbing woman of being on his trail, and I intend to be *very* empty-headed." After she made her way to shore, she added silently. Thank God for the Shaw fortune. It should guarantee her a large suite with portholes.

London, late March, 1885

"America has everything but titles, and I've a hankering to be 'Lady' something. So I'm here to catch me a husband." Sierra smiled brightly at the dozen or so well-dressed people regarding her as if she had just revealed a past career as a dance hall girl. From the horror she saw on their faces and the startled gasps that escaped their lips, her gauche announcement should spread through the social world like a prairie fire.

She surveyed the astounded group as if surprised. "Why are you folks so shocked? Lots of wealthy American women have married titles. At least I'm announcing my intentions up front. And you needn't worry I'll stay here and embarrass all you fancy folks. I intend to take my man home to Paradise Valley and show him off."

"Scandalous," pronounced Lady Kingston, looking around for support.

Her response couldn't have pleased Sierra more. She noticed the Donningtons, an elderly couple she had met only minutes before, silently clutching their empty teacups as if they planned to take them home with them. Ignoring the censure, she continued, "You English bring your daughters to London every spring to find them husbands, don't you?"

Her hostess, Margaret Worthington, wife of the American attaché, chuckled softly. "But English parents usually accompany their daughters, Miss Shaw. Or else a close friend or relative stands in for them. If your father were with you, that would make your intentions slightly less shocking to English society."

"Oh, Daddy was much too busy to jaunt over here. Politics, you know. In any case, he trusts my judgment. When I told him what I wanted he said to choose the pick of the litter," she lied, smiling as if her father's attitude weren't every bit as shocking as her intent.

She sensed, rather than saw, that the little circle had enlarged. Glancing to her left, she found herself under the intent scrutiny of a pair of quizzical hazel eyes. Returning the look with equal interest nearly broke her concentration on the role she was playing. Flecks of gold, gray and green blended and merged in a gaze so sharp she had the unsettling feeling that the mind behind the startling eyes had just stripped every secret from her soul.

For one nervous second, she felt transfixed. Then the man smiled, and her heart set up a nervous rhythm beneath her breastbone. His teeth were very white against sunkissed, clean-shaven skin. With the spell of his scrutiny broken, she became aware of the rest of him. His hair was red! Not bright, orangey red, but the dark russet of wild sumac in autumn. His lashes and thick, arched brows were the same color. The man was handsome, but it was the "knowingness" about him that raised the skin on her nape.

"I don't believe we've been introduced," she said, taking the bull by the horns. She thrust out her gloved hand as if to shake his.

Margaret Worthington came to her aid. "I'm sure I've no idea where my manners have gone. May I present Fitzhugh Kent? Miss Sierra Shaw. Her father's a Senator from the state of Nevada in the United States."

"How clever of them to name a mountain range after you, Miss Shaw," Kent quipped as he turned her hand and lifted it to his lips.

As his mouth brushed her fingers, his warm breath penetrated Sierra's thin kid glove. The fine hairs on her forearm developed a life of their own. Resisting the urge to jerk her fingers from his, she retreated instead to the questionable safety of her new persona. So this was Fitz Kent. She smiled confidingly at those gathered around them. "You see? That's why I want to take one of your Englishmen home with me. They pay such pretty compliments, and an American would never kiss my hand so gallantly."

A trickle of surprised laughter rewarded her. "I do believe I'm going to have a wonderful time in London." She risked looking directly up into Kent's eyes as she answered his question, "I was born the day Nevada was declared a territory. The mountains had been mighty generous to my father, and he wanted to pay his respects."

His bright, intuitive eyes were mocking as he said, "I can't help but observe that Nevada's generosity also provided a Worth gown, Miss Shaw."

Sierra met the subtle challenge and engaged battle. "Aren't you clever, Mr. Kent! And so observant! I didn't want to look like an ignorant Yankee when I arrived in England, so I went to Paris first. Worth is a real fine little man. He reminds me of my grandfather."

Margaret Worthington subsided into a coughing spell. Recovering quickly, she cautioned in a strangled voice, "I must warn you about dear Fitz, Sierra. He's the perfect guest, perfectly dressed, perfectly witty and perfectly charming. One hears he has an obscure post with the government, although no one has ever actually seen him work. But you must never take him seriously or offend him. He wields a rather wicked tongue when he chooses."

Kent protested laughingly, "You wound me, Mrs. Worthington. Have you considered how many engagements I refuse just so I can attend your little gatherings to welcome American visitors?"

"You know I appreciate you, Fitz. Just be kind to Miss Shaw." She turned, directing a welcoming smile toward an overdressed, middle-aged woman. "Lady Naismith. I'm delighted you could be with us this afternoon. May I present Miss Sierra Shaw from the American state of Nevada?" She turned to Sierra. "Lady Muriel Naismith."

The little group had grown, spilling over into the plant-filled bay separated from the left side of the room by velvet hangings held back by ornately tasseled cords.

Muriel Naismith's nasal voice grated on Sierra's ears.

"Isn't that in the western part of America, Miss Shaw?"

"Yes." Sierra anticipated the next question, and she wasn't disappointed.

"Then you must have seen Indians. Tell me, are they as dirty and ignorant as I've heard?"

Concealing delighted laughter, Sierra stepped to the edge of the velvet drape, touched the arm of the dark-haired woman intently examining a lush display of African violets, and drew her into view. "I grew up with Indians in Paradise Valley, ma'am." Smothering a smile of spiteful delight, she tucked her arm around the waist of her companion. "May I introduce you to my aunt, Dolores Shaw? She's here to chaperone me."

Muriel Naismith looked as if she had just swallowed a wiggling trout. Sierra knew her aunt's burgundy silk Worth creation was enhanced by her flawless carriage. With her high cheekbones and straight black hair neatly braided into a coronet, she was striking. Dolores Shaw's warm bronze face was composed, as if she were accustomed to the stares of rude white men and women.

"Oh, dear. Does she speak English?" Lady Naismith said loudly.

"Quite well, thank you. And my hearing is exceptional. Before you inquire, let me assure you I am enjoying my visit thus far and looking forward with pleasure to spending many afternoons exploring your fine museums and conservatories."

Dolores Shaw's diction and pronunciation were more elegant than those of seventy-five percent of the English aristocracy, as was her composure, Sierra thought smugly. She glanced at Fitz Kent, surprising a tiny smile on his lips. He was enjoying Lady Naismith's discomfort, and as if to apologize for his countrywoman's rudeness, he asked courteously, "To which family of The People do you belong, Mrs. Shaw?"

"I am one-half Shoshoni, a tribe of the northwest. My father was a French explorer and trapper, and he and my mother travelled throughout the northern country. Both died when I was quite young. And before Mrs. Naismith inquires, yes, they were married." The twinkle in her dark eyes revealed her amusement at his presumption that she required rescue. "I was raised by Sierra's grandfather, a university professor in St. Louis."

"Aunt Dolores and Uncle Zephath were with my parents when they filed claims in Carson City."

"Claims?" Fitz asked.

"Mining claims. They struck silver before unearthing a mother lode of gold."

"That went well, don't you think, Dolores?" Sierra snuggled against the velvet squabs of the carriage and met her aunt's gaze in the wavering glow from the lamps on either side. The unease on the older woman's usually composed features worried Sierra. "Did something upset you? I was so busy pretending to be a brash American that I couldn't observe the other guests as closely as I'd have liked."

"I very much dislike hearing you flaunting your father's wealth. Otherwise, I saw nothing out of the ordinary, although Mr. Kent seemed to observe you with exceptional interest."

Sierra sighed. "We argued about this all the way from New York. I thought you understood. Since the blackmailer knows Melanie married my father, he'll wonder why I'm here. If I appear to be nothing but a crass husband hunter, he'll think I'm harmless." She leaned forward to pat her aunt's hand.

"This *has* to be better than Daddy charging in with his six-guns blazing. That would send the blackmailer into hiding." She fingered the lace on her frivolous hat as she continued, "This way the only thing anyone will suspect me of is crudeness."

"I don't think Mr. Kent believes you," her aunt insisted.

"He's just afraid I'll replace him as the Season's most entertaining guest. You watch. Everyone will invite me to their lawn parties and dinners, in hopes I'll do or say something outrageous while I'm there. And to introduce me to their eligible sons," Sierra added shrewdly. "This town is overflowing with impoverished aristocrats. The Shaw money will compensate for nearly anything I decide to do . . . even if I eat with my fingers. Besides, Fitz Kent looks as if he spends every waking hour worrying about his appearance. Have you ever seen anyone so . . . so polished-looking in your life?"

She turned away from her aunt's perceptive glance. Sierra had needed only one look into Kent's hazel eyes to know he was capable of seeing through her masquerade. His bright, searching gaze took in every detail of each person and item in the room. She imagined him filing them away for future use. The perfection of his tailoring tended to distract one's attention from the breadth of his shoulders and the wiry grace of his body. On the other hand, his elegant manners and apparent indolence seemed created for a drawing room; she couldn't imagine the man approaching an actual job with any competence.

His elegant grooming both attracted and repelled her. Why did his faultlessly barbered and brushed hair make her want to rumple such perfection . . . ? *Good God! What am I thinking!* "Only a tailor's dummy would wear such a relentlessly starched linen shirt and a matching cravat and pocket handkerchief so discreet they scream extravagance. And he's finicky. Did you see him adjust the crease in his trousers when he sat on the love seat? He nearly crooked his pinky!"

"A man who sees as much as he does could be dangerous, Sierra. You will do well to be on your guard."

The carriage rolled to a stop. Ignoring her aunt's warning, Sierra swivelled toward the door, which swung open as if by magic. "Caleb, if you continue to be such a perfect servant, Queen Victoria will attempt to hire you away from me." She smiled teasingly and placed her hand on the arm of the squarely built young man who had opened the door. Bringing her own groom and horses along had been a necessity. She and Caleb had grown up together, and he was trustworthy; Sierra wanted people she could trust at her back.

"No chance, Sierra. 'Druther be back in Paradise Valley. This place gives me a hemmed-in feelin'."

She patted his shoulder as he turned to assist Dolores to the cobblestones. "I know exactly what you mean. London's nearly as stifling as shipboard. The buildings are too close to each other." Standing in the comparative openness of the street, she suppressed a shudder. Steamship travel might be one of the miracles of the age, but throughout the voyage she had suffered twinges of claustrophobia.

Sierra looked up and down Adelphi Terrace. The address was convenient rather than fashionable, located far enough from Charing Cross railway station to be respectable, but close enough that she could be there quickly if she found it necessary to travel in a hurry. Mayfair and Belgravia, where society lived and entertained, were within a short carriage ride.

Russ, her father's assistant, had been fortunate to find

them anything so acceptable, arriving as he did when families were already moving to town for the Season.

She climbed the shallow steps, smiling wryly as Elkins, the starchy, elderly butler, opened the door at precisely the right moment. Although few well-trained servants were available at this time of year, she never questioned the wonders of unlimited cash.

As if thinking of Russ had materialized him, a tall, lanky figure called to her from the top of the stairs to the left of the narrow foyer. "Thank God you're back early, Sierra. You need to hear this."

Sierra surrendered her pelisse to the butler and ran up the steps to join the gray-haired man. "News? Already? You're a miracle worker." Revealing Melanie's problem to Russ had not been a breach of trust. She'd known him all her life, and he was dedicated to the Senator's career.

"As soon as I arrived, I sent a detective to West Suffolk to the return address on the letter Melanie received. The present occupants denied any knowledge of Geoffrey, even after my man claimed his inquiries had something to do with money. Since Geoffrey's boyhood home was less than twenty miles away, he made inquiries there. Geoffrey's father and his brother died a year ago in a freak hunting accident, and a distant cousin inherited the property in Suffolk, but very little else." He pushed his wire-rimmed glasses back up the bridge of his nose. "Sierra, the cousin claims he never knew any of the Trowbridge family personally. His branch had been transported to Australia."

"Then who else but Geoffrey would know enough to threaten Melanie? Could he truly be alive?"

CHAPTER TWO

Four hours after the attaché's tea, an unobtrusive figure wearing a threadbare sack suit and cheap broken shoes blended into the crowd crossing a busy street leading into Cambridge Circus. Reaching the intersection, he crossed Shaftesbury Avenue and ambled into an alley. Halfway down the shadowy passage he removed a peculiarly shaped key from his pocket and unlocked a door set flush with the moldering stone wall. When the sturdy steel portal swung soundlessly inward, the figure disappeared within.

Inside, the building was surprisingly clean. As the man climbed the stairs to the second floor, another poorly dressed individual descended. "Early tonight, aren't you, Kent?"

Fitz grinned agreement and pulled off his shapeless cap before climbing yet another flight to the third floor, where he entered an unobtrusive door. The portly, balding man hunched over a stack of yellow telegraph paper acknowledged his entrance with a grunt.

"Are all those new, Harrison?"

"Came in not 'arf an 'our ago." He nodded toward a door on his right which muted the sound of a telegraph. "More on t' way, sounds like. Be a bit before I 'ave these deciphered."

Fitz slipped past the scarred oak desk and unlocked the door to Harrison's left. "Bring in the lot as soon as you're done. Might as well put them at the end of the queue." He stepped inside and lit the gas jets before closing the door behind him.

No light from the congested streets below filtered into his spacious office. Unmatching file cabinets, two of them blocking the low, narrow window, covered nearly every foot of wall space. Whitewashed plaster walls showed above the cabinets, and light reflected from the white ceiling. A massive desk built in a U-shape around an ancient leather chair dominated the room.

Contrary to the impression he cultivated, Fitz Kent spent only one evening out of three at dinners, balls and musicales, or gambling at one of the many clubs where he claimed membership. Each night, at varying hours, he reported to his dingy office. "It's all smoke and mirrors," he had once told an associate as they descended the stairs of the run-down building owned by the Old Firm, otherwise known as the British Secret Service.

Not even the most fanciful person would suspect the two floors above a gin shop and a secondhand clothing store of housing anything but prostitutes or decaying furniture. Light never showed in any of the windows, and no signs of activity, legal or illegal, were detectable by the most careful observer. The run-down building coexisted with similar stone and brick structures along both sides of the street, while the bleak neighborhood edged the infamous, ever-widening cesspool of poverty, crime and degeneracy known as Seven Dials.

Fitz removed the ill-fitting jacket and tossed it, along with his cap, atop a file cabinet. Hands in his pockets, he stared moodily at the stack of reports. Within them would be snippets of information from the Transvaal and the Sudan, where British sovereignty balanced on decidedly rocky underpinnings. The Dervishes had annihilated poor Gordon in the Sudan, and Gladstone was under attack by the press and the palace. The fourteen-nation Berlin conference on African affairs the year before had been no help to a continent which bitterly resented the growing governance of more powerful countries.

"Fat bloody chance *they* have," he mused as he eased into his chair and picked up the first report. The countries' dooms had been written in the stars with the discovery of diamonds and valuable minerals. He couldn't afford emotional involvement—his task was sorting information, evaluating which figure or name would be of most value to which department, and attempting to discern the effect of each on the pattern engraved in his mind.

He dropped the paper on the desk and leaned back in his chair. Gold and silver mines. The little American's father was apparently a Midas, as well as a politician. His lips quirked appreciatively as he pictured Miss Shaw's blonde perfection. She was as dainty as a porcelain doll in a shop window. Her pale, elegantly coiffed curls and enormous blue eyes were the stuff of dreams. Yet there was an impudent tilt to the tip of her straight little nose with its faint dusting of freckles, and when she forgot to pout her full lower lip fetchingly, there was a certain sweetness about her mouth. Something didn't ring true about her. He was certain he'd detected sly laughter and . . . calculation?

. . . lurking in the cerulean depths of her eyes.

At the thought, his senses resurrected the scent of violets—wild, not hothouse, elusive and faintly earthy. The sound of her laughter echoed in his ears. Surely such a delectable female needn't buy a husband, titled or not.

Fixing his gaze on the blank, painted panel of the door, he reviewed the encounter with a clinical eye, stripping his mind of any emotional response. The exercise proved more difficult than he expected. The petite American had somehow wormed her way into his subconscious.

21

Finally succeeding in his endeavor, Fitz pushed Sierra Shaw from his thoughts and attended to his messages. Discarding the first as useless information, he saw Adrian Harding's code name on the second. The multilingual viscount had retired from service six months earlier, then married and set out on a round-the-world trip with his bride. Fitz read the decoded words with amusement-laced surprise.

"American Sierra Shaw arriving London. Suspect hidden agenda. Extremely clever but headstrong. May need rescuing."

His first reaction was that the only people requiring rescue were the poor suitors who found themselves "possibles" in her search for a husband.

Had her seemingly naive announcement of her father's wealth been intentionally gauche? What did Adrian mean by "hidden agenda"? Skepticism was Fitz's stock in trade, but Adrian's instincts were sound. Perhaps he should ingratiate himself with Sierra Shaw under the pretense of assisting in her search for a husband . . . purely as a favor to Adrian, of course.

His musings were interrupted by a rapping at the door. "Come in."

A puzzled frown creased Harrison's forehead as he stared at the paper in his hand. "This one don't make sense. Sterling 'asn't worked for the Department since your father died."

"Give it to me." Fitz half rose, reaching across the desk. He was certain his father's death four years earlier had been murder, even though officially the man had died of a heart attack in that holiday hotel. Sterling had worked for Matthew Kent for twenty-five years and been devoted to him. The agent had retired, vowing to continue the search for the woman who had registered at the inn with Matthew the night he died.

Fitz's appointment to his father's post soon after had left him little time to mourn, but he had never abandoned the hope that the truth of his father's death would someday surface.

The decoded message read, "The woman's in Ireland."

Thick fog swirled around the two figures huddled at the base of a stone pedestal on London Bridge. The moisture-filled air revealed a shoulder, then shifted to divulge a stark male silhouette. Rex Haliburton spoke agitatedly. "The Shaw girl's here, I tell you. In England. In London. I saw her name on the passenger list myself."

The voice which came out of the thick mix was cold, instilling fear in the listener. "Please do not shriek. I am aware of her presence. Edgar Donnington mentioned it over the whist table last night. He found her crass references to her father's wealth rather vulgar."

"That American woman has come to dig around. I want out. Right now. I don't care what those railroad shares are worth today or a year from now. If she catches the littlest whiff . . ." the first speaker argued. The sudden touch of his companion's hand at his nape caused him to break off, chilled perspiration forming along his hairline. His employer had no nerves, and he was ruthless. Crossing him was risky, but things were beginning to unravel. He'd been told there would be no danger, that their target was a timid mouse. But now this younger woman, an unknown quantity, had journeyed to England.

"I have been assured she is nothing but a crude social climber, here to buy a titled husband to show off to her common little friends at home."

The disembodied voice failed to reassure Haliburton. "But what if the girl's pretending?" He had appeared in enough second-rate plays to know people weren't always what they seemed. His last role had been that of a dedicated roué tricked by a conspiracy between his wife and his mistress. To Rex's simplistic thinking, the clever story was true to life. He had never trusted women.

Haliburton prided himself on burrowing so far into his roles that he merged his real self with each part. Unfortunately, such mastery had not yet earned him the recognition he felt he deserved, which was why he had accepted a large sum of money from his cold-eyed partner.

"From all reports, she has neither the brains nor the imagination to pretend. Relax. The letter the dear Senator's wife wrote asks for more proof. She wants to 'see' her late husband before she'll believe he escaped the accident, so you're going to America."

The actor drew back from the icy touch and the wintry voice. "She'll know I'm an imposter. She'll have me arrested."

"Nonsense. She's a silly goose. Her caution surprises me, but I hired you in case of just such a contingency. You look enough like my friend Geoffrey to pass as his brother. With a tragic tale of burns and disfigurement and some skillful makeup, she'll believe anything. *If* you're a good enough actor to carry this off."

The aspersion on his skills swept away Haliburton's doubts. "Of *course* I'm good enough," he bragged. In the back of his mind's eye he carried a picture of the cold, barren cell he'd occupied the winter his touring company had attempted to skip town without paying their shot at a boardinghouse. The cast had spent a degrading week in a particularly dank prison. "But what if . . ."

"Calm yourself. It would be most unfortunate for you if the Senator's new wife discovers the future value of that stock before I have it in my hand. You leave for America in a week. Charlie Finn will accompany you to assure you do as you're instructed. He'll give you your final instructions during the boat trip." A mirthless chuckle trickled through the fog. "What is it you theater people say? 'Break a leg.' "

As his employer's muffled footsteps faded into the night, Haliburton crumpled against the railing of London Bridge. Perspiration streamed from his forehead into his eyes; his legs trembled, and he leaned heavily against the cold stone for support. Wiping his face with his handkerchief, he stared down into the lightless water flowing beneath him. "Oh, God! Why did I get into this? Why?"

Pale morning sunshine poured through the sheer gauze curtains covering the tall windows of Sierra's room. Minutes earlier, the maid had deposited a tray bearing a tiny pot of fragrant chocolate on the nightstand beside the bed and pushed back the heavy brocade draperies.

Draining the last of the sweet liquid from a fragile cup, Sierra set it on the saucer and stretched extravagantly, wiggling her toes beneath the sheets. She could become accustomed to such a nicety, even though the practice would probably never transplant to Paradise Valley. The thought brought a smile to her lips.

Theodophilus Shaw's vast fortune could supply any imaginable luxury, but he always remembered his roots. He and his brother Zephath had lived with the barest necessities in the lean-to they'd built for themselves, their wives, and Sierra's two older brothers to live in while they sought shining nuggets. Even after money began to flow into their pockets in an endless stream, their lifestyles could have been described as frugal.

Sierra rubbed her cheek against the herb-scented linen. She had never known want, but extravagance had always been identified as such. The linens at home smelled of fresh air and sunshine, and her senses recalled the wonderful fragrances even as she inhaled the scents of roses and lavender. Her father wasn't a stingy man; he simply abhorred waste. "Be sure you have the proper tools to do the job, and always buy the best . . . but don't waste money on useless whims."

She'd kept that dictum in mind when she approached him about the trip to London for the Season. What if he said no? Surprisingly, it had been he who urged the side trip to Paris for Worth wardrobes for her and for her aunt. "Show 'em we can buy the best, Sierra." His lively blue eyes had twinkled, and his mustache had lifted at the corner in a conspiratorial grin. "And dance your shoes off. Lord knows you've put up with enough foolishness in Washington to deserve some fun."

Love for her father welled up as she recalled the scene. Acting as his hostess for the last six years had taught her much. She'd learned to cope with, and occasionally curb, his frustrating habit of rushing into action without considering the consequences. She'd also learned to separate genuine people from the liars and hangers-on who flocked to the federal feed trough, just as her father had once learned to differentiate promising gold and silver diggings from dead holes.

The comparison reminded her of Adrian Harding and his wife Chloe. During their Washington visit, the British aristocrats had become her friends; Sierra had recognized kindred spirits. When she asked the honeymooning couple for advice concerning a London Season, they had laughed uproariously before admitting they were the last people to ask, since neither of them enjoyed the social scene.

"Just picture yourself changing your dress seven times a day to encounter the same group of people and rehash the same gossip you heard two hours earlier," Chloe had laughingly instructed.

In the end, they had furnished letters of introduction to several relatives and friends. Unable to explain the real reason for her sudden trip, Sierra had referred vaguely to researching family connections. Adrian had eyed her shrewdly, added Fitz Kent's name to the bottom of the brief list, and said, "If you find yourself in a tight spot for any reason, this is your man."

Adrian had seemed sure of Kent's ability.

Was it Adrian's endorsement that made her doubt that the elegant, auburn-haired man was the social ornament he appeared to be, or was her response more personal?

Sierra's stomach protested, and she patted her midsection gently. "Enough of this lazing in bed puzzling about a man I scarcely know. Can't travel far on chocolate, can we?" she lectured herself as she pushed the sheet and quilt to the foot of the bed. She would think no more about the intriguing Englishman.

An hour later, she paced the mews behind the house, impatiently awaiting her mount. Back home at the ranch she would have thrown on wear-softened buckskins and leaped onto her horse bareback before riding off across the pasture.

Halfway around the world from Paradise Valley, she found herself in a deep-rose twill gown especially designed to cover her legs while she rode sidesaddle. Her black, derby-style hat sported a dashing feather the same color as her gown. And she couldn't ride in the park without a groom in attendance.

Washington was straitlaced, but at least there she could occasionally slip away to enjoy the freedom she craved. She didn't dare risk a scandal in Victoria's England.

Caleb emerged from the stable leading two horses. Giving her a leg up onto the sidesaddle, he teased, "Sure hope you enjoy your ride today, Sierra."

Wriggling until she was as comfortable as she was going to get, she responded by reaching down and tugging the ponytail of dark, straight hair that hung between his shoulder blades. "If nothing else, I'll *love* watching people's reaction to a Paiute riding on Rotten Row. Your outfit must be just as uncomfortable for you as mine is for me." Actually, she thought Caleb looked quite dashing in his neat gray jacket and riding breeches.

With the familiarity of a brother, Caleb responded, "Not quite. I'm not wearing a corset." He stepped back just in time to avoid her second grab for his hair. "And I don't have to ride sidesaddle."

Acknowledging both hits, Sierra glanced around the confined area to be sure they were alone, then leaned down and murmured, "While Russ is digging for information about the stock in Suffolk, we can start here in London. Tonight I want you to visit a gin mill in the East End. Melanie recalled Geoffrey mentioning the place on several occasions."

Caleb's dark eyes glinted with laughter. "A pub? You're actually ordering me to spend the evening drinking?"

"You'll ration the mild and bitter if you're to keep a clear enough head to listen for anything we can use. Try to locate some of the regulars. People who've been customers for six years or more."

"Do I get to name names?"

"Look on it as tracking a deer through the forest. You'll

instinctively know what to ask and when to listen. Melanie was married to that good-for-nothing cheat for less than four years, but she says he mentioned The Black Sheep often. Sounds to me as if it was named for him."

"The woman's in Ireland." Sterling's message, after two years' silence, had nagged at Fitz throughout a restless night; now it was imprinted on his brain.

A shoehorn in one hand and a natty brown brogan in the other, he stared at the shoe, absorbed in the memories the message triggered.

After their initial unsuccessful search, Fitz and the retired agent had been pessimistic about Madeleine Dorsey's fate. Why had the woman disappeared? Had she seen anything? She must have. Something that had caused her to stay in hiding all this time. He refused to believe she could be involved in his father's death.

He remembered Sterling's assessment. "Your father was the picture of health. Even his doctor was surprised when he died so suddenly. And the setup was wrong. The innkeeper sent for me as soon as he found Matthew, since my name and where I was staying was written under that date in your father's pocket calendar. The room was too tidy, as if someone had straightened up before I came."

Why had they been unable to locate Madeleine, the charming, independent widow who preferred the role of mistress to wife? That in itself was suspicious, but Fitz knew his father and Madeleine cared for each other. He would have bet his own life on her loyalty. But she had disappeared and hadn't surfaced until now.

During the months following his father's death, the Duke of Cambridge had reorganized the War Office, and Fitz's appointment to his father's position left him with little time to conduct what appeared to be a futile investigation. Assuming the directorship of the unorthodox agency had been a monumental task.

Fitz devoutly wished his father were still sitting behind the scarred desk, humming merrily and shouting with laughter or dismay over each report before shuttling the intelligence to where it would be the most beneficial. He should still be available for Fitz to learn from—to count on at every turn. Matthew Kent shouldn't be dead—not at the age of fifty-five.

Realizing he had spent ten minutes staring at a shoe, he dropped the offending article, which landed with a thump on the Bokhara rug. "Paxton!" he shouted.

The unanswered call echoed through the spacious, high-ceilinged room. "Paxton, I know you're in my dressing room. Get in here!" He fumbled with the buttons of his trousers.

"Have we a problem, sir?" a pained voice inquired.

"I've changed my mind. I'm going riding. Get my boots from wherever you've hidden them." Fitz narrowed his eyes as his valet approached. "I don't care if you *are* in the process of rearranging my clothing so I can't find a blasted thing myself. The boots have to be there someplace."

"Did we arise on the wrong side of the bed this morning, young master?"

Fitz rolled his eyes heavenward and gritted his teeth. Paxton was another legacy from his father—a proper, highly trained gentleman's gentleman whom Fitz had known since he was four. Nothing in the house on Queen Square escaped Paxton's surveillance, and God help even the lowliest servant who failed to do his or her job properly. The valet viewed Fitz with the same critical eye.

"No, damn it, I didn't. I wouldn't dare, not with you

around." Fitz closed his eyes and took a deep breath. "I apologize. A message arrived last night. Sterling has located Mrs. Dorsey."

"Then you are understandably upset, sir. Shall I prepare your travelling valise?"

The oblique inquiry as to whether he would be leaving cut even more deeply into his peace. Paxton's thirst for vengeance was as great as Sterling's. Unfortunately, this was the worst possible time for Fitz to be away; the government was unstable, and he'd already taken leave time a month earlier for a brief sojourn with an accommodating actress in the south of France.

"No, damn it. I don't know where she is in Ireland. Besides, if the Irish Nationalists withdraw their support of the mess in Sudan, which everything indicates could happen momentarily, Gladstone's government will fall. I have to be here in case there's an election." He removed his trousers and handed them to his valet. "A few of us must keep our hands on the tiller, guiding the ship of state."

Paxton wrinkled his long nose and sniffed audibly as he shook imaginary wrinkles from the discarded garment. "Such hyperbole is beneath you, sir. If you'll pardon the comparison, you sound quite like a hero in one of those regrettable serial stories one buys on street corners."

"I'm famous for my cynicism, don't you know?" Fitz replied irritably. Frowning, he slid the discreet gold cufflinks from his sleeves and unbuttoned his linen shirt. "Bring me my riding kit, if you can find it. Otherwise I'll ride off this temper in my smalls."

Glancing up, Fitz saw Paxton's light blue eyes soften as he turned toward the dressing room. The sight took him back to the day his mother died from pneumonia. It had been Paxton who had clasped a grief-stricken seven-year-old to his bony chest and let him cry. His father had been out of the country at the time.

Cursing himself for taking out his frustration on a friend, Fitz shook his head disgustedly. For a few mad moments he considered walking away from everything—his responsibilities to the Crown, the double life he led, and the nagging question of his father's death. He would remove to Kent House and watch black-faced sheep graze by the hour. He would bestir himself only to eat.

A vision of azure blue eyes surrounded by curling, deep umber–colored lashes formed in his mind—the eyes of the blunt little American named after a mountain range. The scent of wild violets seemed to fill his nostrils. Perhaps there was a much more entertaining reason to stay in London. His sixth sense told him Adrian was right. The outwardly guileless young woman concealed a hidden agenda. He'd be an idiot to walk away from a challenge like that.

"Your riding breeches, sir."

CHAPTER THREE

Moments later, impeccably clad in boots, breeches and his favorite tweed hacking jacket, Fitz strode from the house and took the reins of his chestnut gelding from the waiting groom. He eased his pocket watch from his snug-fitting vest, checked the time, and returned the flat gold timepiece to its place before he mounted and urged his mount to a brisk trot, anticipating an early gallop along a deserted Rotten Row.

Upon arrival, he scowled in disgust. Two riders raced toward him, heading toward the bank of the Serpentine. "Damn fools," he muttered. "These paths weren't meant for racing." He ignored the fact that he'd intended to give Chanticleer his head as soon as he reached the trail himself. Instead he reined to one side for them to pass.

As they neared, a young man with a tail of hair streaming above his groom's livery took the lead. The other rider was a tiny, deep rose and gold confection leaning forward intently and riding with exceptional skill. "I would never have expected her of being such a hoyden," he mused. "Brought her groom with her from America, I should say."

On impulse, he raced after them, pulling alongside as they slowed near the water's edge. "Good morning, Miss Shaw. You're an early riser too, I see."

The flushed, laughing face she turned toward him sobered, recognition dawning in her eyes. "Mr. . . . Kent, isn't it? I wouldn't have thought to see *you* out this early." She looked surprised at her own rudeness, then smilingly apologized, "Oh, dear, that wasn't supposed to come out sounding the way it did. I didn't expect to see anyone 'fashionable' here at seven in the morning. This is my groom, Caleb Lonetree," she added.

"Happy to meet you," the young man said, guiding his horse alongside Fitz's and extending his hand.

Without a moment's hesitation at the groom's presumption, Fitz clasped the Indian's strong, callused palm, surprised by the warning pressure in the young man's handshake. "Happy to meet you, Caleb. Senator Shaw must feel reassured to know you're here to watch over his daughter." He tightened and adjusted his grip until his adversary's eyes widened.

The groom tried to retaliate, but Fitz resisted before freeing his fingers with a movement he had learned from an Oriental martial arts expert some years earlier. He suppressed a smile at the surprise in Caleb's eyes.

Turning to Sierra, he realized she had been watching their masculine jockeying for supremacy. The woman couldn't have been unaware of the warning Caleb meant to deliver. Fitz recalled the fleeting expression of amusement in her eyes as she had figuratively thrown Muriel Naismith to the wolves, in the person of her poised, articulate, Indian, aunt.

"It's unusual to meet anyone else at this hour. I often ride early to let Chanticleer race off his oats. May I join you?"

"Perhaps another morning." Sierra's full lower lip curved into a pretty pout and her eyes focused on her fingers as she fumbled with her reins. "I have an early appointment at Lloyd's with someone who is going to explain your ridiculous currency to me." One of the leather strips dropped from her suddenly clumsy fingers. She reached quickly to retrieve it.

Misinterpreting her movements, her mount sidled toward Fitz, brushing against him in the process. He controlled his expression as a familiar shape pressed against his leg through the expensive rose twill. Stepping back mentally, he observed her with professional detachment, ignoring the lures of her haunting fragrance and pretty confusion while she regained control and straightened the rucked folds of her skirt. Only luck and his quick eye allowed Fitz a glimpse of the carved bone knife handle protruding from a flat sheath at the top of her boot.

Filled with sudden, unreasonable annoyance he grated out, "Quite a good idea. After all, you wouldn't want to overpay for an earl when a viscount might be purchased cheaper. I wish you luck."

What was the girl up to—besides boding well to make fools of all the estate-poor bluebloods who would circle her and her fortune like hawks sighting carrion. Did she actually intend to marry one?

Sierra Shaw intrigued him more than ever. She had an Indian bodyguard, a knife in her boot . . . and a very lethal-feeling pistol concealed by the heavy skirts of her riding habit.

"Shall I kill him for you?"

Caleb's low-voiced offer as they rode away penetrated Sierra's surprise at the pain caused by Fitz Kent's insult. When she'd set out to play the role of a forward, title-mad American, she'd known she would be shocking, but why should Fitz Kent's disapproval hurt? She would have to avoid him in the future. Surely it wouldn't be difficult. "Leave him alone, Caleb. I'm sure no one pays any attention to a man like that."

"You're wrong. He's dangerous."

Surprised, she reined in her mount to meet Caleb's dark, opaque gaze. "Don't be ridiculous. It stands to reason he has to be deeper than he appears, but that's no reason to consider him a danger."

"His hands. I was trying to give him a warning, and he broke my grip with some kind of trick. I don't know much about gentlemen, but that one's hands and arms are strong, and he misses nothing. He saw the knife in your boot." Caleb shared his observations calmly, his eyes serious.

A tremor of apprehension rippled through Sierra. She dismissed the sudden crimping of her nerves; she had no time for fears or hesitancy. "He couldn't have."

"I was watching him. His eyes flickered the moment he noticed," he contradicted.

Sierra urged her horse forward, toward the gate to Park Lane. "Even so, he can't be sure I know how to use one." Caleb's snort reached her over the sound of the horses' hooves. "All right, I'll be on my guard around him, but I doubt there's anything to fear. Adrian Harding trusts him." But I don't need him, she told herself.

Caleb shrugged, then continued as if determined to have the last word. "You'll do whatever you want, anyway. You always do. I just hope I don't have to say 'I told you so.'" He guided his horse behind hers.

"Hah!" she shouted over her shoulder as she cantered toward the gate. The encounter had spoiled her morning's outing. She'd looked forward to the exhilaration of riding in the deserted park, away from the constant press of people. Away from worry about finding the blackmailer.

People. London was filled with them, all living within an arm's length of each other, each guarding his or her own small space from encroachment and seizing every opportunity to spread into the territory claimed by the next person.

And always talking. She had never heard so much talk about nothing, even in Washington. No one seemed to listen to anyone else. Except Fitz Kent, who looked at her so intently she had to watch her thoughts in case he could read her mind.

Why did she feel transparent around Fitz Kent? Yesterday his bright, observant gaze had examined her as if she were a painting he was attempting to interpret. The stinging vitality of his lean body reached out to her; when he'd kissed her hand she had felt his touch all the way up her arm—like electricity, that miraculous power source some said would transform civilization. The fragile filaments within the lightbulbs she'd seen demonstrated quivered and glowed with an unearthly light. She wondered if Kent could affect her the same way.

As they dismounted, she turned quickly to Caleb. "You understand what you're to do tonight?"

"Couldn't be plainer. See if anyone knew Geoffrey before he left for America . . . or if they know of anyone who did. Don't look too eager. And don't drink too much." His teeth flashed white against his bronze skin as he grinned at her.

"Be careful," she cautioned.

"I'll be a whole lot safer at The Black Sheep than you'll be at one of those parties you plan to attend. Most of the fancy people I've seen so far look like mountain lions on the hunt for their next meal." Caleb scooped the reins from her and turned to lead the horses to the stable.

Later that morning, as she sorted the growing stack of invitations, Sierra agreed with him. The guests at Margaret's tea yesterday had responded far beyond her expectations. The heavy cream and ivory notepaper associated with good taste had arrived in every imaginable size and fold. Each requested her presence at one event or another.

The sixth such note apologized for such short notice, but begged her to attend a dinner party that evening at the home of Lord and Lady Bennett. Dancing would follow.

Closing her eyes, she visualized the rather bland-appearing woman whose wry sense of humor had been a pleasant surprise. Her husband was a baronet, if Sierra remembered correctly. And Lady Bennett had mentioned a nephew. Sierra sailed the crisp paper across the satiny surface of the marquetry table and rested her forehead on her hands. Deceiving her hosts while she accepted their hospitality disagreed with everything she believed. "Oh, God. It's begun. I'm not sure I can carry this off. I can't lie to these people."

"Your attack of conscience is too late. It might help if you remembered that they apparently suffer no qualms about using your presence for their own purposes," came her aunt's voice from behind her. "Appalling as your behavior was yesterday, you were superb. White man's society is the same all over. If you have beauty and wealth, social gaffes are considered eccentric. And once you have convinced people you're interested only in a husband, no one will suspect you of any other motives." Dolores massaged the rigid muscles at the base of her skull with strong, skilled fingers. "You can't turn back now."

In the dim light of the carriage lamp, Fitz flicked a lazy finger at the speck of dust on the toe of his gleaming black dress shoe. A last minute invitation to join the Bennetts' guests for dancing following a private dinner party hadn't insulted him at all. Missing the meal was a blessing. Their chef had a regrettable tendency to put the same sauce on everything from vegetables to veal.

But his hostess's note had indicated Sierra Shaw was to be present. Fitz smiled wryly, reminding himself he merely wanted a brief, private meeting with the Bennetts' nephew Thomas, who had recently returned from Africa. Matthew Kent had roared with laughter when Fitz had suggested he recruit agents from the ranks of the aristocracy. "My boy, you have a devious mind. Who would ever suspect useless bluebloods of observing anything but the next cocktail or pretty face?"

Fitz had recruited selectively, using intelligence, useful academic interests, political beliefs, and romantic entanglements as criteria. Obviously, one couldn't ask men with wives and full nurseries to take any risk, but several of his recruits had brought back extremely useful information which had come their way while ostensibly vacationing. Only Adrian Harding had encountered difficulties, but those had stemmed from a source connected with his private life.

He had few worries about Thomas Bennett; the man was a respected scientist, consumed with collecting butterflies, so his cover was impeccable. Which brought Sierra Shaw to mind once more.

The carriage rolled to a stop, and Fitz reached for his hat before making sure the ends of the white silk scarf draped around his neck hung properly. It would never do for him to neglect the slightest detail of his fashionable appearance, even at such a minor event. People gossiped about fashion and tailoring. And when they were obsessed with such details, they neglected to pay the slightest attention to his activities. He hoped Miss Shaw was taken in by his facade. Perhaps then she would confide her hidden agenda. Fitz was convinced she had one.

His cynical smile lasted until he surrendered his hat and scarf inside the door.

Lady Bennett bore down on him. "Dear Fitz. I have been positively *counting* on your presence. Lady Lamprey *demanded* I invite the little American heiress at the last minute, since she wanted her son to be among the first to meet her." Her faded brown eyes danced with laughter. "After Miss Shaw accepted, I realized most of my other guests were old crocks, married and twenty years older than she. What could I do but simply *coerce* as many young people as possible to join us for dancing? I refuse to have that poor girl think she must spend the evening in the company of Giles Lamprey. He's nearly certifiable."

Fitz bent to kiss her cheek lightly. "I would never let you down, Georgina. However, the lady and I met yesterday, and she may prefer the idiot's company."

"Never say you've already insulted her, Fitz! How could you? She's a delightfully open little thing. Exquisite."

"And apparently possessed of no other goal in life than buying a titled husband," Fitz said as he tucked her hand in the crook of his arm.

Georgina shook her head resignedly as she allowed him to lead her up the stairs. "You're incorrigible. I quite begin to wonder if you have ever approved of *any* young woman."

"By Jove, I have. Unfortunately, her husband met her first." Chloe Harding's laughing face appeared before his mind's eye. "More intimate knowledge of the lady might have revealed unforgivable flaws, however."

"Just be polite to the little heiress. I cherish no illusions that she and Thomas have a thing in common, but I refuse to allow a guest in my home to be treated rudely.

"Besides, we must encourage friendly relations between our two countries," she added righteously.

They entered the front drawing room, now joined to the public room behind it by opening the pocket doors. The furnishings had been moved into place around the edges of the room, and the heavy rugs removed. "I felt opening the ballroom would be rather pretentious," she explained in response to Fitz's arched eyebrow.

"I'm sure no one complained but the servants, Georgina."

"There. You're being sarcastic again, Fitz."

In one corner, three string players tuned their instruments, the sound scarcely noticeable against the continuous rise and fall of male and female voices. A musical ripple of spontaneous laughter rose in counterpoint, and Fitz unerringly located the source. Sierra Shaw, her pale hair drawn up and back, with several loose curls resting on her bared shoulders, stood in the center of a group of five men. Each appeared mesmerized by the sight and sound of her.

"You hardly need me tonight, Georgina. The lady seems more than adequately entertained." Her husky laughter reached him once more; his body responded viscerally. Fitz struggled to erase a mental image of Sierra Shaw in his arms, her perfect little body straining against him. Flaming hell! What was it about the woman? He was known for judging acclaimed beauties with a cold, critical eye. None had ever caused the slightest fluctuation in his breathing. Porcelain daintiness bored him as a rule. And besides, the last thing he needed in his life was a distraction, particularly a female one.

"Don't be a dolt. That's Giles Lamprey and two of his friends. Birds of a feather, you know. And of course Francis Lancaster and Nigel Brockington. Francis is such a prig. Every time I'm in his company, he makes me feel as if I must apologize for not attending church three times on

Sunday, but Nigel is such a good sort that he makes up for Francis. Go rescue her. We don't want the poor girl to be bored to tears."

Reconciled, Fitz made one last effort. "Why haven't you sent Thomas?"

She gave him a push toward the cluster of black coats surrounding Sierra's burgundy lace–clad figure. "Thomas hasn't arrived. Besides, you're very aware that I don't dare send him out for a newspaper for fear he'll wander off after some silly moth. He promised to be here later, however. Said he'd brought you back a present. Now, go rescue that poor child."

Thomas's trip had apparently been successful. As he crossed the room, Fitz wondered how the little American would react to his arrival. Sierra Shaw might be no deeper than a layer of silk, but she'd mastered the art of juggling the attentions of five men at the same time. At that moment, she raised her ingenuous blue gaze to Nigel Brockington and fluttered lacy eyelashes. Brockington all but leered. Fitz took back his assessment of her depth. The lady knew exactly what she was doing.

"Kent, settle a wager for us," Giles Lamprey called out as he approached.

"Always glad to help inferior intellects, Lamprey . . . after I greet the guest of honor properly," he replied, smiling at Sierra as if they were lifelong friends. "I hope your mentor at Lloyd's was able to disperse the shadows for you this morning, Miss Shaw." Fitz ignored the little stab of guilt brought on by memory of the hurt in her eyes when he'd made his unforgivable comment about purchasing a husband. Why had he struck out at her like that? Surely her marriage plans were no concern of his.

"I told him exactly what I wanted. After much figuring

and explaining, we came up with a figure of twenty thousand pounds. Do you know of any for sale?"

Her innocent smile and soft voice should have robbed her words of sarcasm. Nonetheless, he narrowed his eyes and watched her closely as he replied, "For that amount, you could take your pick, Miss Shaw. Be sure to inspect every available specimen before making your purchase. So many variables in quality, don't you know? You want to buy the best."

Nodding in acknowledgment, she fluttered her lace fan, saying solemnly, "I don't intend to buy a pig in a poke."

"I say, Kent, you're not supposed to talk in riddles none of us understand. 'Tisn't polite," Lamprey complained. "Besides, we need an answer to another question right now. Dunstan here claims members of Travellers don't speak to each other on the premises. Silliest thing I ever heard. You're a member there. Tell him he's been fed a line of rubbish. There's a tenner riding on it."

Fitz swallowed a smile. This would probably be the first time in his dismal life Dunstan ever won a bet. In all seriousness, he answered, "Why should the members speak to each other? They've all travelled five hundred miles or more from London, so each knows all there is to know. Why talk about it? I find the atmosphere rather restful."

Sierra's laughter joined the rest before she commented, "Back home we call that a graveyard."

"Others have already made that comparison, Miss Shaw," Nigel Brockington commented cheerfully. "Besides, the whole world knows Kent never does anything. I can't imagine why he needs rest."

Before Fitz could defend himself, the strains of a lilting waltz burst from the musicians. The tall, dark-haired man who had been listening to the wager and teasing banter with

43

a disapproving expression on his face turned to Sierra and asked, "May I have this dance, Miss Shaw?"

Fitz watched as Francis Lancaster led his partner toward the other couples in the center of the room. Whatever was a prig like Lancaster doing in the company of Lamprey and Dunstan? Or for that matter of Sierra Shaw? The serious-minded banker was at least fifteen years older than the other men. He usually adjourned to the card room at these functions, where, between pontificating on the rise or fall of interest rates and conveying the impression he carried the stability of the country on his shoulders, he recruited funds to battle social ills while his friend Nigel Brockington mingled with the other guests.

Neither could he be the banker who had guided Sierra through the intricacies of the pound sterling. Lancaster and Brockington were both with Child's, on Fleet Street, and Sierra had been engaged at Lloyd's.

For a man who professed disapproval of anything of a frivolous nature, Lancaster acquitted himself well on the dance floor, Fitz decided. But then who wouldn't if partnered with the tiny, graceful American?

He found himself envying the stiff arm clasping Sierra's slender body so properly, and was dismayed by the direction of his thoughts. His hands felt damp inside the formal kid gloves propriety demanded. Fitz wanted to rip them off and rest his fingers intimately against the intricate texture of the lace covering her tiny waist. He wanted to breathe in the fragrance wafting upward from the pale silk of her hair.

"I say. There you are, Fitz."

Relieved at the interruption of such appalling thoughts, Fitz turned to meet the earnest, bespectacled eyes of Thomas Bennett. "Good to see you, old man. Arrived back safely from the Dark Continent, I see. Find *Colotis evippe?*"

"The migration was on, and the few I salvaged had fallen by the wayside. Dead, of course, and not good specimens." He drew Fitz apart from the group still rehashing the vagaries of the Travellers' Club. "This was the first time I've tracked them so far, however. Next year, with any luck, I'll find their wintering ground." Bennett's voice tautened, and a lock of his brown hair fell over his forehead.

"That should be high jinks for one and all," Fitz said dryly. "Then I suppose you'll write an exposé of their activities for one of the scientific journals."

"Laugh if you want, Fitz. Once one gets on the trail of these creatures there's an excitement to equal shadowing a man to discover his secrets."

Fitz smiled at his friend's enthusiasm, and applauded his subtle reference to the work they shared. If only he could lure Thomas Bennett from his fascination with moths and butterflies more often; his powers of observation were extraordinary. "Allow me to take your word that your expeditions are the last remaining true adventures. For myself, I prefer the comforts of England . . . a clean bed, civilized meals, with no lions or snakes popping by to tuck me in at night."

"Go ahead. Make jokes. One of these days you'll give in and join me." Bennett's smile broadened. "I've brought you a little souvenir that should whet your interest."

Fitz looked around to be sure no one could hear. The music had ended; he saw Lancaster leading Sierra toward them. "You shouldn't have, old chap."

"I want you to realize what you're missing. My man will deliver it to your place in the morning. Look it over carefully. I expect to see this particular piece hanging in your study." He squeezed Fitz's arm and walked away.

CHAPTER FOUR

Sierra couldn't remember ever being so uncomfortable. Although he danced well, Francis Lancaster had fixed his dark, deep-set gaze on her face, and was treating even her most innocuous replies to his questions as if it they were a sign of her inferiority. His gaze never wavered, but she felt as if the swell of her breasts revealed by the neckline of her gown was a black mark against her.

During the years she'd acted as her father's political hostess, Sierra had dealt with every imaginable sort of man. Lancaster was a new experience. Never before had anyone attempted to make her feel guilty for her existence.

"Unmarried women require parental supervision, no matter what their age. Your father is extremely remiss in allowing such freedom," he scolded. "It is his duty to teach you your proper place and to exert control over your natural inclinations. Why, a man who was unacquainted with you might completely mistake your morals. I admit that I myself have doubts."

Sierra kept a pleasant smile on her lips and said brightly, "You're a self-righteous throwback to prehistoric times. One wonders why the queen hasn't declared you the Minister of Morality."

Anger flickered in his eyes. "Miss Shaw, look at your life. Your announced intention of taking a titled husband back to America with you is immoral."

Sierra struggled to retain her sense of humor. "Mr. Lancaster, I *do* plan to marry whomever I settle on. The idea of raising a whole passel of little lords and ladies just thrills me, it really does."

"Miss Shaw. You are outrageous." The music stopped. Cold purpose filled his voice as he ordered, "Go back to America immediately and submit yourself to your father's will."

While Fitz Kent's sarcastic dig that morning had hurt, Francis Lancaster's presumptuous order was simply high melodrama. Sierra said lightly, "Even my daddy knows better than to tell me what to do. I'm very spoiled, you know."

Lancaster took her arm none too gently and led her from the floor. "Indeed you are. I know only one other person who is as useless and selfish as you. Unfortunately, he has no title to offer." They came to a stop in front of Fitz Kent. "Miss Shaw is anxious to know you better, Kent. Perhaps you can compare notes on the proper method of selecting dress accessories." He stalked away.

Being decanted figuratively into Fitz Kent's lap didn't suit Sierra at all. She'd journeyed to England to discover who was blackmailing her stepmother, not to unravel the puzzle standing before her in exquisitely cut black broadcloth, attractive as he was. Caleb was right. The man was dangerous. And his smile was devastating.

"Lancaster seemed in a bit of a snit." Fitz's gaze followed the other man as he paid his respects to their hostess.

"I'm afraid I wasn't very diplomatic," she answered without guilt, forgetting for the moment that she had any role to play. "In another minute I would have told him he was a hypocritical jackass. He's the type who has his hand up the chambermaid's skirts while she serves his tea, yet he says *I'm* wicked and willful."

"I wouldn't altogether agree with him, Miss Shaw. Perhaps a trifle spoiled and headstrong, but certainly not wicked."

Sierra drew herself up to her full sixty-two inches and stared daggers at him. "There's an old saying about a pot calling a kettle black, Mr. Kent."

Fitz held out his arms in invitation. "Shall we dance while you critique my frivolous nature? If we stand here arguing much longer, people receive the wrong impression."

"And what might that be?" she demanded as he swept her onto the dance floor.

"The only people I know who argue publicly are lovers and ruffians."

Her annoyance wasn't great enough to overcome the surprising heat of his touch. She felt attached to the hand clasping hers, unable to avoid the hard, gloved palm riding with outward respectability at her waist. A current of warmth seemed to connect the two points. Her feet followed his skilled lead automatically, while her brain swirled. When the knowing sparkle in his eyes penetrated her momentary befuddlement and reminded her of her role, she ventured, "Then it stands to reason one of us must be a ruffian, Mr. Kent." She concentrated on keeping her gaze limpid.

He swirled her in an extravagant turn. "As anyone will tell you, I'm a poor creature much more suited to leisure than to troublemaking. Perhaps you're the ruffian in disguise."

"You're an ass. A British ass." Sierra attempted to ease her fingers from his determined hold. The effort was futile. For the first time, she realized he was nearly a foot taller than she. His indolent stance disguised that fact, as it disguised the strength of his well-proportioned frame.

"Ah, but who knows what the future holds for us if I can

convince you to mend your wicked ways? Perhaps we should join forces. You know . . . Brit and Yank, a sort of hands across the sea arrangement?"

His sunny smile was Sierra's undoing and she laughed, grateful for an outlet for her inner turbulence. "Whatever for?"

"Let me help you search for a titled husband. I know everyone worth knowing, Miss Shaw." He lowered his voice to a mysterious whisper. "Even better, I know everything about them."

"What makes you think I need help, least of all yours?"

"Because I'm the best," he said arrogantly. A devastating smile curved his lips, and his eyes held wicked promises. "Perhaps I can change your mind about your requirements."

"What requirements?" she demanded suspiciously.

"You might decide to bestow your hand on someone who doesn't have a title. Someone like me."

My God, the man's serious, she realized, and found herself tamping down a ripple of excitement that weakened her knees. Dredging up composure, she said coolly, "Queen Victoria will dance the cancan in Piccadilly Circus wearing nothing but her knickers before I'd be that foolish."

Fitz was still chuckling as the dance ended. The ridiculous gauntlet Sierra had thrown down appealed to his competitive spirit. The idea of making her eat her words had sudden appeal. He decided he must be mad. Mad or in love. His amusement vanished. Where had *that* impossible thought come from? Suddenly needing time to adjust to the enormity of his discovery, he looked around and saw Dolores Shaw in conversation with Thomas Bennett and a tall, ungainly, dark-haired man with a formidable beard. He guided Sierra toward them, sharply aware of the curve of her narrow waist beneath his fingers.

"Fitz, you must meet my friend Tony Belville. You'll never believe the astounding coincidence. He's just returned from conducting a horticultural expedition in the Transvaal," Bennett enthused. "And just fancy. Mrs. Shaw is keen on plants also!" As he shepherded the little group farther from the dance floor, Fitz heard Sierra murmur, "What delightful irony. You're about to receive your just desserts . . . a discussion of plant families." The idea didn't dismay him in the least. He wanted very much to talk with Tony Belville, but privately, and not about plants. *Anything* was a welcome diversion from his thoughts of Sierra Shaw.

Sierra's report of the evening's events triggered an argument with her aunt which lasted throughout their drive home and continued as they surrendered their wraps to Elkins before making their way to the stairs.

Dolores clutched the newel post and said flatly, "Kent is intrigued by you. Perhaps he's attracted to women who behave unconventionally, but I doubt it. Therefore we must consider the possibility that he suspects you of not being what you seem, Sierra. Speak to him privately and explain."

Dolores paused, then added cautiously, as if mindful of her niece's stubborn nature, "Adrian said you could trust him."

Still burning from her encounter with Fitz, Sierra countered, "He's a conceited flirt. I wouldn't be surprised if he gossiped worse than a woman." She wrenched off one burgundy lace glove. "You know what would happen if I told him everything. He'd spout masculine superiority and attempt to control my activities. Men always want to be in charge, and I haven't time to stroke the undernourished ego

50

of some idiotic tailor's dummy. I can track this bastard down on my own." Sierra turned her back to her aunt and mounted to the third stair.

"You're being ridiculously naive. If we were in America, you would have no difficulty. But here you're in a different world. You're unfamiliar with the customs, the city, the people . . . with everything."

"People are the same all over," Sierra replied flippantly. "I have Russ and Caleb to help, and there's the inquiry agent Russ . . ."

The door from the kitchen area flew open, banging against the paneled wall. Danny the stableboy stood there panting. Dark red streaks marred the sleeve of his gray jersey. "Miss Shaw, you best come quick. Hit's Caleb."

Sierra flew down the stairs and raced through the door, Dolores close at her heels.

They found Caleb sprawled half on and half off the cushions of the worn settee in the alcove of the roomy, brick-floored kitchen. His hair had escaped the leather thong which secured it at his nape. A rough wool blanket from the stable was wrapped around his shoulders, and blood welled from a jagged cut above his temple.

Sierra bent over him, placing her hand on the smooth bronze skin at the side of his throat. Reassured by the steady throb beneath her fingers, she peered at his forehead. "More light, Dolores. The bleeding has nearly stopped, but this wound looks like it will need stitches."

Kneeling, Sierra lifted Caleb's legs onto the seat, leaving his feet to dangle over the end. "Where did you find him?" she demanded of the stableboy as, careful not to move her friend's neck anymore than necessary, she slipped her hand beneath Caleb's head to explore the back of his skull.

" 'E were layin' jist inside t' door. Looked like 'e'd staggered in and fell down like. 'E let me 'elp 'im in 'ere, then fell all of a 'eap."

She ran competent fingers over Caleb's left arm. "If he doesn't revive soon, we'll have to remove his clothes and check for other injuries. Go upstairs and wake Mr. Tremaine. Send him to me, then go to bed yourself." She unbuttoned Caleb's buckskin jacket and pushed it open, then looked up and smiled her gratitude. "And thanks, Danny. You did just right."

Dolores peered at Caleb's head. "The water in the kettle is hot, and everything I need is here. The potboy cut his hand this morning, so my supplies are in the pantry." She wiped at the blood on his face with a clean cloth.

"You know what a baby Caleb is. Sew him up before he wakes, Aunt Dolores. If he doesn't come to by the time you're finished, we'll call a doctor." Sierra kept a tight rein on the panic threatening to paralyze her. She was closer to Caleb than to her own brothers; his mother had been her nurse, and was now housekeeper at Paradise Valley. They had grown up together, competing at lessons under the tutelage of the stern Easterner her father had imported. Almost from birth, they had raced Indian ponies and dominated the rough-and-tumble play of the other children living on the ranch. If her insistence on bringing him to London had endangered his life, she would never forgive herself.

Russ Tremaine arrived just as the needle pierced Caleb's skin. The Paiute's body contracted and he pulled away from the firm hands pressing his shoulders to the cushioned seat. "Help me hold him, Russ," Sierra ordered.

By the time Dolores completed a neat pattern of stitches at the edge of his hairline, Caleb had abandoned his efforts to escape and lay exhausted against the worn cushions, the only sign of life a revengeful glint in his black eyes.

"You can't have other injuries, Caleb. Not after the way you struggled with us. What happened?" Sierra rotated her weary shoulders as she smiled ruefully at her friend.

"Bushwhacked," he answered flatly. "Just like some damn greenhorn." His anger appeared directed at his own stupidity rather than the cunning of whoever had struck him.

"Where?"

"Halfway home. Most of the streets are illuminated, and I decided to walk. City life doesn't give a man a chance to work up a sweat. Besides I'd watched the way the hackney took when it delivered me." Moving cautiously, he lowered his feet to the floor and pulled himself into a sitting position.

"Home from where?" Russ demanded as he tucked his nightshirt more snugly into his hastily donned britches.

"I sent Caleb to nose around at a gin mill that was a favorite of Geoffrey's," Sierra explained. Turning to Caleb, she asked, "Did anyone there remember him after all these years?"

"Someone must have, or I wouldn't have been ambushed."

"Did you see who hit you?" The brutal attack could have injured Caleb seriously. What if his injuries had proved fatal?

"I only know there were two of them, and they knew what they were doing." Caleb winced at the memory. "I ended up sprawled against the side of a building, and before they ran away, one leaned down behind me so I couldn't see his face and said, 'Go back to America. You got no call to be pokin' around here.' " As if it had just occurred to him, he searched his trousers pockets, his hands coming up empty. "They robbed me!"

"The English don't appear to be very hospitable." Sierra recalled Francis Lancaster ordering her to go home. The coincidence of both messages being delivered the same evening intrigued her. Disregarding her elegant gown, she sank to the floor at Caleb's feet. "What happened at The Black Sheep?"

"I'm hungry. And a glass of milk would taste good," Caleb said petulantly. "English beer tastes the way I always thought cow piss would."

"Dolores will make you a sandwich. If you throw it up after that thump on your head, don't blame me. Start talking." The glance of masculine frustration Caleb shared with Russ didn't escape Sierra's sharp eyes. She knew they took a dim view of her single-mindedness.

Russ pulled over a sturdy kitchen stool and perched on it. "Might as well spill it, son. Now that she knows you won't die, she won't let you sleep till you give her the whole story."

Dolores disappeared into the pantry.

"I don't understand this country. Back home the only reason you would hang out in a place like The Black Sheep is if you wanted to lose at cards or get rolled in the alley." Caleb smiled sheepishly, realizing the latter was exactly what happened. "Anyway, I was kind of surprised. About half the people there were real respectable-looking. Some of 'em were dressed just like those dandies I saw going into the Worthington house the other day. But the rest were the dregs . . . didn't look as if they had the price of a pint on 'em. Now that I think of it, they were mostly drinking gin."

Dolores handed him a glass of milk and a plate with a ham sandwich on it. She wrinkled her nose in distaste. "If you drank any of the gin, this food is your last meal. You will undoubtedly die by morning."

Caleb grinned at her, drank thirstily, then continued, "I wasn't fish or fowl in that crowd, and I could see some of 'em looking at me like I was some kind of freak, so I kept to myself. Just sat at a table in the corner and ordered a pint of bitter."

He paused to chew. Sierra pulled the plate from his fingers. "You've had enough. Talk now. Eat later." His teasing wink filled her with relief. Caleb was himself. If he'd been seriously injured, she would have torn apart the whole East End in her search for the culprits.

"Okay, okay. Just like I figured, curiosity being what it is, nearly everyone in that hellhole made some kind of excuse to come by the table. Some were only being nosy, but a few of the dressier types stopped to talk. They all wanted to know where I was from and why I was there. I received some pretty interesting propositions . . ." He grinned mischievously.

"They didn't!" Sierra and Dolores chorused.

"Oh, didn't they?" Caleb smoothed back his thick straight mane. "None of them had ever seen hair like mine. Hell, one of them actually touched it. He sure didn't like what I promised to do with my knife if he put his hands on me again. Anyway, I laid everything out on the table with anyone who asked. Told them I was looking for someone who might remember Geoffrey. Didn't call him a good-for-nothing crook or anything. In fact, I sort of talked like maybe he had a little windfall coming."

"Not too slick, Caleb. What if you'd met someone he owed money? Even after all these years they'd expect to get paid." Russ had moved his stool closer.

"Never heard anything like that, but one fellow remembered him. Sort of an old rumpot with a round belly and a bald head. His coat was pressed, but its cuffs were frayed and he didn't have a chain for his watch. Kept it loose in his coat pocket. The old sot wouldn't spill any beans until I bought him a drink. He said Geoffrey used to come in with a parson of some kind. After Geoffrey left England, the parson only showed up there once in a blue moon."

"Has he seen the parson lately?" Sierra demanded.

Basking in their attention, Caleb finished his milk in one gulp, licked the white rim from around his mouth, and sighed contentedly. "As a matter of fact, he has. Said he saw him getting out of a carriage on Fleet Street last week."

"Fleet Street?"

"Not far from Amen Corner, and the fellow was still dressed in a dark suit. That's how Freddie decided he must be a preacher." He bent to retrieve the plate Sierra had set on the brick floor beside her, winced at the movement, then looked disgustedly at his flat pocket. "At least there wasn't much for the bushwhackers to steal. I gave Freddie five pounds to send us word if he sees the parson again. That makes me feel better," he said before sinking his strong teeth through the layers of bread and ham.

Later that night, in a shabby boarding room in the theater district, a voice said, "Her agent must be directing the inquiries. That savage hasn't the brains to be behind any intrigue, and she's nothing but a crude slut. Turn around." He inspected the makeup and disguise Rex Haliburton would wear to convince Melanie Shaw he was Geoffrey Trowbridge, tilting the lantern in his hand to peer closely at each detail.

He noted with satisfaction the perspiration running down the section of Haliburton's hairline that was still visible. Such fear would keep him under control. "That mask covering one eye and your cheek is a clever touch. The scar extending past the mask to your temple is particularly effective. You're very good at your craft." The clever disguise drew the eye away from the exposed side of Haliburton's face.

The actor drew himself up as if he had been insulted rather than praised. "My skill was never in question. I assumed that was why you hired me."

"You were hired because you look enough like Geoffrey Trowbridge to be his brother. Any idiot can distort himself with cosmetics."

Although his employer used his icy voice like a whip, Haliburton protested. "See here. This little scheme of yours isn't quite within the law, if you get what I mean. Since I'm the one risking my skin, I deserve a little more . . ."

The cold-eyed man seized his left arm and twisted it behind the actor's back until the bone snapped. At Haliburton's scream of pain, his attacker leaned forward and stared deeply into his eyes. "You may now credit another injury to the explosion. Explain that your arm has never healed properly. Perhaps the simple little widow will shed a tear or two over you." He released his hold.

"You leave with Charlie Finn in two days. He'll have my instructions . . . which you will follow to the letter. Or you won't be paid when you return."

His employer strode through the door of the shabby room and disappeared, and Rex Haliburton shuddered at the pain lancing through his arm. He wasn't naive enough to believe he'd be free after he completed his mission. Unless he did a bunk as soon as the loot was transferred, he would never live to return to England. As he cradled the broken limb with his other hand, he wondered if the American stage might have openings for British actors.

CHAPTER FIVE

Two nights later, Fitz sat at his scarred desk arranging and rearranging decoded reports, sorting information according to departments. Since there had been complaints that isolated bits of information could be useful to several ministries, he occasionally disseminated reports wholesale, enjoying the confusion when totally unrelated material crossed the desks of highly placed personnel.

At present, the nerves of the policy makers were raw and suspicion was rampant. He decided the time was ripe for comic relief. Whatever would the Ministry of Works do with a confidential report on the movement of Bedouins in the Sahara? A fleeting grin crossed his face as he penned instructions to Harrison to make a copy of the report for its second destination before sending the original to its proper recipient. Even if no one else appreciated his humor, he, at least, would enjoy creating a little confusion.

Little enough had been pleasurable the past week. Thomas Bennett's report, hidden behind the nose of a grotesque carved African mask, had contained depressing news. More unrest existed in the Transvaal than anyone suspected. Tony Belville, over lunch at the Travellers' Club, had reinforced this, contributing several useful nuggets of information. Conflict there could continue into the next century, and perhaps beyond, in one form or another.

A half-sheet fell from between two papers earmarked for the Ministry of Transport. Glancing at the decoded words, he leaped to his feet and strode to the door. Throwing it open, he shouted, "Harrison! Why was this mixed with all the other rubbish? When did the message arrive?"

Without lifting his bearded chin from the sheet in front of him, Harrison replied, "The one from Sterling? Arrived late this afternoon. Thought you'd noticed it right off."

"Well I didn't, damn it. You should have sent a messenger to me as soon as you saw his name," Fitz argued, then realized he was being unreasonable. He'd issued no orders concerning Sterling's communiqués. "Flaming hell! It's not your fault." His eyes fell to the neatly printed words. "Irish import due May 12. Will deliver home base." Why would Sterling bring Madeleine Dorsey to Kent House in Suffolk? Only if she knew something.

"Hell and damnation!" Fitz threw himself in his chair, leaned back, and studied the ceiling. He had accepted the fact that his father had been murdered. What frustrated him was not knowing why. And by whom. Somehow, someday, he would know.

Moments later his fertile mind busied itself manufacturing a reason to leave London. His prank with the irrelevant information should surface just before he left to meet with Madeleine. His absence would also be an admission of guilt, but the mix-up would furnish a reason for him to absent himself. Deciding he could lay off the prank to overwork, he wrote a response to Sterling assuring local protection.

That left the matter of Sierra Shaw.

He relived her anger with him that evening at the Bennetts', then he recalled her laughter. Not the shallow, flirtatious giggle of a debutante while peeking coyly upward through darkened lashes, but a warm sound of genuine mirth, delivered as she looked directly into the eyes of her listeners, inviting them to join in.

What was the woman up to? Her purported search for a

titled husband had to be a lie. Such a beautiful young woman, backed by her father's wealth, would have no difficulty attracting any man she wanted—unless she truly coveted a title—and Fitz didn't think that was the case.

Disgusted with this train of thought, he gathered the papers, stacked them in the wire basket on Harrison's desk, and slipped from the building, exiting from the damp alley onto Charing Cross Road. He preferred not to think about what lurked in the puddles he'd splashed through.

" 'Ello, lovey. Be needin' a bit of a tumble?"

The plump, red-haired prostitute's eager hands fumbled at his waist before Fitz could twist away from her. He grasped her wrists tightly, causing her to release the gold watch she'd filched from the sagging pocket of his worn waistcoat. "Good Christ, Sal! You're getting better all the time. Going to take up picking pockets when you get too old to make a living on your back?"

"Ain't thought about it." Her coarse voice dropped to a whisper. "There be a pair of gulls on the street ternight. Fresh t' pluck, as me mam would say. Thought yer'd want to know." She moved away and nodded her head to the right, in the direction of Seven Dials. "Jist a block er so down. Bloody Jacques and Tiny're after 'em."

Sighing, Fitz flipped her several coins and headed in the direction she'd indicated. Sal would knife, cheat or steal from anyone she considered deserving, but she was oddly protective of the innocents who strayed into the East End. Every few months she waylaid Fitz to point out potential victims. He always responded, frequently discovering that most of her charity cases had no desire to be rescued.

Anonymous in his threadbare suit, his shoulders slumped, Fitz travelled the crowded sidewalk at a deceptively rapid pace. From beneath the brim of his battered cap, his sharp gaze swept the squalid area. He ignored the whore delivering her wares while leaning against the front of a deserted storefront and the drunken groups watching or staggering past on the way to further dissipation. The pair he sought could be anywhere by now. They must be obvious, or Sal would have described them in detail.

Slipping through the crowd, he travelled nearly a block before he identified the pair sauntering jauntily along the crowded sidewalk fifty yards ahead. The stocky young man, probably in his early twenties, and his companion, surely no more than a young boy, weren't bothering to disguise their wide-eyed interest in their surroundings. Both were clad in trousers topped by loose jackets of matching rough leather. The boy wore a knit cap pulled down over his ears, even though the evening was pleasant. The older of the pair wore some kind of billed cap, and his hair . . . his black hair was tied at the nape, its length extending well below his shoulders.

Fitz knew their identity even before he accelerated his footsteps. Sierra Shaw and her Indian groom! By all that was holy, if the pair wasn't killed by the time he reached them, he planned to make their death fact. As the two strolled past an alley, two larger figures appeared from nowhere and pulled them into the dark opening.

Fitz broke into a run, dodging several groups of furtive-looking individuals. He avoided the arms of a red-haired whore whose breasts rode high above a tightly laced black corset. A rowdy group of well-dressed youths surging from the door of a disreputable pub nearly carried him with them. The denizens of the streets were a volatile lot. If he called too much attention to his mission, they were likely to turn on him, and then all would be lost. The sound of his own pulse pounded in his ears, muting shouts, raucous laughter, and the off-key music of a motley collection of musicians gathered beneath a street lamp. Fitz heard them all as from a distance.

He was ten feet from the alleyway, the pistol he carried at the small of his back clutched in his sweating hand, when Caleb and Sierra stepped back onto the broken sidewalk. Neither appeared the least bit ruffled, and they continued in their original direction as if they had never been interrupted.

"What the hell?" Fitz paused to glance into the alley. In the diminished angle of light from the flickering gas lamp across the street, he saw what looked like two heaps of discarded clothing attempting to stand.

As they continued their way along the partially lit street, Caleb said disgustedly, "Never knew a town could have so many bushwhackers. Now that I know the rules, it's almost like a game." He turned to stare at a partially dressed young woman who crossed the street to lean into the open door of a hansom cab which had stopped at the curb.

Sierra, scarcely winded from tossing the smaller of the muggers over her shoulder, grinned at him. "You needed my help tonight. The two of them might have nailed you."

"Not a second time. You know, if your father ever learns I took you to a place like this, he'll fire my whole family."

Sierra took his arm, ignoring the exhortations of a scrawny little man peddling the watches hanging inside his black swallowtail coat which had seen better days. "If he should find out, I'll tell him I intended to accompany you whether or not you wanted me, so you came to protect me. Are we far from The Black Sheep?" she asked, exhilarated by their recent encounter.

"Just around this corner. Now remember, let me do the

talking if the parson's here tonight. You'll give yourself away as soon as you open your mouth."

Sierra pulled her cap down more snugly. She hoped the ashes she had rubbed into her face and neck hadn't worn off. She looked down at her hands. The ancient fingerless knit gloves revealed fingernails so thick with grime she doubted she would ever get them clean.

Caleb pulled open the rugged door. The fetid stench of filthy bodies, blended with an acrid pall of smoke and spirits, filled Sierra's nostrils. She fought an overpowering urge to leap back into the street, where at least the miasma passed for fresh air. The noise in The Black Sheep was nearly as overwhelming as the smells. In spite of her discomfort, she shivered with excitement; she was actually inside a London gin hell. Reaching for Caleb's sleeve, she tugged urgently. When he looked back over his shoulder, she mouthed, "How will we find him in this crowd?"

Before she finished speaking, a hand snaked from nowhere to snatch Caleb's other arm, and Sierra kept her hold for fear of losing him in the jostling crowd.

Little light reached the corner booth Freddie Ormsby pushed them into. "Here he is, my good man. The parson I spoke of," he announced with a broad gesture toward the corner of the bench.

The dark figure was nearly indistinguishable from the wall. "What can I do for you good folk?"

A sinking feeling overtook Sierra's spirits. The man's gentle voice sounded like exactly what he claimed to be. A parson. She followed Caleb down onto the bench.

"Do you remember anything about a low-down skunk named Geoffrey Trowbridge?"

Caleb's directness caused the man to lower his head, as if searching his memory. "Geoffrey Trowbridge. Ah, yes. A young man from a privileged background who had gone astray. I tried my best to encourage him to mend his ways. The company here is . . . disastrous to someone with weaknesses."

Freddie Ormsby emitted a snort of disbelief, and the dark-suited figure patted his hand. "You're willful, Freddie, but I have faith you will one day find your way to the light. One day Reverend Booth will welcome you to the Army's fold."

"Trowbridge," Caleb reminded the parson.

"Ah, yes. I suggested he emigrate to America. I don't know whether he took my advice because he intended to turn over a new leaf or because he was fleeing the consequences of some misdeed."

In the village of Upper Whiddlesby, Lady Heloise Lockwood had just finished perusing her morning post. "What an amazing coincidence," she commented dryly, comparing the contents of the recently arrived telegram and the letter written in graceful feminine script lying beside her breakfast plate.

"Wot's up now?" Teapot in hand, Molly O'Day paused at her mistress's shoulder and peered at the correspondence with the familiarity of a long-time servant.

Heloise pointed to the letter. "This is from the young American Adrian wrote about. She very prettily requests my sponsorship for presentation at court. Not an impossibility, even though the lists have been full for months. The telegram is from Fitz Kent, suggesting I hasten to London to keep the very same young lady out of trouble."

"Hmmmph!" Molly thumped the porcelain teapot back onto the silver tray. "That sneaky rascal ain't proper company for decent women. More 'n likely she'll be safe enough if she jist keeps away from the likes of 'im."

"You misunderstand Fitz, Molly. He faces enormous difficulties in a thankless job and acquits himself admirably. But now I've three viewpoints of the American—Adrian's glowing letter about her, Fitz's apprehension, and what I read between the lines of her own note. Intriguing." She lifted the exquisitely embroidered linen napkin beside her plate and patted her lips before rising from her chair. "I believe I must discover the truth for myself. The morning train leaves Cambridge at eight-fifteen, does it not?"

"It *wasn't* a needless risk," Sierra protested to her aunt's back as Dolores knelt to examine a plant budding near the deserted path at Kensington Gardens. "We learned where Geoffrey got the notion of going to America." Dolores stood. Sierra decided their argument over last night's excursion was having little effect on her aunt's enjoyment of the botanical specimens and decorative plantings.

"Caleb is not a reliable investigator in London. You require someone who knows how to proceed in the various sections of the metropolis. Bushwhackers, indeed. Caleb's informant sounds like a ne'er-do-well . . . or a swindler. This Freddie person *had* to have known the man was with the Salvation Army. Their uniform is most distinctive."

She brushed a twig from her skirt and continued, "I still think the best course would be to approach Mr. Kent. Or go to Scotland Yard."

"No," Sierra said firmly. She had every intention of avoiding Fitzhugh Kent in the future. His shrewd, inquisitive eyes missed nothing; she felt as if she were skewered beneath the lens of a microscope. And then there was her inexplicable desire to touch him, to burrow her hands beneath his impeccable tailoring and fastidious perfection to absorb his vitality through her fingertips. The very thought warmed her cheeks. "I don't need help."

"Then prepare yourself for a very long stay. You, Russ and Caleb aren't suited to such a task in a foreign country." Dolores continued along the brick path.

But today, in the middle of a park, with the pale spring sunshine burying itself in the greening branches of trees and shrubs, the soft breeze stirring the curls at her neck, and the earth moist and redolent at her feet, the thought of a prolonged visit held a certain appeal.

No press of people crowded the pathway, and the buildings set cheek by jowl outside the park faded in the distance. She sensed a welcoming, as if it were preordained that she stand in this exact place at this precise moment. Sierra drew a deep breath and looked up at the sky.

She'd sent the inquiry agent back to Suffolk with Russ to ask more specific questions. Sierra envied his trip into the country. "Would that be so very bad?" she answered belatedly.

Dolores's steps quickened, her destination the evergreen topiary at the turn in the path ahead. The gangly figure of Tony Belville approached from another direction.

"Sierra, I love my new sister-in-law, but this is your father's problem, and you should have presented it to him. He would have told the blackmailer to do his worst, and the entire scheme would have dwindled to nothing."

"I don't think so. He would much more likely have barged around like a wounded bull. You know how he gets. And think of poor Melanie if this should become public."

They stopped in front of the yew, which bristled with soft new shoots threatening to distort its sleek swan shape.

"She's tougher than you think, or she wouldn't have survived marriage to Geoffrey Trowbridge. When will you realize you needn't take care of everyone in your family? Let them survive on their own," Dolores hissed before turning a welcoming smile toward Belville.

Fortunately, her aunt and the scientist began to discuss some of the more exotic plants the gardens contained, and Sierra was left to stew. How dare Dolores suggest confiding in a stranger, and a disturbing stranger at that? She would locate the blackmailer herself. Her inquiries had already stirred interest, and her plan to announce she had brought the certificates with her would be sure to draw him into the open like a magnet.

Later that afternoon, his back propped against the pilastered wall of Lord Glenwood's music room, Fitz watched the guests file in. Sierra had not yet arrived, and he wasn't sure what he would do when she did. Last night he could have killed her himself, purely out of panic at her idiotic recklessness. After following her and Caleb into The Black Sheep, he had been able to observe only from a distance. He couldn't imagine why they had risked entering such a place to meet with a soldier in the Salvation Army.

His mystification had deepened after reading the background check he'd requested on Sierra Shaw. The contents caused him to question his own powers of observation.

The woman described in objective terms bore no more similarity to the diminutive blonde beauty invading London society than an American bloodhound resembled a Yorkshire terrier. He damned himself for a blind fool. The blunt man-hunting heiress in search of a title was a far cry from a twenty-five-year-old woman who had successfully acted as Washington hostess for her father for six years, simultaneously supervising the business interests of a cattle empire so vast it was measured in miles rather than acres.

67

The subject of his thoughts, daffodil-yellow silk and quivering ecru lace emphasizing her tiny waist, entered the room. Her head was tilted back, and laughter burbled delightedly from her throat in response to something Devon Carrington had said. Fitz felt the muscle in his left cheek jump. *Bloodyhell!* Carrington, an earl with a more than tidy fortune, wasn't for sale, but the little American might make an exception. Despite his lack of direction, Devon was a man he respected, even though his green eyes caused all the debs to swoon. He was also one of the few informal agents Fitz counted as a friend.

Fitz pushed away from the half-pillar. "Carrington. Miss Shaw. Good to see familiar faces." He assumed the lazy social smile that endeared him to an endless parade of hostesses.

"Surprised to see you here, Fitz. You usually avoid amateur tenors." Carrington's dark brows arched questioningly.

"Lady Glenwood called in an old favor. The singer's her second cousin, and she promised him as many men as doting elderly women in the audience this afternoon." He eyed his friend curiously. "How did she manage you?"

"She told me Miss Shaw would be in attendance."

Fitz took an immediate dislike to the shark-like smile Devon bestowed on his companion.

Sierra's laughter, enhanced by the excellent acoustics, surrounded them. She looked up into Devon's eyes. "We have a word for lies like that in America, but I shouldn't use it in polite company. Do Englishwomen actually believe such nonsense? It's a wonder their fathers don't horsewhip the lot of you."

Her escort smiled devilishly. "You're much more perceptive than those innocent girls just out of the schoolroom.

May I show you the sights of London?"

"Carrington will be much too busy with his hobby, Miss Shaw. Did you know he raises prize-winning dahlias?" Fitz interposed smoothly. "I, on the other hand, promise to leave no alley or byway unexplored. I imagine you'd even enjoy a glimpse of the unpalatable side of life in our fair city."

Suspicion flickered in Sierra's eyes, then disappeared. "Why, Mr. Kent, are you sure you can squeeze me into your schedule? You might not have enough time to visit your tailor."

Fitz smiled at her contemptuous appraisal of his dark brown cashmere suit. "No sacrifice is too great. Particularly when it will further friendly relations between our countries. I wouldn't want you to miss a single exciting excursion." He leaned closer. "Besides, you need my help with your other project."

From the corner of his eye, Fitz snagged Devon's narrowed gaze. Fortunately, the man was acute, more than quick enough to interpret the infinitesimal frown Fitz directed at him.

"Fitz is your man for any task, Miss Shaw." He looked over his shoulder and sighed. "Looks as if the butchered arias are about to start. Shall we take those seats at the end of the last row before Lord Glenwood appropriates one of them for himself?"

Satisfied to have insinuated himself into their company, Fitz followed, maneuvering Sierra into the middle. He was furious he hadn't seen through her masquerade instantly. Then her scent enveloped him and his lower body tightened. Damn her! She was an intriguing mystery, nothing more, nothing less. But what was she up to?

Oblivious to his inner conflict, Sierra inquired, "Is that

Lord Morton with Lady Morton? I met her at the Bennetts' the other evening, but she was accompanied by a different man."

Fitz glanced at Devon and shrugged, leaving him to find a tactful way to explain Lady Morton's butterfly existence. Devon grinned back. "Lady Morton is *never* seen with Lord Morton. They loathe each other. I doubt she's even wished him good day since she presented him with twin sons two years ago. An heir with an identical spare. Now that the line is assured, she rather enjoys variety."

"Publicly?"

"And privately, I'm afraid."

"Back home we have a name for women like her."

Taking pity on Devon, Fitz offered, "Actually, quite honorable rules exist about that sort of thing. Many women aren't pleased with the marriages their families arrange for them. Conversely, some men have difficulty expressing their gratitude to brides whose settlements have just rescued their estates from bankruptcy."

Sierra grinned. "You're making fun of me again. Even though I'm hunting for a titled husband, I'd never marry someone I despise."

"Then it's even more important that you accept my assistance," Fitz pointed out. Suddenly it was imperative that she agree.

Interrupted in the act of settling the silken skirts of her gown more comfortably, she turned to look him full in the eyes. "You know, I believe I will, Mr. Kent. How much will you charge?"

Aware of the possibility that he could drown in the depths of her blue gaze, Fitz teased, "Maybe I'm hoping you'll have to arrange for the queen to do her dance in Piccadilly Circus." She had acquiesced too easily. What prompted her sudden change of heart? He continued, "This will be the sort of challenge I enjoy. Locating the owner of an impoverished title who will welcome you with open arms is the easy part. Finding one you respect is more difficult. And convincing one to return to America with you may be next to impossible." He nodded toward his friend. "Carrington isn't eligible, you know. He has too much money."

"Of course he isn't. I knew that as soon as I met him." Sierra's smile dismissed Devon Carrington as if he were five feet tall, bald and covered with warts. "I've just realized trusting to chance may take too long. Would you bring me a list of possibles tomorrow so we can begin my search right away?"

"I shall appear on your doorstep at eleven in the morning," he said, joining the tepid applause greeting the appearance of a willowy young man whose thin mustache resembled an underfed centipede.

CHAPTER SIX

Tuning out the tenor, Sierra occupied her mind by mulling over her acceptance of Fitz's offer. In a way, she was taking her aunt's advice. Ordinarily, she wouldn't have leaped to such an impulsive decision, but his pointed remarks were too close to her activities the night before. He couldn't possibly know about her visit to The Black Sheep, could he?

The trick would be to keep the man seated next to her so busy searching for the perfect marital candidate that he never stumbled on the real reason for her presence in England. Only four people aside from herself knew of the threat to her father's happiness and career—her aunt, Russ, Caleb and Melanie. And she had no intention of sharing a dark family secret with a stranger, least of all Fitz Kent.

She studied his profile from the corner of her eye. His mahogany lashes were thick and even, like a doll's. A tiny scar broke the line of his right eyebrow, and he had a slight irregularity on the bridge of his otherwise straight nose. The result of an encounter with a hard object? Another scar shone white below the right corner of his lower lip, which tightened each time the soloist soared one half step short of the high note he sought. Rather than marring his features, the imperfections enhanced them.

Even in repose, he looked alert. Fitz Kent might pretend to be nothing more than a tailor's delight, but Caleb's assessment was accurate; he concealed a fit, muscled physique beneath excellent wool and craftsmanship. He also wouldn't back down if she pushed him, and if they should collide . . . Tiny goosebumps rose along her spine at the thought.

The soloist's showy final high note, again slightly flat, drew her back to the present. The tenor bowed, acknowledging the smattering of relieved applause as if the clapping were a tribute. Sierra dropped her hands to her lap for fear of encouraging an encore and murmured, "If he'd been singing back home in Paradise Valley, the wolves in the hills would be howling by now."

Her companions' laughter nearly drowned out the voice of their hostess announcing, "Please be so kind as to repair to the dining room for refreshments."

"If you gentlemen will excuse me, I must see how long my aunt plans to stay." Sierra stood and threaded her way through the crowd, only to discover Dolores besieged by mothers with sons and nephews in tow. Her arrival was greeted by a circle of eager faces, and she resigned herself to the inevitable introductions. Minutes later, she whispered in her aunt's ear, "Oh, God, I can't stand this."

With no end to the parade of eligibles in sight, Sierra felt trapped. Her head pounded and her stomach was in knots. She wondered if her lips could lock in a meaningless curve. "Why do they all seem so young?" she demanded.

"Because they are," Dolores retorted, drawing her away from the crowd of young hopefuls toward a retiring room.

In spite of her headache, Sierra smiled darkly. "I was never that young." She had skipped the customary introduction to society when she became her father's hostess. The years of mingling with mature men who filled positions of power had taught her to view those her own age as immature.

Even Devon Carrington, who appeared to be in his early thirties, gave the appearance of irresponsibility. Fitz Kent was the only man she'd met so far that she suspected of maturity, and possibly even power. She quashed the errant thought. It had no bearing on her present problem.

After her departure, Devon grinned at her retreating back. "Couldn't you think of anything more dashing than dahlias, Fitz? Really, you're losing your touch. She's a fetching little thing, though. Looks as if she's made of spun sugar, and talks 'straight from the hip,' as she would say. All that openness leads a man to wonder what's beneath it." His eyes narrowed, then he smiled again. "Our devious little English girls are safer. They never look you straight in the eye, but they know the rules of the game."

Devon's confession comforted Fitz. "Shouldn't think any of that would matter if one needed money badly enough."

"Which I don't, thank God. Mind you, I plan to stick around for the finale. Should be amusing to see who she finally settles on. If she weren't so insistent on a title, you might try for her yourself. You could toss your job and flee to the United States. Then I could dissipate myself without you disturbing my peace."

"Sorry, old boy. I wouldn't enjoy wearing a dog collar and chain, even if it was gold," Fitz answered lightly. Leave England? He'd as soon throw himself into the Thames, which had been dirtier than ever this spring. His work was his life, as it had been his father's before him.

"Look, she's coming back, and she's acquired an entourage," Devon said. "Locksley's carrying her plate, and Bowden's hefting the wineglass. I don't even know the two sprouts following them. Oh, this is too rich."

"Disappear, Carrington," Fitz ground out.

Devon's left eyebrow quirked upward. "But the fun's

just beginning. I want to watch the lads make asses of themselves."

Fitz smiled confidently. "They won't be around long enough for you to see. I'm getting rid of them. The lady has some questions to answer about her activities."

"Do you think she's here to steal the Crown Jewels?" Devon jibed just before Sierra reached them. Turning, he bent gracefully over her hand. "So glad you've returned so I can take my leave properly, Miss Shaw. I'm scheduled to meet my mother. She's having a crisis of some sort and requires my assistance." With that, he was gone.

Fitz wasted no time. He murmured, "You've certainly been busy." He then stared Locksley into relinquishing the plate of sandwiches and pastries, which he placed on the marble-top table at his side. With another look, he convinced Bowden to surrender custody of the crystal wineglass. This done, he said tersely, "Miss Shaw and I have business." The four backed away, bumping into each other.

Sierra took a cucumber sandwich, which she pretended to nibble before observing, "You're just like a skunk at a picnic."

"Would you mind dispensing with the homespun aphorisms in my company? I doubt you regaled your father's guests with them in Washington," Fitz said, watching her closely. He was gratified to see her fingers tighten on the crustless slivers of bread. A half slice of cucumber slipped slowly from the filling. "Allow me." He caught the pale vegetable between two fingers and dropped it into the vase of spring flowers next to her plate, then pulled out his handkerchief and wiped his glove. The fastidious side of him sighed at the ruined leather.

"Maybe I did." Sierra sank her white teeth into the fillingless sandwich with every appearance of enjoyment.

"You're a cool one, I'll give you that. I was taken in at first." Fitz smiled blandly, gazing about the room as if their conversation were trivial.

"Is that supposed to be a compliment?" She tilted her head to one side and smiled enigmatically before sipping her wine.

Her teasing pose amused him, and he nearly forgot to be annoyed. "You have no idea how much that admission cost me." As if changing the subject, he said, "I suggest you exercise greater care during your explorations of the city."

"My aunt and I explored Kensington Gardens this morning. Surely that's safe enough, and we enjoyed our time there very much. We've been inundated with invitations of all kinds, so I'm afraid I've very little time for sightseeing."

Her eyes were wary now. Justifiably, Fitz thought, because he was about to deliver a warning. "You were fortunate to have had a reliable escort last night. Roughnecks and thieves have a bad habit of pulling unsuspecting pedestrians into alleys. Some quite nasty crimes have taken place in that kind of situation."

Favoring him with an ingenuous smile, she said, "My father warned me about the exact same thing before I came to London. He also said the varmints I'd meet in society would be much more dangerous than those on the streets."

"One should always take care, Miss Shaw. Even experienced people have been caught off guard, in or out of society. Of course, some parts of London are more dangerous than others." Fitz watched for a flicker of acknowledgment in her wide blue eyes. When he saw none, his reluctant admiration grew. She and her groom had fought off two men and walked away. She was good. Damn good.

The American attaché's wife joined them, smiling

broadly. "I see that my little party managed to launch you socially, Sierra." She turned toward him. "Good to see you again, Fitz." Her voice lowered. "Wasn't the tenor perfectly dreadful?"

Sierra's spontaneous laughter rang out, and Margaret Worthington joined her before they embarked on an animated conversation. Fitz wondered why he had failed to pick up on their friendship during the tea at the attaché's residence.

Fitz's life had never been carefree. His father had trained him for the family business at a young age by outlining hypothetical household problems and challenging him to accumulate enough facts to present a solution. He was an observer, aware of everything that occurred around him, an expert at reading body language and correlating the subsequent impressions to what he heard. Until he met Sierra Shaw. Was her masquerade really that flawless? Or had he been so blinded by his attraction that he overlooked the obvious?

How wonderful it would be to concentrate instead on his body's response to her scent, to the husky, slightly breathy quality of her voice, to the fluid grace of her hands as she described someone she'd met to her friend.

"I must rush. I promised Hal I would be home in plenty of time to dress for a particularly dreary dinner party. Please call one day next week and tell me how your quest is progressing, Sierra." Mrs. Worthington slanted a smile at Fitz. "I've scheduled another tea for new arrivals a week from Friday, Fitz. Perhaps you'll meet someone of interest. May I count on you?"

"But of course. I won't promise to *like* any of them, however. The American sense of humor appears to be an acquired taste. Your countrymen take too much pleasure in misleading simple Englishmen.”

"I've never thought of you as simple, Fitz. You never appear to be out of your depth." She turned to Sierra and urged, "You must enlist Fitz to help you in your search. He knows simply everyone, and can tell you which men to avoid."

If Fitz hadn't been watching closely, he would have missed the brief, horrified expression Sierra tried to hide at Margaret Worthington's use of the term "search." "You appear appalled, Miss Shaw."

"I'm afraid I was wondering who sold that unfortunate dress to the overweight lady talking with our hostess." Soft color crept up her cheeks. As if embarrassed, she supplied hurriedly, "I apologize. My daddy taught me it was rude even to *think* such unkind things. He impressed that on me just before he made me promise never to lie, but his second commandment has always been easier to follow than the first."

Fitz grinned, amused by her quick diversion of his question and convenient adaptation of her father's dictums. "I'm reassured to hear of your steadfast dedication to the truth, Miss Shaw."

His quick, slashing grin had nearly been her undoing. In spite of the cat and mouse game he played, for that brief instant, she had trusted him. Now he was making fun of her, and she had no choice but to pretend she hadn't the slightest idea what he implied. He had investigated her past and somehow knew where she had been last night. What else did he know? She felt as if she were suffocating, and clutched her glass convulsively.

"My dear Miss Shaw, you've a disconcerting habit of disappearing into your thoughts in my company. You'll never bring one of our impoverished sprigs up to scratch if you don't converse with a little more spirit."

His words wrenched her thoughts back to the present. "I'm practicing. Aunt Dolores says I speak too freely."

Fitz pried her fingers from around the empty wineglass and set it on the table. "I assure you, talk of gold and silver mines is never amiss. With your wealth, the young men and their families will gladly overlook your Yankee upbringing. You could have hair on your chin and a dreadful squint, and no one would notice. It's rather too bad you didn't think to arrange for a presentation. The royal stamp of approval would be the final touch."

"What a delightful coincidence. I received a telegram today from Lady Heloise Lockwood. Adrian Harding referred me to her, and she's agreed to sponsor me. I expect her in town tomorrow afternoon." Glancing up, Sierra glimpsed Fitz's brilliant hazel eyes brimming with mirth. What could he possibly find so amusing?

"I'm going to get a book from the library and read myself to sleep, Aunt Dolores. I'll see you at breakfast." Sierra desperately needed to take her mind off a day which certainly had not progressed to her advantage. The conversation with Fitz Kent that afternoon had replayed in her thoughts throughout an interminable dinner with the Earl of Shipham and his countess, providing a background to bad food, decaying surroundings and the disgusting attentions of the Shipham heir. The viscount had appeared to have spent the afternoon inspecting the wine cellar.

The gas sconces in the narrow hall were turned low as Sierra made her way to the little library she and Russ used as an office. She pushed open the door and reached for a match from the small brass box attached to the wall on her right. In the light from behind, she could just make out the gloomy painting of a forest scene which hung between the tall windows.

The odor of burning candle reached her nostrils at the same time she felt, rather than saw, a movement to the left of the picture. Crouching, she slipped her derringer from its holster above her ankle and demanded, "Who's there?"

The heavy drapery billowed in response. Evading furniture by memory, Sierra raced across the room and snatched back the pleated velvet with her left hand, the small gun steady in her right. Only garden-scented darkness greeted her through the open lower sash. Faint moonlight illuminated the emptiness of the tidy little balcony. From the corner of her eye, she saw movement atop the brick wall at the back of the small garden, then nothing.

"I will be damned," she murmured delightedly as she pulled down the sash and fastened the latch. She struck a match and lit the lamp. In the circle of light she saw the papers she'd left neatly secured beneath a paperweight spread across the mahogany surface. Drops of candle wax pooled next to one sheet.

Sierra smiled with satisfaction. Their inquiries had rattled someone enough for them to come investigating. Her smile widened as she extinguished the light, all thoughts of reading matter banished from her mind. As she crossed the room toward the hall, she bent to tuck the little pistol back into its holster. "Curiosity is a terrible thing. You come close another time, and we'll be waiting for you."

Sierra's amazing announcement played and replayed in his thoughts as Fitz mounted the stairs to his office. He would give anything to see her face when she met the redoubtable Heloise. To the uninitiated, the woman was a terrifying old tartar; she'd tear holes in the little American's masquerade within an hour of meeting her. He thanked his stars that their shared profession had established a soft spot for him in the noble lady's heart.

When Fitz entered the outer office, Harrison peered over his glasses at him, a brusque jerk of his head to the left his only acknowledgement of the presence of a small, wiry figure with a cap pulled down over his face. Fitz nodded at his visitor, gathered an untidy stack of messages from the basket on Harrison's desk, and waved his hand for the caller to follow him.

"Didn't expect to see you this month. Come into my office." His casual words covered the quickening of his pulse at the sight of the agent who reported happenings in the northern English countryside. The farms and villages were prosperous; no major labor unrest had surfaced in years.

Mickleby was simply a precaution. His cartage business took him from place to place, and the man had a genius for sensing anything out of the ordinary. Fitz shut the door behind him, dropped the papers on the spotted blotter, and took his place behind the desk, gesturing toward the worn leather chair opposite.

"What's brought you to London?" he asked.

Mickleby pushed the cap high on his forehead, revealing small, close-set eyes and a thin nose that veered to one side. "Strange goin's on in your own briar patch, for sure. Never did run into so many people askin' questions."

"Describe both. The people and the questions," Fitz prompted sharply. Inquisitive visitors in the vicinity of Kent House would be disastrous. Madeleine Dorsey was due there in a matter of days.

"A couple of missionary-lookin' types been askin' about you. Wantin' ter know why you don't live on yer farm all the time, like. Your bailiff talked round and about, tellin' 'em about your fine Lunnon ways. Sort of give 'em the idea you was a bit of a nancy-boy, if you must know."

Fitz swallowed a smile. Judson had been at his post since before his birth. What the man didn't know about his own and his father's clandestine activities could be inscribed on the head of a pin. And he hated inquisitive outsiders even under normal circumstances. "Any indication why they're poking around?"

"Looked as if they were tryin' ter get the lay of the land, so to speak. Made themselves right at home in the village, pretendin' they're there ter organize a new Methodist church. Yer know how many's left Chapel in the last year? Forty-seven! People're ripe for somethin' a bit more stiff, looks like. Chapel's bin gettin' a little loose and easy for some folk."

"Judson mentioned something of the sort in his last report. Maybe these two hope I'll join their movement."

"Not after wot Judson told 'em." The network of wrinkles decorating the man's face creased into a smile.

"I must remember to thank him." Mickleby enjoyed dragging out a tale, and Fitz knew he had held the most revealing information for last.

"They asked about your father, too."

Fitz straightened in his chair. "What did they want to know?"

"What he'd done in Lunnon, mostly. Just sort of nosy-like."

"What did Judson tell them?"

The little man smiled slyly. "Said he went ter town ter tup the ladies."

"Clever. We sound like a pair of real Johnnies." He spun his chair around and stared fixedly at the small locked file cabinet tucked in the corner. "Thank you for bringing this to me, Mickleby. I appreciate the information."

"Didn't say I was finished. There's more. A furrin bloke came through the village last week. Talked real slow-like. Said he were interested in your sheep, then allowed as how he were lookin' to buy breedin' stock fer some American." The carter extended his workbooted feet in front of him and stared intently at the toe of the left one.

Fitz bit down on his impatience and fed him the question he wanted. "Did he say what part of America?"

"Out west somewhere. Funny soundin' name. Nee-vah-dah. He sort a' leaned on the middle part. Said it's an Indian name."

Coincidences of this sort delighted Fitz. "Did he mention the name of the man he worked for?"

"Some kind a' politician. Man's rich as a king." His attitude clearly expressed his disrespect for either condition.

Fitz had no doubt as to the identity of the man's employer. "What else did he have to say?"

Mickleby's shoe-button eyes glinted with pleasure, as if he had reached his favorite part of the story. "He were askin' 'bout the Trowbridge family."

Fitz's sixth sense began waving flags. "Was he now."

"Judson said 'twas sad ter speak the truth for once. He tol' him the only one left was that fellow from Australia, then sent him ower ter the old Trowbridge place."

"Judson has an extremely delicate conscience," Fitz commented.

"Ayeh." Mickleby rose and pulled his cap down his forehead, preparatory to leaving. "Anyways, Judson and me thought you ought ter know. Didn't your pa have dealings with a Trowbridge?"

"He did, to my everlasting regret." Fitz rose and leaned

over the desk to shake Mickleby's hand. "I can follow up on the fellow from this end. He's probably straightforward as far as the sheep go, but the Trowbridge inquiries intrigue me. Have you a place to stay tonight?"

"With me daughter and her husband. They've a bit of a place above his bakery."

"Give Jocelyn my regards then. And thanks."

Fitz tilted the swivel chair as far back as possible and propped his crossed ankles on his desk. Bloody hell. The agent, if that's what he really was, had undoubtedly arrived with Sierra Shaw. A report of Geoffrey Trowbridge's fatal accident was in the heavy metal file cabinet in the corner— along with any information even remotely connected to Matthew Kent's death.

Fitz's feet hit the floor with a thump. He wanted to find a board and beat himself over the head with it. The report on Sierra had indicated that Geoffrey's widow had married an American Senator. What an idiot he had been not to make the connection immediately. He hastily scribbled an order asking Harrison to send for verification, but he already knew the name of the Senator. There really was no such thing as coincidence.

In a small, but luxuriously appointed library across town, the most recent letter from Senator Shaw's wife sailed into the cheerful fire in the grate. The heavy linen stationery balanced on the red-hot coals for a matter of seconds, then burst into flame.

"Damn that bitch! After three months of excuses she tells me she doesn't have her *papers* in Washington. The slut left them in the safe in Paradise Valley, and it will take *weeks* to travel there. I want them *now!*" The inkstand followed the letter into the flames. He leaped to his feet, sending the heavy desk chair slamming into the paneled wall behind it. He swept his arm across the desktop, scattering papers and supplies. A crystal paperweight shattered against the brick hearth.

The sound seemed to break the man's tension. He braced both arms on the desk. "The biggest coup ever to occur in the market is within my grasp. I've planned. I've eliminated people. I've waited for the time to be ripe, and now I *will not* lose." He clenched his fingers into tight fists, the tendons at his wrists bulging from the strain.

CHAPTER SEVEN

"Someone searched the library last night," Sierra announced, closing the door of her aunt's room behind her. "Whoever it was escaped out the window just as I entered."

"What's missing?"

Sierra padded over to sit at the foot of the bed. Her aunt's ability to awaken instantly never ceased to surprise her. "Nothing. Whoever it was couldn't have learned anything. The desk held only the invitations we've accepted."

Dolores sat very straight, her braided hair as neat as if it had never touched a pillow. "That could put you in danger."

"I'll alter my schedule. Arriving late to parties is more fashionable here. Caleb can drive the carriage on roundabout routes." Sierra drew her knees up to her chin and wrapped her arms around her legs. "Maybe I'll skip a few engagements. God knows I don't enjoy this society routine. I did so much entertaining in Washington I could sleepwalk through most of these affairs."

Her aunt smiled. "You could if you didn't have to remember to say something ill-bred at least once during each function."

"If you say 'I told you so' one more time I'll tell Caleb to scalp you. The masquerade will be even more difficult after Lady Lockwood arrives, particularly if she's able to arrange a presentation. Women of her generation shock easily, and I can't repay her kindness in such a fashion." She rested her forehead on her knees and turned her face away from her aunt.

"There's something else you might as well know. Fitz Kent offered to assist me in my husband search. Since I don't dare tell him the truth, I accepted."

When Sierra looked up, she saw laughter in the depths of her aunt's eyes. Dolores's lips curved. "The spirits have carried my petitions to Yahweh!" Her aunt's serenity was a family legend, yet the woman had tears rolling down her cheeks.

"Aunt Dolores . . ."

Her reply came between bursts of hilarity. "You have laid yourself open to ridicule from these people. And now you're about to be paid back. Oh, how I wish your brothers could be here to see a real Lady correct you." She mopped at her tears with the linen sheet as her composure returned. "And they will *never* believe an English gentleman actually furnished you with a list of prospective husbands to inspect—as if you were buying calico at the general store!"

Sierra seized a petit point pillow from the foot of the bed and threw it at her aunt. "This is *not* funny. I shall be under severe strain!"

Her aunt's hilarity switched to solemnity as quickly as it took to wink her damp lashes. "You're spoiled. In the past, you've treated any number of fine young men cavalierly. Each of them went on to marry young women who at least *pretended* to be less capable than they were, while you've occupied yourself becoming indispensable to your father and to your family."

"That's ridiculous . . ."

Dolores rested her capable fingers on Sierra's arm. "My dear, any number of American men in powerful positions are terrified of you. How do you think lesser men feel?" Sierra lifted her head and looked into her aunt's eyes, searching for, and finding, the love and compassion which had been offered her freely as long as she could remember. "You're making that up."

"Did you ever notice that no one, *no one,* ever refuses an invitation to your father's house?"

Baffled by such a simple question, Sierra responded, "My father's a very influential man. People realize that."

"I love your father, Sierra, but he's only human, and he makes mistakes the same as anyone else. When you set out to be his hostess, you were determined to be perfect. *You* made each function perfect. *You* limited the guest lists to the select few people involved with whatever issue was most important at the moment." Dolores spoke slowly, as if teaching the alphabet to a three-year-old. "And if you had not headed him off on countless occasions, his own bluster would have kept him from success. Look what you're doing right now."

Sierra still couldn't see the point. "If you gather the most important voices on an issue in one room, you encourage discussion. Think how much time that saves . . ."

"Exactly," her aunt interrupted. "You set up a climate for accomplishment. *You* were the key, not your father. He has simply benefitted from your instincts."

"None of that was due to me. My father is the person with the vote," Sierra argued.

Dolores threw back the covers and swung her legs to the floor, then reached for the wrapper on a nearby chair. "He's also old enough to take care of himself. Besides, he has a wife now."

"This is the last time." Sierra responded defensively. "When this is over I'm going back to Paradise Valley and stay forever."

Dolores tugged the bellpull to signal the maid, then came to kneel in front of her niece. "Where you'll still hold the reins." An uncharacteristic giggle escaped her lips. "I've no doubt you'll settle this business for Melanie, but I find myself half hoping that along the way you fall in love with one of these Englishman, a strong-minded one who loves you but who refuses to allow you to run his life. Then, for once, you'll be compelled to direct your considerable talents toward settling your *own* affairs."

Her aunt's words floated at the edge of Sierra's thoughts three hours later as she inspected the sheet of foolscap Fitz Kent presented with great ceremony. She had nearly cancelled their meeting. Now that his exhilarating presence filled the drawing room, she wished she had followed her first impulse. His bright gaze seemed to mock and tease her. The cursed list was still warm from his hand. The skin at her nape felt both hot and cold at the same time.

"You appear displeased, Miss Shaw." Even his voice taunted. "Surely you weren't hoping I would forget our meeting."

Goaded by his sarcasm, she blurted, "No. No . . . that is, taking you up on this offer is the first impulsive thing I've done for years." Rather than meet his eyes, she scanned the dozen or so names written in slashing script.

"Pity. One's first instincts are frequently best." He came to stand beside her, his gaze fixed on the list. "You may not be impressed by several of these at first glance, but they're all sound men. I included Carrington, although he'd never acquiesce to your plan to take him to America like a lapdog. He's an earl, and he seems attracted, but he's too well-set financially. Do you fancy being a Countess? You could settle here."

Desperate to escape the sharp, citrus scent of his cologne, Sierra turned away to sit on a slipper chair lit by sun sifting through the filmy underdrapes. "Devon Carrington thinks I'm an attractive freak. He'd only marry me if he hadn't a penny to his name. And he'd still tend to give orders. The man I marry must understand that I am in charge of both my money and my own life," she said irritably.

"Come now, Miss Shaw. You're not buying a pet pug, you know."

His patronizing tone of voice goaded her into speaking without thinking. "Don't you dare condescend to me! If you recall, I didn't ask for your assistance. The offer was yours." The challenge she saw in his eyes as he walked toward her brought Sierra to her feet. Her first instinct was to retreat, but she had never before backed away from a confrontation, and she refused to start now.

"I couldn't resist tweaking your independence, Yank," he said softly, his voice belying the civilized menace of his stance. Without breaking eye contact, he pulled the list from her suddenly lifeless fingers. "Have you any other particular requirements? I must be aware of your specific requirements, so I can scratch any unqualified candidates before we waste time discussing them."

His resonant voice was so close to her ear her heart skipped a beat. Her gaze still locked with his, Sierra said stumblingly, "Age. I mean . . . not *too* old. But then . . . not too young, either. I doubt I'd be comfortable . . . married to someone who was younger than I." When he stepped even closer, she held her ground.

"How young is too young?" he queried, settling his hands on her shoulders.

"I'm twenty-five," she blurted, her mind occupied with deciding whether his eyes were more green than brown, or perhaps gray. The subtle tweed of his suit matched his bright gaze. A corner of her mind wondered fancifully if the cloth had been woven with him in mind. Perhaps if she looked at him more closely she could decide which color his eyes really favored. Her shoulders tingled beneath his touch.

"So old? That tears it for young Hensley. Too bad. He was the most promising of the lot. Not a penny to his name, and a moldering old ruin of a mansion to prop up." He grazed her cheek with the tip of one finger. "Whatever has your father been about to keep you on the shelf this long?"

Improbably, the words weren't an insult. His caressing baritone could have tempted a nun to forsake her vows. His breath stirred the curls piled loosely atop her head, and Sierra felt compelled to answer honestly, if only to hear him speak again.

"He's been urging me to marry for years. No one seems to . . . suit." Helplessly, she tilted her face to him as he lowered his head and brushed his lips across hers. Not only did she feel their smooth warmth, in an obscure corner of her mind she thought she heard a sound when they touched hers—a sharp crackle like taffeta petticoats in winter sizzled through her bloodstream.

His arms closed around her and she rose to her toes as if drawn upward by marionette strings. Enough of these electrical sparks, and she would glow.

Common sense warned Fitz that if he had any sense at all he would flee. Deep within his soul, he couldn't believe such a passionate, beautiful woman intended to settle for an unknown milksop who would give her control of their life together. She'd be miserable.

He ignored the voice of reason and gathered her closer with one arm, cupping her slender neck with his other hand. The silky texture of her skin and the rapid pulse beneath radiated through his fingers and raised his own heartbeat.

The intense blue of her eyes nearly disappeared as her pupils dilated. He kissed her again, lingeringly, her response heating his blood. Pulling back an infinitesimal distance, he said, "Close your eyes."

She stiffened for a heartbeat, then yielded when he tightened his grasp. Pleased by the little victory, he smoothed his fingers over the curling fringe of her lashes before pressing a gentle kiss to each eyelid. "Very obedient," he murmured.

"Why, you . . . you . . ." She glared angrily and shoved against his chest with considerable force.

He chuckled. Ignoring her struggles, he clamped her against him. "If you learned compliance, you'd be an acceptable wife for *any* man. Close your eyes again, love."

Fitz expected her resistance, but she fit in his arms so perfectly he pretended not to notice. Instead, he concentrated on gently nibbling at her full lower lip, tracing the curve with the tip of his tongue as he held her in the curve of his body. He sensed the moment she became aware of his arousal.

She stilled. "Don't do this . . ."

Seizing the opportunity, Fitz slipped his tongue between her lips. The taste of her flooded his senses, and his resolve not to soothe his inner confusion with a punishing kiss faltered. She was fragile and soft in his arms, and he wanted to drown in her scent, to luxuriate in the textures of her mouth as she allowed him greater access. He caressed her nape and plunged his fingers into the silken mass of her hair.

Seconds later, he sensed, rather than felt, subtle movement at his ankle. Swallowing a smile, he broke the kiss and swung her around. Crossing one arm over her heaving breasts, he pinioned her arms, while the other anchored her hips against him so tightly she was unable to move her legs.

He blew gently into her ear, then dipped his tongue teasingly into the intricate whorls before saying, "Don't try to play your Indian tricks on me, sweetheart. I know them all."

"Let me go, you low-down bastard!" Even though she knew the move was futile, Sierra arched her back, heaving her hips away from him as far as she could. For the first time, she felt grateful for the padded wire frame holding her skirts away from her. Her body's treacherous reaction to the hard pressure against her belly had surprised her. If she hadn't acted when she did, she would have surrendered to the seductive persistence of his kisses. But his warmth still surrounded her. She felt his steady heartbeat against her shoulder. Held as she was, escape was impossible. If she could free her arms . . .

He murmured teasingly, his breath brushing her ear, "I think I can guess why you've never married, Miss Shaw. You humiliate your suitors by Indian-wrestling them. Did you ever think of proposing to that groom of yours? I'll wager he could take you two out of three."

Damn him! He wasn't even breathing fast. "Don't be ridiculous. Caleb's like a brother." She wrenched her shoulders forward unsuccessfully. "Besides, his people would never accept me as his wife." Giving in to the inevitable, she ceased struggling, inwardly bemoaning the arrogance that had led her to ignore Caleb's warning concerning Fitzhugh Kent. The man was dangerous, all right, but his physical strength wasn't the real hazard. She was perilously attracted. To worsen the situation, she realized her wits were scattered. "All right, you win."

"What do I win?" His lips brushed her ear.

She shuddered. "Damn you, I don't even know what it is you want!" she spat between clenched teeth. Why was he baiting her? From their first encounter, he'd laughed at her and questioned her every statement. Now he'd capped his persecution by kissing her. Her mouth relived the feel of his lips, and a quiver of need shook her. "I promise to behave. Now will you take your filthy hands off me?"

"I'm not sure your promises are worth a great deal," he responded, tightening his hold.

"My word is as honorable as any *man's*."

"I'll try to remember that in the future, my sweet, but before I release you, I want to know your real purpose in London. God knows you need a husband, preferably one with experience taming lions, but I refuse to believe you need to buy one. Your ruse is good, but only a simpleton would believe you."

Sierra nearly told him the truth, but she had no way of knowing how far she could trust Fitz Kent. "Are you calling me a liar?"

His gust of laughter brushed her neck. And then she was free. By the time she turned around, he had moved to lean against the door. His eyes held a determined light, and his lean jaw was set. "You, young lady, are a frustrating mix of intelligence and feminine subterfuge. My instincts warn me you're poking into something over your head, which means at some point you're going to require rescuing. Why do I suspect the task will fall to me?"

He rested his hand on the crystal knob. "If I discover you putting your pert little nose where it doesn't belong, I'll jerk you back by your corset strings and ship you off to your father so fast you won't have time to pack. Perhaps I'll even stoop to notifying him through official channels. I hope he's man enough to give you the spanking you should have had twenty years ago."

Rage and shock held Sierra rigid with anger. No one had ever threatened her before. "You have no authority over me. You can't keep me from so much as crossing the street. Get out of my house, Brit!"

"You underestimate me, Yank. Until you explain your activities since arriving in London, don't be surprised when you look over your shoulder and see me." With an impudent salute and an even more impudent grin, he was gone.

Sierra restrained herself from kicking the paneled door which closed quietly behind him. The man had actually given her an ultimatum. She hurled a piece of wax fruit instead. The impact, followed by the thud as it fell to the floor, was unsatisfying.

Sinking onto the leather ottoman, she rested her chin on her hands. What did he know of "official channels" or following her? "He's bluffing. He has to be," she murmured. She ran the tip of her index finger over her lower lip, remembering his kiss and the drenching pleasure of being held close to his hard, muscular body.

She weakened at the memory. Annoyed with herself, she sprang to her feet to ring for Atkins. "Mr. Tremaine was to return this morning. Have you seen him?" she asked when he appeared.

"I believe he is in the library, Miss Shaw. Shall I summon him?"

Instinctively stiffening beneath the butler's superior stare, Sierra wondered if she should have checked her appearance in the oval mirror above the fireplace before summoning him. Pretending nonchalance, she said dismissively, "That's not necessary. I'll go to him."

With that she swept past and turned down the hall, sneaking a surreptitious glance toward the mirror over the mantel as she passed. Her cheeks were flushed and a pale lock of hair hung loose in back. She willed her hands to stay at her sides until she reached the library door, out of Atkins's sight, then pushed the curl into place before knocking.

Russ's voice bidding her to enter was familiar and dear, and in her vulnerable state she felt a strong surge of homesickness. Fitz Kent's words had her doubting the success of her mission, and she badly needed reassurance. She turned the knob and slipped inside.

"Sierra, I was hoping you'd have time for me. That stiff-assed butler said you couldn't be disturbed." Russ rose from behind the desk and pulled a leather-upholstered chair closer to the one in which he'd been seated. "I killed several birds with one stone while I was in Suffolk. Look at these figures."

Sierra sank gratefully into the seat, warmed by his familiar presence. "*Any* kind of news will be an improvement over the false leads that have shown up during the last few days."

"First off, the agent put me on to a place that raises the best-looking black-faced Suffolk sheep you ever saw. Their wool is short, but it's high-quality, and they're also good meat. They're hardy and breed easily. The bailiff is agreeable to selling a small starter flock. I was thinking that hilly section near the Paiute village would be perfect for grazing sheep."

Sierra accepted the sheet of figures and reached for more paper and a pencil. Working with numbers and talking business calmed her jangled nerves. Even though the sheep's presence could create animosity amongst the other ranchers, they would enable the Paiutes to become self-supporting. She'd have to devise a plan to soothe ruffled feathers. Distracted from the problem which had sent her scurrying for safety, she tabled the project for later study. "This is excellent, Russ, but that wasn't why I sent you there."

Russ's embarrassed smile peeked from beneath his drooping mustache. "Sorry, I got so excited about the sheep I wandered off track. Nobody in East *or* West Suffolk wants to talk about Geoffrey Trowbridge. Finally, I went to the vicar in the same village where I found the sheep. He was cagey about talking, but he sent me to Mrs. Beecham, who was the local schoolteacher ten years ago. *She* sure didn't have a problem gossiping."

"She couldn't have taught Geoffrey. He'd have attended Eton or Harrow. But as a teacher, she'd be aware of everything in the area." Sierra leaned forward eagerly. "Has she seen him?"

"Seems right after she retired, Geoffrey went through the village like a dose of salts, pushing shares in a railroad scheme that couldn't lose, and she bought five hundred pounds' worth, using the better part of a nest egg she'd inherited from her mother."

He rifled through his briefcase and offered her a creased sheet of paper. "In fact, everyone on this list bought five or more shares. They're all ordinary folk who hoped to bolster their savings. They trusted that son of a bitch. Then the project was cancelled. Trowbridge disappeared, and so did the money."

Sierra looked at the names. Russ had identified each of the people by their status in life. "He even stole from the vicar! Russ, no wonder Geoffrey had to get out of England. He must have conned everyone he knew!"

Russ grinned even wider. "And then some. Seems after he disappeared, his father and brother tracked down every buyer they could find, intending to repay some of the money to make up for good old Geoffrey. They would have bankrupted themselves if some bank in London hadn't stepped in and bought back the shares at half value."

Sierra leaned forward in her chair in her excitement. "Russ, the blackmail letter demands Melanie's shares. What if the venture's become viable? If, somehow, Geoffrey is still alive, he'd do almost anything to get Melanie's shares back."

Rubbing his neck with one big hand, Russ leaned back in the chair. "Doesn't have to be Geoffrey. What if he had partners who were even more crooked than he was? They'd do a hell of a lot more than 'almost anything.' "

Sierra was delighted with Russ's discovery. *Take that, Mr. Kent. I don't either need your help.* "As far as we knew, the shares were worthless, but since the blackmailer demanded them, I brought the certificates along in case we needed to use them as bait. I put them in a lockbox at Lloyd's for safekeeping. If Melanie received a response to her first letter, she was to write back that she'd left the shares at the ranch. I wanted to delay a showdown as long as possible."

"You want me to go to the bank and bring them here?"

"No. I don't want those certificates anywhere near me. There's no safe in this house, and while we were out last night, someone searched this very desk. First I have to be sure Melanie's shares are for the same venture as those Geoffrey sold the townspeople in Suffolk. We could be talking about two different schemes." Excitement flooded Sierra. "If they're the same, whoever holds the bulk of them would already have control. Why else would someone be so desperate to acquire Geoffrey's?"

Russ's weathered face crinkled with amusement. "After I

left Mrs. Beecham's, I went back to see the vicar. Seems he feels he was 'rightfully punished for his attempt to gather up earthly treasures.' Said he'd kept one of the shares. Framed it and put it on the wall of his study to remind him never to give in to the sin of greed again."

"What was the name of the company?" Sierra demanded.

"He was cagey about that. Wouldn't let me see the certificate. I didn't like to be too pushy."

She thought for a moment, then said, "I'm going there myself. I'll take a sample with me to compare to his. And while I'm in Suffolk, I'll check out those sheep."

CHAPTER EIGHT

"I'm truly in your debt, Heloise. I wouldn't miss this for all the jewels in the Tower," Fitz said as he assisted Lady Lockwood from his carriage that afternoon.

"Indeed. Must I infer that your protégé has become even more unmanageable in the short time since you wired me?" Heloise adjusted the sleeves of her black brocade jacket to meet the hems of her black gloves, concealing any hint of the cuffs of her starched linen blouse. Her steel-beaded reticule hung precisely from her right arm. She cast a severe look at him as they ascended the shallow stairs. "One assumes your interest in this young woman is entirely impersonal, of course."

Fitz regarded her cautiously. How much should he tell the old martinet? "Actually, my interest is extremely personal. Her employee's been in Suffolk inquiring about Geoffrey Trowbridge." *And I can still taste her lips.* His astounding physical response to Sierra Shaw intruded on what was an intriguing puzzle, a puzzle that might or might not shed light on the mystery of his father's murder.

"I recall being quite amazed that your father had been taken in by that scoundrel," she said, frowning. Sierra's butler swung open the door, and she stepped over the threshold and extended her card between two black-gloved fingers, addressing the servant imperiously. "Miss Shaw is expecting me. Don't dawdle."

Following close behind, Fitz swallowed his laughter. He suspected that until now Atkins had regarded employment by the Americans as an insult to his consequence. Heloise's visit should elevate his employers' status considerably in his eyes, not to mention furnishing bragging rights with other butlers. "You needn't bother to announce me, Atkins. I'm with this lady."

The butler, a stunned expression on his face, ushered them into a sparsely furnished anteroom and departed carrying a silver tray with Heloise's card precisely in the center.

Fitz grinned at his companion. "The fellow looked happy as a grig. He probably hasn't been properly snubbed in weeks."

"Do not attempt to divert me. Geoffrey Trowbridge was a blackguard. He swindled your father and nearly bankrupted his own parents. What connection can this Shaw woman have with him?" she demanded.

"I believe we can safely assume that Geoffrey didn't undergo a religious conversion and emigrate to America with the intention of converting the Indian population to Christianity," Fitz temporized, rising to pace the little room. He paused to rearrange the bric-a-brac on an ornately carved shelf.

"Surely he couldn't have seduced this young woman. One would scarcely expect her to request a presentation if she were searching for a father for her child," Heloise said to his back.

The obscene vision of Sierra as a victim of Trowbridge's oily charm infuriated Fitz. He responded stiffly, "Sierra Shaw's stepmother is Geoffrey's widow. She has no idea I am in possession of that fact, or that I'm aware her man of business, accompanied by a detective, has been in Suffolk making inquiries."

"Fascinating. May I assume that this young woman is very beautiful?"

"What in hell does . . ."

Atkins appeared in the doorway. "Miss Shaw and her aunt will see you now."

Heloise arose, and Fitz, grateful to avoid confirming her accurate speculation that part of his interest in Sierra could be personal, trailed behind her dignified exit. He was eager to witness the meeting of two dominant, resourceful women. Her comment about Sierra's appearance had been out of character, but then so was the twinkle which had lurked in her shrewd dark eyes.

He lingered in the hall, listening to the voices within. Sierra's first words froze him in place. "Howdy, Lady Lockwood. You're right kind to come to London so quickly. Meet my aunt, Mrs. Dolores Shaw."

Her hearty, bogus homespun speech surpassed any social gaffes she had made so far. Why? Fitz hurried into the room in time to see Sierra lead Heloise to a chair near the fire. "Please sit here, ma'am. It's right chilly today. Never saw such a climate. Tea should be here quick as scat. Do you want a little something in it to warm you?"

She looked very tiny next to Heloise, who was taller even than Dolores Shaw. Fitz had never before seen Sierra in this ersatz frontier mode, and he realized he preferred her when she was either lying to him or defying him. "I hope the man brings enough for four," he said, taking advantage of the pause to enter the room. The expression on Sierra's face didn't disappoint. She looked as if she had swallowed a lemon. Whole.

Sierra nearly knocked over the fire screen she was adjusting for her guest's comfort. How dare Fitz Kent show his face after his behavior this morning? How dare he insinuate himself into Lady Lockwood's visit as if he had been invited? How dare he look so utterly wicked and handsome at the same time? Damn him!

Fitz Kent was . . . intrusive. Sierra wanted to shout the word, as if it were the worst insult she could think of, but she didn't dare; she needed a favor from him. But first she must make amends to Lady Lockwood for bringing her here under false pretenses. Originally, she had planned to pretend a sudden aversion to the idea of a presentation and apologize prettily. Her overuse of folksy Americanisms had been a last-minute inspiration, one she'd assumed would convince this awe-inspiring lady of her unsuitability. But she hadn't counted on Fitz's presence.

Gritting her teeth and hoping her cheeks weren't as red as they felt, she smiled and said, "Mr. Kent. I don't remember sending you an invitation, but here you are, like a skunk at a picnic. Have you met Lady Heloise Lockwood?"

"I have known Fitz since he had spots. He wasn't at all impressive," said Heloise, seating herself. Her rigid spine was inches from the button-tufted back of the chair.

"Now, Lady Lockwood, surely that was some other callow youth," Fitz protested. "I was never spotty."

"My memory is excellent, Fitz. Pray recall that you are here on my sufferance. Do sit down and do not interrupt. Miss Shaw and I have issues to discuss." She waved her hand imperiously.

Fitz greeted Dolores Shaw, then settled on the brocade-upholstered settee.

Heloise wasted no time. "I have initiated inquiries through Victoria's staff, Miss Shaw. Your name can be added to the list for the last drawing room. However, before I proceed any further, I must satisfy myself as to your suitability. Adrian Harding's recommendation, although helpful, is hardly sufficient."

The arrogant statement couldn't have suited Sierra's purposes more completely. She took a deep breath, and said, "Why, shore thing, ma'am! You wouldn't want to buy a pig in a poke, then dress it up like a sow's ear to parade in front of the Queen." Sierra strode to the empty chair opposite her guest and threw herself gracelessly onto its stiff upholstery. "Usually, my daddy's money'll grease any wheels that squeak. Funny what stock people put in gold and silver. The whole world sits up and takes notice." Ignoring her aunt's indrawn breath and the gleam in Fitz Kent's hazel eyes, she watched the autocratic old lady for a reaction.

"Several of my acquaintances have mentioned meeting you, Miss Shaw. I am surprised they failed to make reference to the extent of your vulgarity, so I assume this lapse has a purpose." She fixed a hawk-like gaze on Sierra and continued, "You might be surprised to learn that none of them referred to your wealth except in passing. London society is accustomed to opening its ranks to wealthy Americans. I suspect you have already discovered, however, that even gold won't redeem blatant crudeness."

Heloise leaned forward. "My friends' observations concerned your refreshing openness. If you had been this uncouth prior to today, I should have been informed. Are you attempting to persuade me to withdraw my assistance?"

If Lady Lockwood had hit her in the stomach, Sierra could not have been more dumbfounded. Her fruitless mental search for a response was interrupted by a discreet rap on the parlor door and the arrival of the tea cart. She nearly threw her arms around Atkins's neck in gratitude.

During the lull in the conversation, Sierra was burningly conscious of Lady Lockwood's speculative looks. Only years of exposure to Washington society kept her from squirming. She felt as if she were part of a stage performance as she dispensed tea and thin sandwiches for her aunt.

"I have never been so embarrassed in my life," Dolores hissed as Sierra handed her a flowered cup and saucer.

Scarcely moving her lips, Sierra murmured, "I'll fix it." Carefully avoiding Fitz Kent's eyes, she addressed their aristocratic guest. "I must apologize for inconveniencing you, Lady Lockwood. Just this morning I realized I've little time to squander on preparations for a presentation."

Heloise's gaze held steady for an instant, then dropped to the steam rising from her teacup. "A sensible decision, my dear. You've been out in American society for . . . over six years now, isn't it? Propping ostrich feathers in your hair and kissing the air above the hand of a queen your country wouldn't accept if she arrived on a gold platter seems hypocritical."

Stunned, Sierra blurted, "How did you . . . ?"

Heloise glanced at Dolores Shaw's relieved countenance, then frowned at Fitz. "I am current with events and people in many places for a variety of reasons. No doubt you are unaware that I have business interests of my own throughout the world."

"Why do I allow myself to think I can ever get ahead of you?" Fitz mumbled as he examined the watercress sandwich he held between his thumb and forefinger.

The cryptic exchange caused Sierra to watch them narrowly. Just how much did either of them know about her?

"Precisely," Lady Lockwood told him. "You may leave, Fitz. The entertaining portion of the afternoon has passed, and I'm sure you have many useful tasks requiring your attention. I wish to speak with our hostess and her aunt privately."

Mystified, Sierra watched Fitz rise and bid a graceful farewell to her aunt. He moved toward the door, then turned to Sierra, his expression both mocking and regretful. "Good luck, Miss Shaw. I don't recall anyone ever besting the old girl, but you might give her a run for her money. Pity to miss the fireworks." He turned to Heloise. "My carriage will wait to convey you home, Lady Lockwood."

Sierra couldn't believe the ramrod-straight old autocrat had just ordered Fitz Kent from the premises. The woman had insinuated herself into Sierra's affairs without so much as a by-your-leave. And Sierra still needed a favor from Fitz. She sprang to her feet and hurried to the door to call after his retreating figure, "Mr. Kent, can you call tomorrow morning? We've business to discuss."

He nodded agreement, winked roguishly, and disappeared out the door.

"Please sit down, Miss Shaw. I dislike dawdling, and I've an engagement for dinner this evening." Heloise waved her hand toward Sierra's chair. "One fails to see what business dealings you might have with Mr. Kent."

I wonder the same about the two of you, she thought. Obviously, Fitz hadn't told Lady Lockwood of her acceptance of his offer to screen marriage candidates. Sierra decided in favor of honesty—up to a point.

"Ma'am, I realize my abrupt change of intention might lend the impression I'm somewhat flighty," Sierra said. "I assure you that is not the case."

She looked at her aunt, hoping for assistance. Dolores shrugged her shoulders as if to say, "You dug this hole. Climb out on your own."

Heloise set down her plate and brushed her fingers together to remove nonexistent crumbs before answering. "I am gratified to see that you have dispensed with your masquerade. One need only observe your present manners and your aunt's demeanor to assume you employed such crudeness for a very good reason."

Smiling involuntarily, Sierra replied, "Most people I've met appear to expect a few rough edges."

Dolores spoke for the first time. "People are much more surprised that *I* speak properly, since their expectations of me are lower. I'm an oddity," she said, her tone implying that the English were the *true* oddities.

"I make no apologies for my countrymen," Heloise responded briskly. "They are insular at best. However, this still does not explain why an intelligent young woman would intentionally appear vulgar."

Sierra cast an anguished glance at her aunt, who finally came to her rescue, offering the explanation they'd concocted for just such an occasion. "My niece has been under considerable pressure from her father to marry. As you may have already noticed, Sierra is quite independent. She feels no urgency to marry at this particular time, but before coming here she assured her father she would consider seriously any offer from a gentleman she could respect."

Heloise's harsh bark of laughter rang through the room. "So that's why she flaunts her father's millions and pretends to be a title-struck American."

"By claiming I'm only interested in a title, and an impoverished one at that, no man worth having will offer for me, so I can honestly tell my father I didn't receive an acceptable proposal," Sierra said, grateful to her guest for understanding so quickly. She offered her father silent apologies. Theodophilus Shaw was a romantic. To him, love—not economics, not heirs, not even expediency—was the only reason to marry. "Meanwhile, I can see all the sights I've read about."

Heloise rose and shook out her severely cut skirts. "Personally, I find spinsterhood vastly preferable to marriage with a fortune-hunting cretin." She extended her hand first to Dolores Shaw, then to Sierra. "This has been highly entertaining. Young Fitz was of the opinion your husband search masked some nefarious motive, but then, he is suspicious by nature. I shall reassure him your masquerade is purely self-serving."

Sierra apologized a second time as she accompanied her guest to the foyer. "I'm sorry for any inconvenience, Lady Lockwood. Truly, I didn't decide to dispense with a presentation until this morning."

"No need to don sackcloth and ashes. I had already planned a visit to town to talk with my man of business and to fulfill several social obligations." As Heloise accepted her cape from Atkins, she added, "Although I attend few social events, we shall undoubtedly encounter each other at some affair or another."

"I look forward to seeing you again," Sierra said with honesty.

After the door closed behind her guest, Sierra leaned against it and heaved a sigh of relief.

Immediately upon returning home, Fitz dispatched a parlor maid for Paxton, shut himself in his study and began to pace the soft-hued Aubusson carpet from edge to edge. His path led him to the hideous carved mask Thomas Bennett had brought from Africa. The souvenir, a surprisingly compatible accent in the rather Spartan room, frowned down at him from beside the Adam fireplace. When the door opened, he returned to his desk.

"Did you require anything in particular, sir?" His valet's tone indicated barely restrained annoyance at the interruption of his schedule.

"Are any pressing household brouhahas in progress, Paxton?"

The elderly man stiffened. "As you are well aware, sir, I do not encourage any sort of upheaval. Have you a complaint?"

Fitz grinned at him. Paxton's umbrage was reassuring; the man looked on the slightest irregularity in his domain as a personal slight. "Just checking. I have a task requiring your assistance until I can recruit enough personnel to keep her under surveillance."

"Quite so. May I inquire as to the nature of the duties?"

"You're to shadow Miss Shaw, the little American." He bent over his desk and scribbled her address on a scrap of paper. As he handed him the information he said, "Starting tonight. She has accepted an invitation to Endersby's ball this evening. When I arrive, you're free to leave. I'll locate her in the ballroom and take over. If she should leave before I arrive, send a messenger to me there."

Paxton folded the paper precisely before tucking it into his coat pocket. "I take it this is a matter of importance?"

Fitz massaged the back of his neck. Sometime between breakfast and tea, Sierra had dropped the ridiculous idea of a presentation, and he'd noticed an anticipatory twinkle in her eyes that afternoon. Perhaps Heloise had been able to pry out something. "Damned if I know for sure. Her man of business made inquiries around Home Base concerning Geoffrey Trowbridge. Remember that railroad business?"

"Indeed, sir. Your father was quite disgusted with his own naiveté concerning the affair."

"Everyone's judgment lapses at some point. But that was over five years ago. Why is an American picking at the scab on that particular wound after all this time?" He pulled a book from the shelf and opened it, revealing a hollowed-out interior filled with coins and paper bills of all denominations. He offered a healthy selection to Paxton. "Here. In case you have to hire horses or travel to Scotland. The woman is liable to do anything."

A hesitant knock at the door brought Fitz's head up. "Yes?"

"There's a real *Lady* come to call," the maid announced in an awed voice as she peered around the edge of the door. "L-L-Lady Lockwood!"

Fitz grinned at the expression on his man's face. "Don't look so horrified, Paxton. Kate appears to be more than up to the occasion." He turned to the maid and said gently, "She won't bite. She just *appears* fierce," he lied. "Show Lady Lockwood in, will you, Kate?"

Heloise swept past the maid, pausing only to nod in response to Paxton's respectful bow as he exited. "Isn't that your father's valet?" she inquired.

"And now mine," he replied, lifting the stopper from a decanter. "Sherry?"

"I prefer brandy," she said, seating herself in the carved wooden chair across from his desk.

For the first time in their acquaintance, Fitz heard frustration in Heloise's voice. "Am I to assume Miss Shaw did not take you into her confidence?" Fitz asked, handing her the fragile snifter.

Heloise sipped gratefully. "*Such* a devious young woman. Adrian's letter lauded her sickeningly. He particularly stressed her integrity. I offered Miss Shaw an open invitation to enlist my assistance." She smiled ruefully. "In the end, I heard a ridiculous tarradiddle concerning her father pushing her to marry. She professes to be against the notion, which is why she's here in London behaving like the

Western heroine in a cheap American novel . . . attempting to insure no one worthy will propose." She drained her glass and handed it to Fitz. "The girl is clearly up to something."

"My sentiments exactly. And my instincts tell me at least a part of the 'something' is imminent," Fitz replied worriedly. He splashed another dollop of brandy into her glass. "That's why I've just sent Paxton to take the first watch." He set his own drink on the desk and removed a slim book from an inner pocket of his jacket. Opening it, he scanned a list of names. "I'm calling in experienced agents to shadow the little darling."

"Stop pouring over that page and mumbling to yourself. You sound like a cat fretting over her only kitten. Before this proceeds any further, you must tell me everything," Heloise commanded. "Including whether or not your intentions are honorable."

Fitz looked up in surprise. *Damn the old woman!* He'd forgotten how very acute she was. "Now, see here, Heloise . . ."

"You're blushing, my boy. I quite thought you had lost the ability in the cradle. Sit down." She pointed at the wing chair directly beneath an elaborate sconce. "I cannot wait to hear how the activities of this young woman can affect the well-being of the British Empire."

"Dear heaven," Sierra murmured to her aunt as the receiving line inched forward that evening. "When Father remarried, I thought I was free of social misery, that Melanie would take over all that. Now look at me."

"Stop tugging at the bodice of your gown. Your décolletage is quite modest compared to what I have noticed so far, and the gown is lovely. The blue matches your eyes," Dolores said serenely. "Must I remind you that *you* were the one who insisted on chasing over here and slaying your father's dragons for him?"

Sierra frowned as she smoothed her lace gloves between the fingers of her left hand and moved forward six inches. "I didn't feel I had any choice. And I *am* making progress." Leaning closer, she whispered, "Remember, we must leave by midnight."

The smooth skin around Dolores's mouth tightened. "Just because I helped you deflect Lady Lockwood this afternoon doesn't mean I approve of your venturing out again with Caleb tonight."

"I know this could be another false lead, but Freddie's message swore he'd found the genuine article. I can't ignore the possibility." Exhilaration filled Sierra. She didn't doubt Geoffrey was dead. If she could discover who was using his identity, one way or another she would defuse him. Then her father's happiness would be secure—and she could live her life as she pleased. When a niggling voice in her subconscious demanded to know what, precisely, that was, Sierra ignored it. She needed to concentrate on the present.

The obstacle of asking Fitz for an invitation to Kent House to evaluate his sheep remained, but such a request was the only valid reason to visit the shire where Geoffrey had cozened dozens of innocent people into purchasing shares in a railroad that was never built.

She didn't want to owe Fitz Kent. He might decide to call in his marker.

Please, Freddie, don't fob off another substitute on us.

CHAPTER NINE

Sierra took a deep breath and moved forward to greet Lord and Lady Endersby. "Thanks for the invite! You folks have all been so friendly I swear it's almost like being back home." She deliberately gave each of them a hearty handshake, reveling in their shocked expressions.

As she and her aunt descended the marble stairs to the ballroom, Sierra gave the Endersbys full credit for ignoring her gauche behavior. They had responded like purebreds.

She chalked her overdone masquerade up to awe at her surroundings. For the first time, she was truly impressed. Nothing she had ever imagined could compare to such elegance. Eight gaslit crystal chandeliers and dozens of sparkling crystal wall sconces spread refracted light over figured silk–paneled walls and a gleaming parquet dance floor. Around the edges of the room, clusters of gilt-trimmed, velvet-seated chairs offered respite for nondancers.

Although accustomed to diplomatic and official Washington entertainments, Sierra was fair-minded enough to admit that her nation's emerging culture couldn't compare with the grandeur around her.

Except for one thing. In America, she would never have found it necessary to pretend politeness to Francis Lancaster. Bearing down on her in the company of Nigel Brockington, the cadaverous-looking banker squelched Nigel's cheerful pleasantries and led her toward the dance floor before she could refuse without making a scene. She looked around for her aunt, and saw her already on the dance floor with Tony Belville. With no help available from that quarter, she resigned herself to another lecture.

"I particularly looked forward to this evening in hopes I would see you, Miss Shaw." His dark head bent toward her as if sharing momentous news. "I want to assure you I hold no hard feelings for your outburst the other evening."

Sierra nearly stepped on his foot. "That's mighty big of you," she drawled, gratified when he blinked and his neck reddened.

"Nigel pointed out that I might have been a trifle judgmental," he acknowledged as he drew her onto the dance floor and into his formal embrace. "Your background and the social climate of your country are quite different. I was raised to adhere to much stricter standards."

The backhanded apology startled Sierra into missing a step. Slipping back into the rhythm of the sprightly waltz, she glanced upward. His cold, dark eyes were hooded, but the lines of disapproval which had creased his sallow cheeks during their last encounter had smoothed into a feeble attempt at a smile. *Now* what was she supposed to say? Lancaster saved her from a hasty decision.

"I may have appeared overbearing because I am aware of the pitfalls awaiting visitors to our country. Am I incorrect to suspect that you have a reason other than marriage for your visit here?"

The heavy musk of his cologne, the same he had worn the other evening, burned in Sierra's nostrils and she felt slightly queasy. She widened her eyes to disguise her dismay. "Why, I haven't the littlest old idea what that could be, Mr. Lancaster. All I want is a titled husband to show off to my friends at home. Surely that's enough to occupy any woman's inferior mind."

The skin around his thin mouth tightened before his cheeks creased in a travesty of a smile. "I must say, your openness is commendable, Miss Shaw. Many young ladies mask their real intentions beneath social platitudes. You, I can see, have no secrets."

"Oh, I have secrets aplenty, but I believe in the direct approach when I set my sights on something." Sierra smiled confidingly.

The music ended, and as he accompanied her toward her aunt, Lancaster leaned down and whispered, "I just want you to know, Miss Shaw, that Nigel and I stand your servants should you find yourself in any difficulty."

"You're real sweet to offer, Mr. Lancaster, but I can't imagine needing help. I've always taken care of myself." Sierra fumed inwardly. Because she was small and delicately made, people tended to treat her as if she were incapable, both mentally and physically. Throughout her adolescence, she had taught her father and brothers the hard way that she could fend for herself. Ever since she had beaten Caleb at arm wrestling when she was nine, he had been a believer.

"Do you mind if I take her off your hands, Lancaster?"

The voice came from behind them, and Sierra smothered a ripple of awareness. She wasn't up to verbal sparring with Fitz Kent tonight; she'd yet to erase the searing memory of his kiss. And he'd witnessed her awful performance with Lady Lockwood. How could she invite herself to his farm in Suffolk without revealing how very much he unsettled her? "*Must* you speak of me as if I were a litter of unwanted puppies?" she demanded after Lancaster walked stiffly away.

Tiny laugh lines fanned from the corners of his eyes. "I was thinking more along the lines of the barn cat's kittens. They're usually half-wild." His lips curved in a lazy, teasing smile. "Are you engaged for the dinner dance?"

"I'm not at all sure we'll stay that long. Aunt Dolores

thinks she might be getting a sick headache," she lied smoothly.

The music had resumed, and couples were pushing past them to reach the dance floor. He drew her along with them, his hand warm at the small of her back. Sierra craved his touch, but wanted to evade it at the same time. She felt almost dizzy. "If you wish to stay, I can arrange for someone else to escort your aunt home, then deliver you later myself. It would be a pity to miss one moment of your first London ball, particularly since you're looking so lovely that all the other ladies are gnashing their teeth."

The direct compliment dizzied her, but only for a moment. She pulled away from his touch, but the mixed scents of his citrus cologne and the starch from his shirt still reached her nostrils. Fighting their influence, she said, "I appreciate the compliment, even though I doubt the other ladies have much to worry about. My aunt becomes quite nauseated. She'll need me with her."

"What if I promised to make it my mission to insure your complete enjoyment of every stolen moment?" he tempted.

Sierra half-closed her eyes as she met the sleepy challenge of his gaze. The bastard looked as if he were about to kiss her again. Right here in the middle of a ball. She wanted . . . damn it, she wanted him to do just that.

What was it about him? She despised men who looked as if they spent their entire day polishing their appearance; from the way he looked tonight, she wouldn't be surprised to learn Fitz Kent had been born shod, brushed, groomed—and dressed in white tie and tails. She needed her wits back; she thought he looked wonderful. "You'd only spend the evening pressing me to tell you whatever guilty secret you think I'm hiding. Go flirt with an attractive widow."

"Not a bad idea." He looked over her shoulder. "I see Lucy Haines-Dermott over there with Carrington's crowd. She complains of loneliness."

His easy diversion and speculative comment brought Sierra's blood to the boiling point. He had no right to sound quite so interested. "By all means, don't waste another minute." She walked away from him, her movements so brisk she felt her dress improver sway beneath its burden of dusty blue silk and Russian lace. In another hour she and Dolores could make their excuses and depart. Meanwhile, she had better reinforce her pretense of looking for a titled husband.

Shortly after midnight, Fitz slipped through the open French doors at the far end of the ballroom. The sounds of music and laughter followed him as he walked quickly across the terrace to merge with the shadows of the shrubbery. Minutes later he exited a side gate in the ivy-covered brick wall and whistled softly. His carriage, which had been waiting in the narrow alley, rolled toward him. Before the coachman came to a stop, Fitz called instructions in a low voice and swung into the leather-lined interior. His sixth sense, which he never ignored, had warned him to prepare for a hasty departure this evening.

As he shed formal dress and donned the dark trousers and knit jersey he pulled from the cabinet beneath the seat, Fitz chuckled. When Dolores Shaw left, she had looked no more ill than he himself felt, which was surprisingly exhilarated. Sierra, on the other hand, had appeared flushed after an encounter with Lord Asquith, one of London's biggest bounders. Since Fitz had the greatest confidence in her ability to leave the sod in an unconscious heap if necessary, he thought it more likely some other adventure was on tap for the evening.

He pulled a disreputable cap down to his ears and slipped his feet into scarred low boots just as the carriage pulled up at the end of the alley behind Adelphi Terrace. After assuring himself the slim, razor-sharp blade resided in its sheath inside his left boot and adjusting the flat handle of its twin in the webbed case beneath his knit sleeve, Fitz slid a revolver into the back of his waistband and spoke to the coachman through the window above the seat. At his murmured command, the carriage pulled down the street, pausing in the shadow of a brick wall.

He exited the coach and slipped through the shadows until he reached the shrubbery surrounding the mews behind Sierra's rented house. The waning crescent moon provided sufficient light to reveal any movement at the back entrance. Now all he had to do was wait.

Fifteen minutes after his arrival, the door swung open. Two roughly clad figures slipped down the brick stairs and stopped not ten feet from his hiding place.

"Shall we take a hackney?" Sierra's voice came to him faintly through the moisture-laden mist.

"Too risky. I've scouted the way. We want to sneak up on the bastard to make sure he's alone before we show ourselves." The second speaker's thick tail of hair was all Fitz needed to verify his identity.

"Then what are we waiting for?"

Fitz remained in place until the pair rounded the corner of the stable, heading toward the alley he had traversed moments before. He savored the sight of Sierra's hips swaying beneath the edge of the rough jacket. Did she really think she fooled anyone? The woman walked like a temptress; even the stiff, asymmetrical skirts fashion dictated couldn't disguise the fact. He followed soundlessly. What on earth was the precocious pair up to this time?

At the end of the alley he gestured to his coachman and faded into the shadows behind Sierra and her Indian friend. The next twenty minutes were a revelation. During the short time he'd been in residence, Caleb had apparently memorized this section of London. Fitz had forgotten most of these alleys existed. No sooner would they emerge from the middle of one block of buildings than the fast-moving pair darted across the street into yet another dark, narrow opening. Where in bloody hell were they going? He spotted his carriage pausing hesitantly at the end of the block and hurried to give the coachman further instructions, then set off in pursuit once more.

Light appeared at the intersection ahead. A dray loaded with cartons and barrels rolled past. Thunder rolled lazily above, adding to the din. When Fitz paused to assure himself which direction they had taken at the end of the alley, the thunderous roar of a locomotive and the hiss of escaping steam split the night. He needed no map to tell him where he was.

Why in God's name were they at Charing Cross station?

"I thought we were to meet him in the railway station," Sierra shouted, slowing her pace as Caleb continued past the impressive columned entrance on the opposite side of the street. There was little need to speak softly. The sound of the train pulling out nearly deafened her.

"Nope, he mentioned a cul-de-sac along here somewhere." He pushed her into a shadowed doorway. "Stay put while I look around. We want to approach from the back."

Sierra padded after him in her soft moccasins. "Not on your life. If you run into an ambush, you'll need me." She ignored his grumbling, concentrating instead on the darkened buildings to her right as they traversed another block. In the thin light of the street lamps, she saw layers of soot covering the buildings, the walkways and the streets. Sierra wondered how people could live in such noise and filth.

Caleb stopped and pulled her into the shadow of a doorway. "There's the entrance," he whispered, gesturing ahead. "Freddie's man'll expect us to come in from Charing Cross Road like a pair of stupid Americans. We'll cut through that alley back there and get the lay of the land from behind." He nodded his head toward the narrow opening behind them. "Better have your knife ready, just in case."

"You blockhead, I've had my hand on the hilt ever since we set out." Although her heart sank, Sierra followed him toward the dismal-looking passage. No reflection of lights in the distance or from nearby lamps leavened the blackness ahead. "Lead on."

Distant thunder sounded, stronger this time. "Oh, fine," Sierra murmured beneath her breath. "Pitch dark and a storm coming."

Not for all the tea in England would she have admitted that the inky passage turned her insides to jelly. Freddie's message had assured them the informant was the disgruntled valet Geoffrey had left behind to cope with the landlord and a host of angry creditors. Sierra hoped the man could supply the names of Geoffrey's friends. But why had he insisted on meeting them in the dead of night on a deserted street? Her moccasined foot slid on an unidentifiable wet patch. "Ugh!" She grabbed at the rough stone wall.

"Shhh . . ." Caleb hissed.

"Shhh yourself," she retorted beneath her breath. They were nearly to the end of the alley. She focused on the dim light ahead. Caleb's shadow blended left, and she hurried to follow.

120

"Well, just *damn!*" Caleb breathed disgustedly.

Sierra peered past his shoulder. Ahead, wavering lamp-light washed over the cul-de-sac. She counted six huddled shadows watching the entrance. Waiting for them.

Caleb turned, silently urging her back through the alley they just travelled. Her foot encountered a patch of gravel, dislodging small pebbles which scattered like buckshot. The sound was amplified in the enclosed space. Shouts sounded behind them.

"Damn it all! Run, Sierra." Glancing left and right without breaking stride, Caleb seized her arm and pushed her ahead. "Turn right when you reach the street. If we can . . ."

A shadow separated from the wall beside them. A hard hand shot from the darkness to grip Sierra's other arm. Fitz Kent's voice warned, "We'll never make it across the road to the station. Run like hell . . . and watch out for that lamppost."

Lifted from both sides, her feet flying over the brick side-walk, Sierra remembered Fitz's threat to follow her. She heard shouts from behind, and risked a glance over her shoulder. "We're not losing them!"

"At least we're far enough ahead that we can choose where we want to fight," Fitz said.

To her annoyance, he didn't sound as if he were exerting himself. And where had he found such disreputable clothing? "Caleb will know the best place," she shouted, determined to relegate him to the role of intruder.

Long black hair flew back from Caleb's face. "Two alleys down. On the left," he instructed breathlessly. "Piles of trash . . . behind the pub. Great ambush."

Their pursuers' shouts followed them. Caleb steered the trio around a group of amazed pedestrians. Everyone from dustmen to finely dressed aristocrats inhabited the streets. Why did no one offer to help? Americans would have, Sierra was sure.

She risked another look over her shoulder. "They're gaining on us," she panted. "Caleb and I can handle this, Fitz. Stay out of the way."

His grip on her arm tightened. "You, young lady, are going to keep right on running through to the next street and the first bobby you see. Caleb and I will hold them off."

Sierra ignored him. The opening to the alley loomed on their left and they swerved in. Ahead, halfway through on the right, was a mountainous pile of refuse jutting out from the wall. The piercing stench of fish and rotting food trapped in the narrow, dark passage caused her eyes to water, and she blinked rapidly to clear them. When both men released her, she followed the dark shadow that was Caleb around the open side of the sprawling mountain.

Fitz's hand rode at the base of her spine. Ten feet past the untidy barrier he slapped her rump, pushing her ahead. "Get going," he ordered.

The familiarity brought Sierra up short. She took a deep breath, then exhaled and said sharply, "Step aside, Brit, you're in the way." She pushed past him toward the edge of the foul-smelling mound and crouched close to the narrow opening. Fitz Kent had no business interfering.

Rough voices, their sound magnified in the confines of the alley, sounded from the other side of the impromptu barrier. Glancing over her shoulder through the dimness, she saw two amorphous shadows positioned on either side. Fitz and Caleb were in place.

Their pursuers' shouts fell briefly to a murmur. Then stealthy footsteps echoed in the narrow gap, and she crept closer, forcing herself to wait until she felt the attacker's disgusting breath on her face. Swinging her right leg in front of the thug, she reached for his arm. He stumbled, cursing, and she pulled his off-balance body forward, using his own momentum to tumble him past her. The solid crack of knuckles hitting flesh that followed nearly distracted her from dealing with the next miscreant, who was close behind.

Her second victim gasped as his cohort's shadow disappeared, and Sierra seized his shoulder and sent him to follow his friend. A third ruffian, more cautious than his fellows, paused. Seconds later, his head extended past the opening. Raising her right hand, Sierra struck sharply at the angle where his shoulder met his neck. Before he fell, she used his momentum to tumble him along his way to Caleb.

Her heart beat with exhilaration. She was having a wonderful time.

The voices of the last three echoed through the opening. "I don' hear nuffing. Bert and Louie allus yells and screams when they does in toffs," a querulous voice declared.

"Fings don't sound right to me, neither. Alphie, go along t' wall ter check. We wasn't s'posed ter make much to-do. Doan want t' bring ta rozzers down on us."

After much grumbling, hesitant footsteps eased through the passage. Sierra thrust out her foot once more, but the solid ankle didn't budge. She grabbed for an arm, and her hand met hard, unmoving muscle. The ruffian's free hand pulled her into a suffocating, one-armed hug. The man was huge. Frantic, she kicked at his legs. *Oh, God. I might as well have kicked the wall!* He clutched her so tightly against his greasy jacket she could taste the mixed odors of fish and rancid grease. *Where in God's name were Caleb and Fitz?*

CHAPTER TEN

A muffled shriek reached Fitz's ears. Sierra! A massive shadow blocked the narrow passage around the mound of refuse where she'd crouched. He leaped over the unconscious bodies and approached cautiously. In the dim light, Fitz could see Sierra struggling in the grasp of a giant. Surely there couldn't be many people in London that large. He tamped down his panic, swallowed his fear for her and clutched his hands at his sides.

"Alphie, you promised me you'd stay out of trouble," Fitz said, striving to sound bored. Sensing movement beside him, he seized Caleb's wrist, holding him back. If startled, the giant could snap Sierra's neck as if it were a wheat stem.

After a brief silence, a rough voice answered, " 'Oo's that? 'Oo's talkin' ta me?"

Fitz tightened his hold on Caleb. "You should know me, Alphie. Remember that ugly incident when the *Mary Angelica* was unloading? I told the rozzers to release you after you promised to behave. Now you're disappointing me. Let the boy go."

"I'm 'elpin' me family. Besides, 'tain't no boy."

Ignoring this last, Fitz released Caleb and stepped closer. "Why are you and your brothers chasing us?"

"Don' know why." Alphie's voice sounded confused, but he continued stoutly, "Bert said to. I allus does wot Bert says. Wot yer want wi' 'er?"

"*He* knows things I want *him* to share." Sidling closer to the simpleminded giant in the darkness, he slipped his knife from beneath his cuff and, praying his hand wouldn't shake, pressed the long, narrow blade along the giant's chin. "Put *him* down, Alphie. I don't want to hurt you."

Alphie lifted his ham-like hand from Sierra's head. After what seemed like an eternity, he lowered her body until her moccasined feet touched the ground. As she leaped out of range of Alphie's hands, Fitz bit back a shout of relief.

"Yer won't 'urt me, will yer? Mam don't like it above 'alf when I bleeds."

From the corner of his eye, Fitz saw Caleb move toward Sierra. His last encounter with Alphie had proved the man harmless, incapable of anything but following orders, but he didn't believe in taking anything for granted. Keeping the knife flat against Alphie's throat, he demanded, "Did Bert say who hired him?"

"Never did." The man's second chin quivered against the knife blade. "Yer ain't gonna stick me, are yer?"

Fitz felt like a school-yard bully. He pressed the knife more firmly against the quaking flesh. "I think you do know, Alphie. Bert talks all the time when he has a job in the wind. I'll bet he mentioned a name." Lightning flashed overhead, the sharp crack of sound penetrating the opening between the two buildings.

Silence followed, a silence disturbed by rainfall, the shuffling of Alphie's feet and faint stirrings from the three bodies heaped alongside the wall. The brothers who had sent Alphie through the narrow opening appeared to have vanished at the sound of Fitz's voice.

"I finks it were some bloke from ta church."

"Give me a name," Fitz demanded.

" 'Ta Parson. 'At's 'oo. 'Ta Parson."

Fitz heard a gasp. Alphie's response meant something to either Sierra or Caleb. His arms ached from reaching above his head to threaten a man who outweighed him by at least eight stone. "I'm going to let you go, Alphie. But if I catch you making mischief with your brothers again, I'll have to lock you all up." He hardened his voice. "You know I'll do that, don't you?" He slipped the knife back into its sheath.

"Me mam wouldn't like 'at."

The fear in the man's voice amused Fitz. "If I hear of any more trouble, you're as good as in the dock. Alphie, there was no woman in this alley tonight. Just two men and a boy. Tell your brothers that's who got the best of them."

"No woman?"

"No woman. Remember that." He hardened his voice. "Now get along with you."

As he watched Alphie retreat, Fitz nurtured a hope of someday meeting "Mam," a woman who had birthed five violent, larcenous sons and one simple giant who feared her. When the sound of shuffling feet faded, he turned briskly back to Caleb and Sierra. Silently, he shepherded them ahead of him through the alley and across the next street. The pair was uncharacteristically quiet, which worried him. Lightning flashed again.

"My carriage should be waiting just one street over," he said, drawing them into yet another alley. "My coachman followed me while I was trailing you. I waved him off somewhere along here."

Sierra pulled free of his hold. "Caleb and I will find our way back on our own."

The insistent look she slanted toward her friend released the anger that had been simmering beneath the surface since his first sight of the pair streaking toward him. He locked his fingers around her arm and said between his teeth, "I don't think so. Now's as good a time as any for a jolly visit, don't you think?" When she didn't respond, he steered her toward the patch of light at the end of the alley, leaving Caleb to follow.

Thunder rolled through the sky, and sudden, slanting rain at their backs drove them toward the waiting coach. "Fitting," Fitz muttered as he thrust the pair ahead of him into the dark interior. He followed, pulling the door closed behind him.

He barked Sierra's address through the hatch, then lit the carriage lamps. Fighting for his customary control, Fitz studied the faces opposite him in the thin light. Caleb's expression was wary; Sierra's thunderous frown matched the storm now raging outside.

"I don't suppose you would like to share the reason six thugs were set upon the two of you," he asked tightly.

Sierra glared at him from beneath the checkered cap pulled down over her forehead. Fitz eyed the buckskin jacket and trousers, then the fringed moccasins on her slender feet. When she didn't answer, he said offhandedly, "Perhaps it was your costume they disliked. Your hat doesn't match."

Her eyes were pools of temper as she yanked the cap from her head, releasing the silver-blonde braid coiled beneath it. The thick plait fell forward over her chest. "Only a fop like you would notice a thing like that." She lifted her chin defiantly, flounced further back onto the seat and crossed her ankles. "Caleb and I were to meet someone. There must have been a misunderstanding," she muttered evasively.

Fitz narrowed his eyes, glancing briefly at Caleb. The Indian's face was closed and expressionless, revealing nothing. How many years had Sierra been leading her friend around by the nose? Why did he allow it? "You work incredibly fast, Miss Shaw. You've been in London how

127

long . . . nearly two weeks? And you've already alienated some of the most feared toughs in the East End." He propped his right foot against the seat beside Sierra's thigh. "Alphie and his brothers hire out only to the highest bidder. They're not very bright, but they're efficient. Do you know what they'd have done to you if they'd caught you?" The thought sent a shudder through him.

"We didn't need your help. We could have escaped on our own," she said airily, tossing the braid back over her shoulder.

Fitz saw the flicker of disagreement in Caleb's dark eyes. "You little fool! You needed me. The two of you wouldn't have been enough against Alphie's brothers, who aren't as slow as he is, and Alphie could have broken you like a twig. It's fortunate that I've dealt with them before."

"They didn't capture us," she said mutinously, edging closer to Caleb.

"What was Alphie doing? Teaching you the waltz?" At her wince, he demanded, "What are you up to?"

"Nothing that concerns you. It's a family matter."

A violent crack of lightning chose that moment to strike close by. The horses whinnied in fright; the coach rocked precariously. "I became a player in your little games when I joined your *other* little scheme. Prowling the streets in this weather is not my favorite pastime."

"Then don't do it! None of this is your business. Caleb and I can handle ourselves!" Tears of rage glimmered in Sierra's eyes. Her hands fisted in her lap. Her lips moved again, but a heavy roll of thunder drowned out her words.

What the devil had the girl got herself into? And why did he care? The answer to that question shook him to the soles of his battered boots. Ignoring the weakness, he countered, "Sierra, you're a little fool! This is the second time I've found you two wandering unsavory streets. Are you trying to get yourself killed?"

He watched so closely for her reaction that he nearly missed Caleb's surprised expression.

Sierra said loftily, "You made that point days ago with your thinly veiled references to the dangers of London streets after dark, Mr. Kent. One *must* wonder, of course, what kind of business took *you* to Seven Dials on that first occasion. We both know your motivation this evening was simply a natural tendency to interfere." She looked at him intently. "And then there's your close acquaintance with Alphie. Were you schoolmates?"

Fitz repressed the beginnings of a smile he hadn't known was available. "We met under rather unusual circumstances. I was merely a passerby, but found the opportunity to help the poor soul. Pathetic as he is, he's the best of a bad lot."

The coach rolled to a stop, rocking slightly. Rain pounded on the roof. Sierra shot him a disbelieving look and reached across Caleb to unlatch the door. Her voice hard, she said, "I don't believe that, anymore than I need your help or your meddling. And . . . and . . . you don't have my permission to call me by my given name. Good night, Mr. Kent."

With that she nudged Caleb, who scrambled out behind her.

Fitz watched her delectable trousered derriere disappear through the door. She'd escaped in the nick of time. Otherwise he would have had to strangle her. He rapped twice on the roof and blew out the lanterns. If one had a tendency toward melancholy, a dark carriage on a rainy night provided the ideal atmosphere.

"Fat chance you'll get an invitation to look at his sheep

after that encounter," Caleb quipped as he stood shivering in the rain outside the kitchen entrance, waiting for Sierra to unlock the door.

The portal swung inward noiselessly. She slipped through to the scullery, where Caleb joined her. The two shook themselves like wet dogs before peeling off their jackets. The pungent odor of damp leather filled the utilitarian cubbyhole.

Sheep were the last thing in Sierra's mind. She rubbed absently at her upper arm where Fitz had gripped her; she would have bruises tomorrow. The man was more dangerous than she'd imagined. How foolish she'd been to think the only threat from him was to her emotions. His banked anger when he questioned them in the coach had been terrifying. Still, she had no intention of revealing the humiliation her father and stepmother faced—if, by some malignant irony, Geoffrey were really alive. The secret belonged to those who loved her father best. Those who would die to protect him.

Yet for one brief, uncontrolled moment she'd wanted to confide in Fitzhugh Kent. She thanked God she'd had the will to resist. Not for anything would she put herself in debt to Fitz Kent. He would ride roughshod over her . . . and the glitter in his bright, knowing eyes promised something more. The man could ensnare her and own her if she didn't maintain her guard. Sierra had no intention of allowing any man to dominate her.

Realizing her thoughts had strayed from Caleb's teasing reminder, she slipped off her damp moccasins and pushed past him into the kitchen. A gaslight near the stove burned low. Turning, she beckoned to him. "I have one of the certificates here. The rest are still at the bank. Tomorrow I'm going to Suffolk to find out if the shares the villagers bought are the same."

"What time are we leaving?" Caleb whispered.

"*We're* not going. I am. Alone. Not even Dolores will know until after I've left. I'll leave her a note telling her to cancel my social engagements. She can say I have the flu. You'll stay here to maintain the appearance of the lie."

"No!" Caleb shouted. Lowering his voice at her sharp signal, he continued furiously, "You're not travelling alone in a foreign country. Look what happened tonight. We were set up, and Alphie and his brothers meant business. Better we stick around and find out who gave them their orders."

Sierra refused to think of the danger they'd escaped. If she did, she'd have to admit how much she'd welcomed Fitz's help. "If the world thinks I'm ill, no one will expect to see me. Not even Fitz Kent. Wes and the investigator have gone to the Scottish town listed on the stock to see if anyone there knows anything, so you're needed here for window dressing," she said patiently. "Caleb, these certificates might lead to the blackmailer. I must know why he wants the stock before I can eliminate the threat to Melanie and my father. I'll be safe. I promise."

If she arrived in Suffolk in the disguise she had planned, no one would be able to describe her to Fitz Kent, she told herself smugly.

While she was there, she could hire a carriage and drive past his fields to look at the sheep Russ was so enthusiastic about.

Fitz kicked the gleaming surface of the umbrella stand. "Damnation! Serves her right for staying out till all hours in the rain." He stared at the faint scuff mark on the brass while doubt nibbled at the edge of his thoughts. "If she's truly ill."

Last night's storm had passed, but the rain continued to fall—a thoroughly English rain, slowing traffic, turning the gutters into miniature rivers, and fraying the tempers of people like himself. He knew he was being unreasonable, but Sierra Shaw didn't strike him as someone who would come down with a cold after something so trivial as being doused by a summer storm. Yet he'd been turned away at the door by that damned stiff-rumped butler.

"Paxton!" he shouted, the sound echoing through the paneled foyer.

He was about to repeat the summons when his valet appeared, stopping not two feet from him. Paxton stared at the scuffed umbrella stand. "My, we are in a temper, aren't we? May I assist you in some way?"

Fitz ignored the man's sarcasm. "Who watched the Shaw house last night?"

"Twickerton was there until dawn, when Hornsby relieved him."

"Have you heard anything from either of them?" Fitz demanded.

"One would assume Twickerton would send word if anything unusual occurred, and Hornsby is still there," Paxton said dryly.

"Of course," Fitz said, pulling his Burberry from the hall tree and shoving his arms into the sleeves. The finger of doubt niggling at his intelligence had grown into a hand. "What a stupid idiot I am! She's gone. Sure as I'm standing here, she's taken off on her own. That's why she's 'indisposed.' But where would she go?" He retrieved his umbrella, then stopped in the act of reaching for the doorknob.

Paxton surveyed him calmly, then said, "Doubtless you neglected to inquire of him a list of people who have left the premises from Hornsby. Might I remind you that the young lady is extremely inventive."

Not bothering to respond, Fitz strode out the door, his thoughts churning. He hailed a cab and climbed in. Throughout the short ride, he tried to imagine Sierra Shaw's possible destination. Leaving the cab at the end of the street, he approached the rented house cautiously, then stopped short of the entrance and whistled shrilly. Hornsby appeared from the shrubbery. "Mr. Kent, sir. Weren't you 'ere less than an 'our ago?"

Fitz led the rotund, bewhiskered operative behind the dripping hedge. "Have you a list of everyone who's left the house today?"

Hornsby fumbled in the pocket of his rain gear for his notebook. Finally successful in his search, he thumbed the soggy pages. " 'Ere we go. Not much 'appenin'." He offered the book.

Scanning the notes, Fitz demanded, "Have any of the residents left?"

"Not likely. Not in this. Hit's a proper gusher." He thumbed another page over the first. " 'Ere now. Saw a widow lady come out of the alley in back."

"A widow? All in black? With a heavy veil?"

"A little 'un. All draped like t' fun'ral was takin' place today. She were on foot."

"That was this morning?" Fitz demanded. His agile mind worked on the possibilities. She could have . . .

"On the dot of nine. She were 'urryin', like she had someplace important to go," Hornsby said stoutly.

"Was she carrying anything?"

"A carpetbag."

Fitz eyed the end of the terrace, where another hedge obscured the alley. Where had she gone? His mind grappled with the possibilities. "The train," he said decisively. "Carry on. I'll want a precise description of everyone who calls or leaves the house." He clapped Hornsby on the shoulder and set out on foot.

By the time Fitz arrived home, his trousers were wet to the knee and he still had no idea of Sierra's destination. He'd poured over the list of train destinations covering a two-hour period, and none had any connection with his knowledge of Sierra Shaw.

The problem would have to wait. He'd a train of his own to catch. He disposed of his wet outerwear and hurried up-stairs.

"Your bath is drawn, Mr. Fitz. And your travelling bag is packed. I left it in the dressing room," Paxton announced as he strode into his room.

Fitz had long given up trying to figure out how his valet anticipated his needs. "My thanks, Paxton. The train leaves at four-thirty, so I've time for a light meal."

"That is all arranged, sir." The valet accepted Fitz's tweed jacket and awaited the matching trousers.

Fitz said abruptly, "She's gone. I'm positive she's wearing widow's weeds."

A discreet cough was the only indication of Paxton's interest.

"The stubborn wench toddled off on her merry way to points unknown. The butler said she was in bed with a cold, which is fiction. Where could she have gone?" Fitz demanded.

"I'm sure I've no idea, young sir. Miss Shaw appears to be an extremely resourceful young woman, if I may say so."

Fitz stepped out of his damp trousers and jammed them onto his valet's extended arm. "Quite. Keep in touch with the surveillance, Paxton, and if she returns while I'm away, lock her up somehow. I can't put off this journey to Suffolk."

Sierra stepped off the train in St. Swithin's Vale. Other than to ask directions, she fended off the services of the porter who leaped to her aid and found her way to the small inn three doors from the station. The fewer people she spoke with, the fewer who would remember her.

The village was small but prosperous-looking. Two boys raced hoops down the street as she reached the door of the inn, and she paused to watch them, scanning the street for the church as she did so, and filing away in her mind the direction she must take. Upon entering the inn, she was greeted by a dyspeptic individual who grudgingly registered her under the name of Mrs. Alexander Pope. She'd neglected to prepare an alias, and supposed that would do as well as any. Her status as a widow eliminated any question about the acceptability of her travelling alone, which was why she had chosen the disguise. As for the false name, the innkeeper was obviously not a student of literature.

After depositing her carpetbag on the rickety straight chair next to the uncomfortable-looking bed, she removed her heavy veil and rinsed her face and hands with water from the chipped pitcher on the washstand.

This done, she donned the clinging black once more and set out, locking the door carefully behind her. The church's steeple led her to the outskirts of the village, past the stone walls of a little cemetery accessible only by a lych gate beside the church. On the other side stood the vicarage, built of the same weathered stone as the church and the wall. The little complex looked as if it had stood there for centuries.

Her knock at the vicarage door was answered by the tiniest lady she had ever seen, who inquired in a small, whispery voice, "May I help you?"

"I'd like to speak with Mr. Pettigrew if I might," she said softly. "I'm Mrs. Alexander Pope, and I wish to speak with him."

The tiny lady drew her inside and led her across the hall to an open doorway. "My husband is working in the garden. If you'll take a seat in his study, I'll make sure he's with you directly." With that she bustled away, her starched skirts crackling.

"This seems too easy," Sierra mumbled as she entered the crowded little room. A quick survey revealed stacks of what appeared to be sermon notes covering every inch of the desk, and books were everywhere—on the chairs, on the floor, and even on the octagonal table in the corner. "Russ said the vicar hung the framed certificate in his office, so it has to be here somewhere." The limp widow's garb eased the task of slipping between the two burdened chairs to the side wall.

The certificate hung between the vicar's seminary diploma and a framed picture of six young children. His? Her heart beat faster as she dragged her gaze back to the stock certificate. Her hands searched her reticule for the carefully folded share she'd hidden in its folds. She was sure they were identical.

"Are you admiring the scrollwork on my folly, Mrs. Pope?"

The booming voice nearly frightened her out of her half-boots. She turned guiltily, and choked out, "I was just . . . looking . . ."

Surely this man couldn't be the husband of the wisp of a woman who had answered the door. He was over six feet tall and built like a barrel, with full silver muttonchop whiskers below a luxuriant head of matching hair.

"That pretty piece of paper is the most expensive piece of artwork I shall ever possess," he said, buttoning the cuffs of his frayed white shirt. He had obviously stopped to wash the soil from his hands, but a damp, muddy stain graced the front of his shirt. "Most people around here know not to stare at the thing, and I never point it out to visitors."

Sierra pretended surprise. "The certificate looks like an investment issue. Surely it has value."

"Not worth the paper and the fancy drawings," the vicar said jovially as he removed an untidy stack of books from the chair across from the desk. "I keep it there to remind myself of the one time I succumbed to the notion that such a thing as 'easy money' exists. 'Twas a painful lesson." He edged his way behind the desk, dislodging a sheaf of papers covered with cramped writing in the process. "Please sit down. Mrs. Pettigrew said you wanted to talk with me."

The door swung open and the tiny lady entered carrying a tea tray that looked too heavy for her wrists. She walked to the octagonal table and serenely nudged the tower of books with her elbow until it crashed to the floor, then set the tray in its place. "Fresh scones, Oliver. Your favorites," she said economically, then bustled out the door.

Mr. Pettigrew stepped over the tumble of books and poured tea from the sturdy brown pot into heavy crockery cups. "Milk and sugar, Mrs. Pope?"

"Just sugar, thank you," Sierra responded. "One lump."

He delivered the sturdy cup and held out the plate of scones. When Sierra declined, he carried his own cup and the serving plate to his desk. As he sat he fixed an unnerving green stare on Sierra and said, "What else would you like to know about that stock certificate, Mrs. Pope? That *was* your reason for this visit, was it not?"

137

CHAPTER ELEVEN

"How . . . why would you think that?" Sierra stuttered, astounded by his directness.

Mr. Pettigrew answered cheerfully, "You're the second American to come to the village in a month. The last one pretended to ignore my mention of the stock, but I couldn't mistake his interest. I tend to be perverse, Mrs. Pope. I told a small falsehood. I said I never showed the certificate to people." He spooned jam onto a scone and took a large bite, chewed fiercely and choked out, "Don't like coincidence." He shook his head, as if disappointed in her.

Sierra appreciated his directness. Lifting her veil, she settled it over her hat and leaned forward in her chair. "Russ, the man who was here, is my employee, Vicar. He didn't mean to mislead you . . . he's really a very honest man." She sipped the nearly black tea. It was strong enough to stand without the cup, and she felt her eyes widen.

"You needn't finish that if it's too strong. I like my tea with hair on it, and my wife forgot to bring water to dilute yours." He sipped his own with relish, then said, "Why are you so interested in the stock?"

"Because my stepmother was once married to the person who sold them hereabouts." She reached into her reticule and pulled out the certificate. "He left her five hundred shares when he died."

Booming laughter flowed from the vicar's throat. He shook so hard he had to set his cup on the littered desk. When he recovered, he said, "Poor Geoffrey never overcame the wickedness in his nature. I pity your stepmother.

Was she left in very bad straits?"

"She married my father, who is quite wealthy, and since I was coming to London for the Season, Melanie asked me to look into the venture more fully. All the stock exchange could tell us is that the railroad project was cancelled and the stock worthless."

"You're going to a great deal of trouble over this, Mrs. Pope." His green eyes twinkled merrily. "By the way, I find your choice of names delightful. May I hope to know your real identity one day?"

Sierra's cheeks heated with guilt and embarrassment. The vicar was as sharp a rascal as she'd ever encountered. "I'm not really a widow, but I wanted to travel alone, so the alias seemed practical. Since we now have most of our cards on the table, Vicar, can you tell me more about this venture?"

"The principals were going to build a rail line in Scotland, one that would cut many hours between two manufacturing cities." He shook his head. "I wish I could tell you the names, but they escape me. I fear I've succumbed to the sin of denial in respect to the entire affair," he said, leaning back in his chair.

"When word got out that the project was cancelled, Geoffrey's family was willing to sacrifice their fortune to recompense their friends and neighbors. For some reason, Child's Bank in London offered to redeem the certificates. You see, the venture wasn't a sham. If the railroad had been built, the shares would have paid handsomely. The problem was that Geoffrey had a reputation for taking part in . . . shall we say, less than honorable schemes in the past." He looked at his certificate and sighed. "I kept that sample as a reminder of my own folly."

"Did anyone in the village buy a noticeably large number

of shares?" Sierra knew there was something more behind the story of the investment. Else why would the blackmailer demand the certificates?

The vicar sighed. "Matthew Kent bought five hundred. He said he'd investigated the company and that the venture was sound, in spite of the fact that Geoffrey had the selling of the shares. For once, the boy appeared to be connected with something legitimate. I suppose he wanted to encourage him." He grinned merrily. "And of course there was the lure of easy money."

Matthew Kent. Could he . . . ? "Who is Matthew Kent, Mr. Pettigrew?"

"He owned most of the northwest corner of Suffolk. Inherited it from his wife, who died well over twenty years ago. Matthew had some kind of government post in London, but he spent a great deal of time here. He and his son loved Kent House." The vicar picked up the last scone and smiled reminiscently.

"You speak in past tense. What happened to Mr. Kent?" Sierra asked.

Swallowing hastily, he replied, "Heart attack. He died suddenly, just days after the Child's offer. Pity. He was in the prime of life, and very fit, but when the Lord builds his kingdom, He doesn't pluck only the broken flowers from the garden."

This last philosophical nugget went unheard. Sierra's mind was in a whirl. Could Matthew Kent's death be connected? What had happened to his shares? The blackmail letter had arrived soon after Melanie married her father. Like Mr. Pettigrew, Sierra didn't care for coincidence either. "Had he sold his stock to Child's?" she asked.

"His death and a break-in at Kent House right after the

funeral overshadowed the shares. After all, most people got money back, so . . ."

Sierra broke in, "A burglary? Was anything taken?" She sat forward on her chair, clutching the wooden arms so tightly her fingers cramped.

Mr. Pettigrew looked surprised at her interest. "Nothing of much value. Several rooms were heavily damaged, though, so his son postponed his mourning to put his home back into order."

"Then what did he do, Mr. Pettigrew?" Sierra wasn't sure why she asked, because she thought she already knew the answer, but she found herself holding her breath as she awaited his answer.

"I believe young Fitz assumed the position his father held with the government, although I can't tell you what he does. Doesn't seem to have a strict work schedule, as he comes up here at odd times. But that's government employment for you," he said jocularly. He eyed the empty plate with a certain sadness.

Sensing the vicar had told her everything he could, Sierra thanked her host and moved toward the door. She needed time to think.

By the time she finished a plain, but excellent, early dinner in the inn's little dining room, she knew she couldn't leave without investigating Kent House, even though there was probably nothing to find. She wandered the village in the dusk, subtly acquiring information about the location of Fitz's estate. She intended to break into his home.

The man both frustrated and fascinated her. He had insinuated himself into her life, yet she knew nothing about him—except for her growing need to be near him. Battling with him energized her.

At times he seemed to toy with her, but his eyes promised more. His kiss and the memory of his touch caused her heart to beat faster. The man wasn't at all what he seemed. Since fate had thrust him into her inquiry, she would grasp the opportunity to discover more about the man behind the mask.

The stall of the dark bay gelding she rented was in the rear of the livery stable, where a tall door, wide enough to accommodate a single rider, opened to the rutted alley. Slipping out during the night would present no problems.

She returned to her room to wait.

The position of the moon and the chiming of the clock in the village bell tower tolled midnight. Clad in the buckskins she had tucked in her carpetbag at the last minute, Sierra slipped from the inn and gathered her horse from the livery. No one roused as she led him to the outskirts of the village before mounting and urging him to a trot in the direction of Kent House. "If I don't find Kent House, at least I'll have had a nice moonlit ride," she murmured as she set out along the deserted road.

It was almost too easy. The dark outline of the stone walls surrounding the manor house grounds loomed sooner than she had expected, and she slowed the gelding to a walk. Just inside the entrance, she dismounted and led her mount behind a yew hedge, where she tethered him to a gnarled tree trunk. "Be a good boy and stay quiet. I'll be back," she whispered, digging an apple from her pocket and offering it.

The scents of damp earth and early spring flowers followed her as she slipped along the drive toward the rambling stone house in the distance. The shadowed night was silent. Grateful for the moonlight, she circled the house, looking for an entrance. Spotting the leaded, diamond-shaped panes of a pair of French doors, she flattened herself against the side of the house and peered inside. The ghostly outlines of bookshelves showed along one wall. The room appeared to be either a library or study, the first place she would want to investigate. *Jackpot!* she thought, amazed at her luck.

She stood very still, listening. The only sound was her own even breathing. Moving very cautiously, she slid the blade of her knife down the crease between the doors. The doors weren't locked! Before she could draw her hand back, the latch opened and one side of the door swung open an inch.

For one breathless moment, she froze in place, staring at the opening. Then she recalled how far out in the country she was. Deciding the door was probably never locked, she slipped inside and pulled it closed, listening for the latch to catch.

A quick search of the room revealed a heavy desk in front of a dresser-like outline along the inside wall. She untied the tiny safety lantern from the thong at her waist, set it on the desk, and reached for the tin of matches in her pocket. Before she could open the lid, she was seized from behind. The tin fell to the parquet floor with a hollow sound as strong, ruthless arms wrapped around her. Before she could kick at her attacker, one of his legs hooked around her ankles. Sierra fell backward, sending him to the floor beneath her.

A wad of fabric stuffed into her mouth stifled the scream that rose in her throat, and her heart stuttered as he rolled on top of her. For the first time in her life, Sierra felt helpless.

The lithe, muscular body beneath him writhed, struggling to free itself. Beneath his fingers, supple, rough-surfaced leather shifted and pulled over unexpected softness. To his horror, Fitz's lower body hardened as he grappled with his captive. Damn it, he needed light, but any sign of occupancy would frighten away the people he expected momentarily.

Maintaining a firm hold on the wriggling form, he inched and rolled his captive toward the long rectangle of moonlight spilling through the doors. Then he inhaled deeply, and recognition hit him—wild violets, tanned leather and Sierra Shaw.

"Damn you, Sierra!" he whispered vehemently. "I can't light a lamp. Will you promise not to scream if I remove the gag from your mouth?" Her struggles ceased abruptly. After a pause, her chin moved up and down against his chest.

Keeping her legs clamped between his, he removed the wadded handkerchief from her mouth. Picturing her tongue moistening her dry lips, he repressed the urge to take over the appealing chore himself, but now wasn't the time to relieve his body's demands. "What happened to your widow's weeds?" he murmured.

"They're in my room at the inn," she snapped defiantly.

"You reckless little fool. I nearly shot you outright."

"Well, how was I to know you slept in your study! Besides, you're supposed to be in London."

He smiled in the dark. "Ordering flowers and delicacies for delivery to the indisposed Miss Shaw, I suppose. Sorry, my dear. Not my style."

"Would you please get off me?" She strained against his hold. "Your . . . knee . . . is poking me."

He chuckled his admiration of her delicate euphemism for that part of his body which was pressing into her belly. He rolled to his side and released her. "I was rather enjoying myself," he murmured.

"Don't be vulgar," she retorted. "What are you doing here?"

Her knit cap had pulled loose, and her braid was undone. Moonlight shining through the pale strands gave the effect of a halo he suspected Sierra would have difficulty earning. He grinned.

At that particular moment, Fitz wished Sterling and Madeleine a million miles away, leaving him the rest of the night to ravish the disgruntled beauty next to him. "Must I apologize for being present in my own home when you decide to commit a bit of burgling? What in bloody hell were you looking for?"

He held up one hand as if to fend her off. "No . . . let me guess. Your father isn't really wealthy. You support yourself and your entourage by relieving the wealthy of their surplus."

"Don't be ridiculous! I've never broken into a house before . . . well, maybe into the kitchen in Paradise Valley, but that was just for cook's roly-polies to share with Caleb and the others while we practiced night raiding."

"Then what are you after? Was that paper I heard crackle inside your jacket?"

"Nothing. Nothing at all." She edged away from him.

He caught her upper arm and held her still while he searched. Her body was warm and soft beneath the buckskin, and the thrust of her breast against his hand nearly made him forget his original purpose. Then his fingers found the crisp parchment in the inner pocket. "What have we here?" He pulled out his find and unfolded it.

Fending off her attempts to reclaim the paper, he tilted it into the path of the moon's radiance. The flowing print and intricately scrolled border swam together in front of his eyes, but he knew immediately what he held. The blood froze in his veins. "Is this why you came here? In hopes of finding more of these?"

She stilled, as if sensing his sudden anger. "No. That is, I came to see the vicar. I wanted to see if his certificate was the same as this one. He said . . ."

"He told you I had a whole packet of the little bastards, bequeathed to me by my father." Fitz's thoughts whirled, remembering his father's skepticism concerning the demise of the railroad project. "You're not the first person to break in and search. Unfortunately for you, I don't keep them here." How did Sierra come by the share he held? Why was she trying to locate more? And why the elaborate masquerade? Surely Child's would be a better source of information. Her body warmth clung to the paper. Her scent filled his nostrils, distracting him from the puzzle of the railroad shares.

Sierra shrugged and inched away from him toward the shadows. "I don't know what I hoped to find. Why didn't your father redeem his when he had the chance?"

Her body seemed almost ethereal, the moonlight highlighting her curves and burrowing darkly into the subtle valleys. Fitz realized he'd lost interest in the worthless shares. "Frankly, he was curious as to why the family and the bank were in such a rush to stifle the scandal. He'd planned to investigate further, but then he died without telling me what he suspected." He lazily clasped his fingers around her upper arm. "How badly do you want to see my certificates?" With that he pulled her across the polished parquet into his arms.

At his sudden movement and the change in his voice, Sierra's heart stuttered. She fought the familiar dizziness as he locked her against his hard body. The day had been too full of surprises; how was she to have guessed the stock would lead her to Fitz Kent? "Let me go!" she demanded breathlessly. The feel of his lips nibbling the rim of her ear was exquisite torture.

"No." His lips grazed the line of her jaw.

"I don't . . . want this." Sierra's stumbling attempt to speak trickled to nothing as he covered her mouth with his.

Moments later he broke the stinging contact to whisper, "But I do." Then his lips descended once more.

His kiss drew her into a vortex of spinning color and heat. Sierra threw her arms around him and clung, as if to keep from twirling off into space. She met his ruthless lips and demanding tongue as an equal, her need as great as his. The feel of his muscles stretching and flexing beneath her fingers as he pulled her closely into the cradle of his hips fed her hunger to explore further.

Even as she luxuriated in the extravagant passion of his embrace, she damned Fitz for the ease with which he bent her to his will. He shifted against the hard parquet, his lips slanting against hers as he drew her atop him. Heat pooled low in her body, responding to the press of his hips. Alarm bells rang in her head. This was madness. She was in his house, caught in the act of breaking in, and she was at his mercy. She struggled to pull away from his avid lips.

"Stop." She levered herself upward, reluctantly pulling the lower half of her body as far from him as possible. In spite of her precarious situation, Sierra wanted nothing more than to nestle closer to that intriguing hardness. "Please, Fitz."

"If you don't stop wiggling like that, I won't have any choice but to please you very much," he murmured, his voice thick and his words slurred. He pulled her back against him.

Sierra lay still, absorbing the solid, rapid beat of his heart. She felt her hair loose against her neck and wondered when she had lost the rawhide thong from the end of her braid. As if sensing her thoughts, Fitz's fingers slipped restlessly through her tumbled curls. His arousal throbbed against her leg.

She had grown up in a household of men. Overheard conversations and her own knowledge of stock breeding had left her with few illusions about the mechanics of sex. But she hadn't realized how delicious close contact with an intriguing, unequivocally male body could be. "I've no doubt we could please each other immensely, but we mustn't," she answered candidly.

"Why not?" he demanded, nuzzling beneath her chin. His warm tongue burrowed into the little indentation between her collarbones.

"Please. Don't." Sierra pleaded. His second assault on her senses weakened her resolve. "You're . . ."

"Arousing you?" he teased, his lips joining his tongue.

"Damn it, Fitz, do you expect me to fall into your arms like a doxy?"

A chuckle shook his hard chest. "That's exactly what happened. You came here and forced yourself on me. I'm perfectly innocent." He slid one hand between them and caressed her breast.

Shuddering with pleasure, Sierra bit back a smile and pulled away from his touch. "No," she protested. Bracing her left knee on the floor, she tried to rise just as a shadow fell over the rectangle of moonlight surrounding them. Arresting her movement with one hand, she reversed and threw herself back on Fitz's chest. His arms came around her immediately, pulling her close to resume his assault on her neck with his warm, clever mouth.

"Stop that, you randy bastard! There's someone outside the French doors."

Fitz cursed silently and comprehensively. Sterling was to have delivered Madeleine two hours ago, and he chose now of all times to arrive. On the other hand, Sierra's advent hadn't been precisely well-timed, either. "Stop hissing in my ear," he whispered. "I've been waiting for them. Why the hell else did you think I was sitting here in the dark?" He kissed the tip of her nose and reluctantly moved her to one side. The wrinkled certificate crinkled beneath his hand, and he stuffed it into her fingers.

"Strange kind of guests," she muttered. "No one civilized arrives after midnight."

"May I remind you that the clock in the hall struck one just moments before you broke into my house?" he responded, gathering his feet beneath him. "For once in your life, do as you're told and stay in the background. I'd rather you didn't see these people, but it's too late now."

Standing, he slipped out of the light and moved cautiously to the French doors, where he peered around the heavy drape he'd pulled aside earlier. Satisfied there were only two figures crouched behind the marble statue at the edge of the terrace, he unlatched the door, pulling it inward.

Moments later a heavily draped feminine form slipped through, closely followed by a tall, cadaverous figure. Sterling's hatchet-cut profile was nearly as familiar as his own.

"Fitz?" Sterling whispered as he peered into the shadows.

"Wait till I close these," Fitz instructed. He latched the door securely behind his visitors, then pulled the heavy, lined drapery closed, fussing with the edge closest to him.

Satisfied the close-woven brocade covered the doors completely, he struck a match and lit the gas sconce on the wall behind him.

The thin light revealed Madeleine Dorsey, her head and shoulders covered by a heavy shawl. Sterling stood beside the library table, his gaze locked on Sierra, half-kneeling on the hearth. "Who's she?" he demanded.

"An American. When she broke in earlier, she wasn't aware I was expecting visitors," Fitz explained dryly.

"Broke in!" Madeleine cried.

Fitz crossed the room and raised her hand to his lips. "It's a long story. Quite boring, actually." He lifted the shawl from her head, revealing her coronet of silver hair. "You're looking even more beautiful than I remembered. How are you, Madeleine?" He'd very much wanted her for a stepmother. If his father had lived . . .

"Fitz," she murmured with delight, pulling her hand free and leaning into his body for a brief embrace. "It's been too long."

"I have to leave," Sterling said, shifting from one foot to the other. "I'm fairly certain we weren't followed, but I don't want to risk anyone seeing me near here. If I hurry, I can be the other side of Cambridge by dawn."

Fitz shook his hand. "Thanks, old friend. I'll fill you in on everything when I get back to town."

"Good enough. A closed coach will arrive for Madeleine shortly after noon tomorrow. You'll know the driver." He cast another curious look at Sierra, then slipped behind the drapery and let himself out.

The exhaustion on Madeleine's features tugged at Fitz's heart. He'd been truthful when he'd complimented her—she would be beautiful if she lived to one hundred—but the woman looked as if she'd been living too long on nerves.

"You must be dead on your feet, Madeleine. I'll show you to your room now. We needn't talk until morning. Can I get you anything to eat or drink?" From the corner of his eye he saw Sierra's puzzled expression. "I've forgotten my manners. Madeleine, this is Sierra Shaw, from America. Madam Dorsey is a close friend of my family, Sierra."

The two women greeted each other warily, Madeleine eyeing Sierra's bizarre clothing before saying, "Just show me where I'm to sleep, Fitz. And if I might have a small glass of brandy to take up with me?"

As he splashed the amber liquid into a small snifter, Fitz wondered how much information about his guest would satisfy Sierra's curiosity. Her single-minded pursuit of the railroad shares didn't necessarily mean she was in any way connected to the nebulous scenario he'd built concerning his father's death. Only Madeleine could tell him the details of his father's last day on earth.

CHAPTER TWELVE

Before ushering his guest from the room, Fitz ordered Sierra to remain until he returned. "We haven't finished our discussion."

"Discussion indeed," she said, staring at the closing door. Sierra debated whether or not to obey. Fitz's guests had rescued her from herself. Never before had she felt such attraction to a man. In the past the few men who'd kissed her had professed deep feelings—but she had eventually discovered that each had more interest in her father's wealth and power than in her. Fitz hadn't professed or promised anything; he had merely kissed her until she yearned for more. Damn him.

Why did his beautiful guest arrive so clandestinely? Who was she, and who was the man who accompanied her? An aura of competence surrounded the attenuated man, and he and Fitz had communicated with few words, as if they knew each other well. She wandered idly to the sideboard and poured herself a snifter of brandy. Cupping the glass between her hands, she stared up at the portrait over the fireplace. The resemblance was so striking that Sierra smiled before sipping from her glass. Fitz's mother. The artist must have been half in love with his subject, an auburn-haired beauty half-turned toward the viewer, her gown of soft sea foam–colored silk draping a slender body, and her bright hazel eyes glowed with vitality.

Absorbed in the painting, she didn't hear the door open and close. "People said she brought life into a room when she entered. My father and I were shattered when she died of influenza. I was just a boy." Fitz's voice was grave. "In his later years, my father met Madeleine. She's not at all like my mother, but she's a lovely woman. I'd hoped they would marry because my father needed a wife he could turn to for peace. She refused, because of the danger of his profession, but they continued to be lovers."

"What did your father do?" Sierra asked. The vicar had told her that Fitz had followed in his father's footsteps.

"That's a deep, dark secret," Fitz said lightly. He poured whiskey into a small crystal tumbler and leaned against the sideboard. "Certainly not one I'd share with a common housebreaker," he said, arching an appraising brow.

Sierra returned his cynical look and raised her glass as if toasting him. "Surely not common."

"Perhaps not, but a housebreaker just the same." Fitz sipped his whiskey, then demanded, "Why are you tracking those certificates?"

"What business is it of yours?" Keeping her eyes blank, she looked at him, encountered the purposeful expression on his face, and lowered her gaze to her glass. He was leaving her very little leeway for lies.

"You made it my business when you entered my house."

"The certificates are connected with a personal family matter," she countered.

"Tell me. I'm known for my discretion. As long as there's no connection to my own investigations, the tale will travel no further than the deepest recesses of my brain. Trust me, Sierra." Fitz drained his glass and walked toward her.

Sierra edged toward the door. She had to escape. This Fitz Kent was a different man from the one she'd known in London. His eyes were dark and compelling and his expression serious. She had an unwelcome vision of herself telling him everything.

Never. He already affected her more than she'd ever allowed another soul. In desperation, she demanded, "Give me a good reason why I should trust you."

"Because the Queen does."

Fitz watched Sierra's round-eyed surprise become narrow-eyed suspicion before she replied flippantly, "And I'm Grover Cleveland's Secretary of State."

He answered dryly, "I never said I was important. I just said the Queen has confidence in me. You'd be amazed at the secrets I carry around in my head. See how much I'm trusting you?"

"Trusting me? With what?"

"Why, with the knowledge that I've a secret life." He crossed the room to a comfortable chair and sat. "Surely you've heard what a worthless sod I am. Have you the slightest notion how carefully I've built that reputation?"

Sierra's expression remained skeptical. "I *have* wondered why someone as arrogant as you is content to have the world think you useless. Are you playing some kind of a game with society?"

"I'm wounded. You saw right through my little charade." Fitz held the back of his hand to his forehead dramatically. Sierra, with her native shrewdness, had picked up on his masquerade, even though she didn't suspect the reason for it. "Really, my dear, I can help you. Tell me why you're so obsessed with the shares."

"I can't. The secret isn't mine," she responded tightly.

"Then I suppose I shall have to summon the constable," he murmured as he rose from his seat.

"Don't be ridiculous," Sierra snapped, crossing to set

her empty glass on his desk. "You'll never be able to convince anyone I broke into your house." She snatched her dark cap from the faded Oriental rug and crossed to the French doors. "Just one thing. I have no intention of maintaining an acquaintance with you. You've interfered in my life for the last time." She pushed the drape to one side.

Reluctant for her to leave quite yet, Fitz said, "Go ahead. Run. You'll be much safer in London reviewing a swarm of poverty-stricken aristocrats. Have you turned up any possibles?"

She paused, her hand on the brass handle, and dashed his hope of a negative reply by retorting, "Dozens. And they're all quite eager to marry me *and* to come to America. By the way, not one of the eligibles from that list you gave me is acceptable."

"Maybe you'll have to settle for an ordinary Englishman after all," Fitz teased, ignoring the voice of caution in his brain.

Sierra's color rose; her eyes twinkled like mischievous sapphires. She swung the door inward before responding, "I'm looking for a title, not perfection. What's the good of taking home an Englishman if he's a Mister like everyone else in America?" Stepping through, she slammed the door behind her so firmly the panes rattled in their lead framework.

Safe in her dark room at the shabby hotel, Sierra stripped off her buckskins and tossed them into the corner, then jerked her nightgown over her head impatiently. How stupid could she be? Her body still shuddered at the memory of Fitz's touch. Even though he'd appeared distant when he returned from showing his guest to her room, her senses had still thrummed with the passion of his embrace not half an hour earlier.

For one brief moment, she'd wavered. She had nearly told him everything. Everything about the blackmailer and why she was determined to expose him. But Fitz had looked exhausted.

Although he was alert, his eyes were shadowed, as if he'd missed a quantity of sleep. Whatever the reason, he appeared already burdened with his own nightmares, and her well-honed desire for secrecy had held her back.

Then he'd begun to pry. In the past, she had withstood the blandishments of powerful Washington lobbyists, senators and congressmen fishing for information or access to her father. Now, in the dark of night, she wondered if this time she hadn't been too stubborn. She desperately needed a dispassionate viewpoint from outside the family.

Disgusted with such weakness, Sierra snatched the coverlet back and threw herself on the narrow bed. Damn Fitz Kent and his confidence! He'd assumed her uninhibited response to his kisses meant she was ready to unburden herself.

Heading off scandal was her primary mission. She wanted only to locate the bastard, expose him, and go home. Home to Paradise Valley. She would solve this problem by herself and leave. And yet . . . How much easier would it be with Fitz's help? He was an enigma; she had ascertained that his teasing facade disguised a bright, insightful intellect. But what if he . . . if they . . .

She punched the flat pillow and folded it double, propping her head so she could watch the pre-dawn light gather outside the room's single window. The decision would be easier if she could forget the sensual storm that swept over her when Fitz Kent held her in his arms. She fisted her fingers and struck the mattress by her side. "No!"

She needed to go home, back to the mountains and valleys and streams and fresh, invigorating air. Back to managing the business side of both the ranch and her father's mining interests. Back to something she understood much better than this inexplicable attraction to Fitz Kent. And she would. Just as soon as she discovered the identity of the blackmailer.

As the sun rose, she murmured, over and over, the litany she'd recited to herself during the claustrophobic journey across the Atlantic. "After this I'll be free."

Shortly after sunrise, Fitz jerked a heavy fisherman's sweater over his head and hurried down the stairs to breakfast with Madeleine. He intended to pull every detail of the day his father died from her memory. Perhaps the task would clear his senses of the scent and feel of Sierra Shaw.

Why did he allow such a stubborn, wrongheaded woman to dominate his thoughts? He grinned wryly. Her obsession with worthless railroad stock might be puzzling, but there was no mystery about her effect on him. Fitz stopped in the hall outside the dining room and adjusted his twill slacks, which had suddenly become uncomfortable.

Women had always been important to Fitz, but only as fascinating dilemmas, and only if they accepted from the outset of any sexual liaison that marriage was not written into the script of his life. Sierra Shaw attracted him as no other woman had yet done.

Common sense told him her purported search for a noble husband was a red herring, a flashy facade to cover her real purpose for coming to London. Why did his instinct's message please him so much? But what would her presence have to do with a cancelled railroad venture?

"Ah, Fitz. You remembered our breakfast engagement."

Madeleine's rich voice greeted him from the doorway of the sunny, paneled breakfast room. "Your other . . . guest last night was so intriguing that I feared you might forget," she teased. Her eyes were clear and rested, and Fitz was struck again by her soothing presence.

He smiled as he gallantly took her arm to lead her to a chair. "Intriguing describes Miss Shaw perfectly. Unfortunately, I offended her so deeply that she vanished into the night." Fitz eased the chair forward and waited until his guest seated herself on the brocade-cushioned seat. He squeezed her shoulder reassuringly.

"I know what you want from me, Fitz. But surely the discussion can wait until we've eaten." She smiled, lips curving pensively. "However, I'm still curious about Miss Shaw. I couldn't miss a certain . . . vibration between you. Did my arrival interrupt something?"

Her innocent question triggered a burst of laughter. Collapsing in his chair, Fitz answered candidly, "A great deal more than I'd anticipated when the evening began. Miss Shaw wasn't invited last night. She broke in, hoping to find those old railroad shares Father bought."

His cook's daughter, a fresh-faced girl in her twenties, entered the room and set crystal plates of fresh pineapple slices and strawberries in front of each of them. Madeleine stared at him with surprise. "How odd. Matthew spoke of that investment during dinner the night he died." She took a deep breath and continued, "Perhaps I should tell you what you want to know now, while I have the courage. I'm not proud of how I reacted, but Matthew's death was a terrible shock.

"When I returned to the room, he was lying across the bed. A pillow lay beside his head." Her voice thickened with anguish. "I saw two glasses on the bedside table, and I knew I would be suspected of . . . murdering him. After all, I wasn't his wife, and we'd registered as a couple." She clenched her fork tightly. "So I packed one of the tumblers in my valise . . . and I disappeared."

Triumph flooded Fitz's mind. Madeline's description of the scene reinforced his suspicions. His father *had* been murdered. There had been someone with him before he died. Someone who had drugged him and then suffocated him. Who? He inquired carefully, "Do you recall exactly what he said about the railroad scheme?"

Chaos ruled the docks in New York City. Those with loved ones about to embark cried. Those greeting long-unseen friends laughed and cried. Stevedores loading and unloading cargo ships and porters unable to keep track of their employers cursed colorfully. Rex Haliburton, cradling his broken arm to one side and clutching a heavy carpetbag in his good hand, ignored the chaos as he raced toward the tangle of transportation awaiting travellers escaping the invigorating mix on the docks. The carpetbag thumped against his leg.

Unashamedly emphasizing his upper-class British speech and respectable appearance, he commandeered the nearest hackney by intimidating the harried gentleman who was about to enter. Looking back, he saw the thug-like figure of Charlie Finn some twenty yards behind. As he swung up into the worn interior of the cab, he shouted to one of New York's finest, who was attempting to maintain some sort of order, "That man running toward us just tried to pick my pocket!"

Without inquiring why a pickpocket would pursue a victim who could describe him, the policeman waved his billy club in Charlie Finn's face and seized his arm.

159

"The theater district," Rex Haliburton shouted to the cabbie. He fell back against the sour-smelling squabs and proceeded to count the bills he had removed from Charlie Finn's money belt. Surely an actor of his talents would be able to find both work and a way to fade into the milieu that was the stage in New York City.

By the time the morning train delivered her to London, Sierra's fertile brain had devised a plan, and her spirits had risen accordingly. They plunged when she slipped through the door leading from the servants' staircase and came face-to-face with her aunt in the hall outside her bedroom. "I . . . I was coming to find you as soon as I changed," she mumbled apologetically.

"Don't you ever disappear like that again!" Dolores ordered her. Looking around quickly, she grasped Sierra's arm, opened the bedroom door, and drew her inside. She slammed the door behind them.

Sierra sighed. "I knew you wouldn't approve. That's why I left a note, and why I was so careful to insure no one saw me." Her brocade carpetbag felt as if it were full of rocks. She dropped the luggage to the carpet at her feet.

"I had the devil's own time keeping the maids out of your room. Sierra, you *cannot* ask me to lie to our servants. I feel squeamish enough about lying to strangers." She pulled the bell rope. "Get out of that ridiculous masquerade while I order hot water and a meal. I shall tell the staff you've just made a miraculous recovery." As she left the room to intercept the maid, she added, "We'll talk later."

Sierra pulled off the claustrophobic veil and dropped it to the floor. Next she eased the combs and pins from her hair, sighing as the weight of her curls fell from the cluster at her nape. "She has every reason to be upset," Sierra reminded herself. It *had* been underhanded to sneak off as she had, she admitted, wrestling with the jet buttons down the front of her bodice. She unfastened her heavy crepe skirt and petticoats and let them fall, then stepped out of them distastefully.

Moments later, all evidence of her masquerade stuffed into a hatbox and pushed to the back of the wardrobe shelf, Sierra tied the satin ribbons of her peignoir and peeked around the edge of the heavy lace underdrape. The same man who had been out there the day before lurked two houses down, this time disguised as a street sweeper. Was he someone Fitz had sent to watch her? "We'll have the cleanest cobbles in London at this rate," she observed as her aunt entered.

Dolores carried a breakfast tray and was followed by a sturdy maid with a scuttle of coal in one hand and a brass jug of hot water in the other.

For the first time, Sierra noticed the fire in the grate. Her room was overly warm, and she was about to protest the maid's efforts to add fuel to the glowing coals when Dolores spoke. "That will do, Edwina. I doubt Miss Sierra will require as much heat now that she's feeling better."

Edwina bobbed her head in acquiescence and left the room. "Yes, and that's another debt you owe me. Because you were supposed to be in bed with chills and fever, I kept this room so warm that whenever the door opened, heat simply rolled out. And I had to drink more tea than I've imbibed in my whole lifetime to preserve the fiction that you were in here. Why aren't invalids served coffee like civilized people?" Dolores demanded irritably.

"My dear, I never gave all those details a thought. I'm so sorry," Sierra apologized. She wrapped her arms around her aunt.

"You can make up for it by washing your face and hands and telling me what happened while you eat your coddled eggs and junket. And don't complain about the menu. Mrs. Shaughnessy has decreed that's all you can have to eat for another twenty-four hours."

Sierra moaned and obeyed. "Only Russ would hire a cook who thinks she's a doctor," she mumbled from behind the lavender-scented towel.

"Stop complaining and tell me what happened. Did you discover anything?"

As she drew her chair up to the octagonal table set before the windows, Sierra delivered a carefully edited version of her adventures. "The vicar's certificate is identical, and you'll never guess who owns still more of them . . ."

At the end of her recital, she fumed, "I sailed all the way across the Atlantic Ocean to protect my father and Melanie, and that . . . that overbearing oaf tries to horn in on my plans. As he himself would probably say, not bloody likely."

Dolores leaned back in the chaise where she'd seated herself during Sierra's recital. "Why must you be so independent, Sierra? Kent might be a great help. Remember, he has a strong incentive. His father lost a great deal of money when that railroad scheme failed."

Sierra jumped to her feet and strode to the window. She peered out at the street sweeper, even more positive he worked for Fitz. "I'll do very well on my own. Unfortunately, I must preserve my husband-hunting image while I search for the blackmailer." She wondered how anyone could seriously consider marriage to one of the inbred, poverty-stricken puppies who pursued her so diligently.

If she were truly looking for a husband, she wanted someone who could match her wit for wit and will for will, someone who challenged her, who made her pulses race, someone who . . .

Dear God. She'd want someone like Fitzhugh Kent. The realization was stunning. Light-headed, she reached for the bedpost, clutching the smooth wood until her knuckles turned white.

"Sierra, are you ill?"

Pushing her discovery into the recesses of her mind, Sierra forced a smile to her lips and shook her head in denial. "Not at all, Dolores, I've just been struck with a perfectly marvelous idea," she lied. Actually, the idea had come to her on the train ride from Suffolk. Straightening, she hurried to the wardrobe. "I'm going out. Would you send word to Caleb to bring the carriage around?" She leafed through the padded hangers, pushing aside one gown after another. Finally selecting a marine blue walking dress, she said, "And would you ask Atkins to obtain Lady Heloise Lockwood's address for me?"

Late that evening, Fitz stepped from the last train of the day. Since he was alone in his compartment, he had changed his clothing while the train passed through the outskirts of London. None of the porters or the conductor recognized him as the exquisitely dressed gentleman who had boarded four hours earlier.

Despite his appearance, Fitz found a hackney driver willing to deliver his luggage to his home before he set out on foot for Cambridge Circus. His nostrils, fresh from the purity of Suffolk air, at first took exception to the city odors of horse excrement, chimney smoke, sluggish sewers and massed humanity, but after ten minutes he scarcely registered the change. If asked, he would have said he smelled wild violets, so awash was his mind with thoughts of Sierra.

He'd seen confusion in her eyes before she slipped out

into the predawn darkness. For a moment, she'd looked as if he had struck her. Then her expression had hardened, and her posture became resolute. As if she were fighting an inner battle.

Nimbly avoiding the outstretched hands of two beggars on crutches, Fitz pushed his way through a gathering of revelers on a street corner, all the while keeping an eye out in case the crippled pair had cast aside their disabilities to follow him. The tweed cap pulled low over his eyes and the threadbare sweater and corduroys he usually wore on the farm should proclaim his poverty to the world. Besides, his essence of sheep blended nicely with the amalgam surrounding him.

Without slowing, Fitz slapped away the furtive touch of the pickpocket who jostled against him before turning into the alley off Charing Cross. As he unlocked the discreet door, he murmured to himself, "Damn her! She's up to her ears in this thing. I wonder if that agent she brought along has any influence with her. He sounds like a sensible chap."

"Talking to yourself again, Kent?" demanded the portly, ill-dressed man descending the first flight of stairs. "Too much of that and they cashier a fella, don't you know?"

Fitz laughed, answering, "Shouldn't think I'd be that lucky, old man," and continued up the stairs, buried in his thoughts. *Flaming hell! I should never have let Sierra leave by herself. Who knows what she'll get into.* At least one person had been murdered already. As he swung open the door he said, "Harrison, I need three men for instructions soonest. Will you be free to code a message to Scotland in about ten minutes?"

"Sure thing, guv." The decoder pushed a heavy white envelope across the desk. "This just arrived for you. Through official channels."

Fitz scooped up the elegant missive and turned toward his office. Pulling off his cap, he stared at the copperplate handwriting with quick recognition. "What the . . ." he muttered as he sank into his chair and thumbed open the flap.

My dear Fitz,

I feel constrained to tell you your American friend just left. I have been convinced to lend the use of my safe deposit box at Child's Bank to safeguard five hundred shares of railroad stock, thereby encouraging her to keep me informed as to her progress. The entire scheme sounds enormously cloth-headed. Since I promised I would not betray her to you, this is all the information I can honorably furnish. Please take whatever steps are necessary to protect her. I find her quite single-minded, impulsive and refreshing. My dear boy, whatever have you done to put her into such a furor?

Heloise Lockwood

After his first rush of annoyance faded, Fitz smiled involuntarily. He had wondered how many certificates Sierra possessed. And where she'd come by them. Why wouldn't she announce their supposed safety at her own bank, instead of using Heloise's box? Whatever the reason, it was obvious she trusted Heloise more than she did him. She and the aristocratic Lady Lockwood must appreciate each other's more flamboyant characteristics.

A discreet rap at the door interrupted his musings. At his low-voiced "Come in," three disparate but anonymous-looking men entered. As the door closed behind them, Fitz said, "One of you is travelling to the wilds of Scotland. Draw straws, gentlemen."

CHAPTER THIRTEEN

The next evening, Sierra wished for the hundredth time that she had mastered the nuances of a fan. Opting to work with what she had, she offered Francis Lancaster her most flirtatious smile and fluttered her eyelashes. His usual disapproving expression softened to one of near-civility as he stopped in front of her. Standing at his side, Nigel Brockington greeted her sunnily, his rather plain features lit by his wide smile and frankly admiring blue gaze. "By Jove, Miss Shaw, I'm glad to see you. Didn't I hear you were out of commission with the flu that's going around?"

"Surely that was mere idle gossip," Lancaster said ponderously. "Miss Shaw appears to be in the best of health."

Laughter bubbled very near to the surface at Lancaster's version of a lavish compliment. He was simply socially inept, and she had no idea why he sought her out repeatedly, unless it was for the opportunity to suggest she return to America. During her return trip from Suffolk the day before, she'd considered this propensity of his at great length. Rightly or wrongly, she had pinpointed Lancaster as a candidate for villain, and the idea had given root to the plan already in motion.

The large envelope she'd stored in Lady Lockwood's safe deposit box was empty, but she'd taken great pains to tell everyone she met that she'd placed railroad shares at Child's for safekeeping. Word should have spread throughout the room by now.

Thinking of the shares inevitably reminded her of her midnight encounter with Fitz Kent. The memory heated her skin, and parts of her that she preferred not to think about felt achy.

The puzzled expressions on the faces of the two men towering over her reminded her they expected some sort of response. *Oh, dear.* She leaned toward them conspiratorially, conscious of the flattering blonde lace outlining her bare shoulders and trimming the low neckline of her gown. "Don't tell a soul, but I spent two days catching up on sleep. Your parties here start so late I never return home till the morning hours. Since I ride every morning at seven, I haven't been getting enough rest. My aunt said I've been trying to push three pounds of mush into a two-pound sack and ordered me to bed."

Sierra glanced around the crowded room. "How do you two keep up this pace? Don't you have to be at the bank early every morning?"

Brockington threw his arms out in a helpless gesture. "Surely you've heard of bankers' hours, Miss Shaw. I can't speak for Francis, but I sleep until the very last minute every morning. Few of us have your penchant for fresh air and exercise that early."

"Cowardly, Brockington." Fitz's voice, from right behind her, caused Sierra's hand to jerk, nearly spilling the glass of champagne she'd been nursing throughout the evening. "If early rides are why Miss Shaw is as attractive and glowing with health as she is, maybe there's some point in exercise after all. I must try it sometime."

Cursing his habit of popping up behind her, Sierra turned to eye him narrowly. Fitz had been in the park that first morning she and Caleb had set out, and she'd seen him in the distance on several occasions since then. Why did he persist in enhancing his reputation for uselessness? Exactly what *were* his duties with the government?

"And destroy your image, Kent?" Brockington said, pretending horror. "You're such an inspiration to us all."

Fitz sipped from his own glass and shrugged. "You know the old saying, 'Give a dog a bad name . . .' " His hazel gaze flicked carelessly from one man to the other, then lighted on Sierra. "It's much the same for a woman. Once people view her as a shallow twit, she's buried with the label. Even if she suddenly devotes herself to something serious, such as finance."

Sierra tilted her head flirtatiously and teased, "Surely you're not talking about *me*, Mr. Kent? If I were thinking of changing my ways, finance would be the refuge furthest from my mind. All those numbers would be too much for the female brain."

"Miss Shaw, you're charming just as you are. But why are you wasting your time with three commoners? Shouldn't you be in pursuit of some agreeable young sprig from a noble tree?"

Sierra met his bright, brittle glance with a glare of her own. Why did his gibes about her false husband hunt hurt so much? Tears pricked at the backs of her eyes. Without even excusing herself, she fled.

Slipping silently through the shadows into an alley from Fleet Street toward four that morning, Fitz felt more and more annoyed with Sierra Shaw. So far, his search of the area surrounding Child's Bank had been fruitless. He'd found only a few protected doorways and interesting niches where an enterprising watcher could settle in for the night—and his own people occupied two of them.

He almost missed the figure crouched in a basement entrance, nearly indiscernible in the dimness. Fitz edged behind the dustbin haphazardly angled toward the stairwell, then reached through the iron bars fencing the entrance to tap Caleb's shoulder lightly.

The Paiute slid his knife from its sheath and tensed. Fitz touched his shoulder again, this time adding a reassuring squeeze. Caleb's head raised cautiously above the stone border, his dark eyes alert in the faint light from the street.

Fitz whispered, "I didn't mean to embarrass you, old chap. If it's any comfort, I've been sneaking up on people without a sound since I was just a little nipper."

"Jesus! You nearly got yourself scalped!" Caleb mouthed softly.

"Fancy a red one, do you?"

Ignoring his quip, Caleb demanded, "How did you find me?"

Fitz hunkered down into the angle between the building and the cobbled alley, wishing the only shelter available was somewhere other than behind a foul-smelling dustbin. "I'd love to say I tracked you here from Miss Shaw's house, but you probably wouldn't believe that." An unbelieving snort from the entry confirmed his guess. "I tried to think like your pretty employer and decided I'd stake out the bank where I'd just stowed worthless shares."

"I suppose you also know who I am watching for." Caleb's voice revealed nothing, and Fitz was sure the Indian's features were as impassive as his inflectionless whisper.

He answered, "We share the acquaintance of several people with access to Child's." When Caleb didn't respond, Fitz continued, "I imagine she's a bit of a handful to work for. You really shouldn't allow her to send you out on these fool's errands in a strange city."

"Maybe this isn't a fool's errand. No one would dare touch the deposit box during the working day. He has to make his move at night," Caleb responded doggedly.

Fitz rolled onto the balls of his feet and rested his chin against his bent knees. "Possibly. But what if you've the wrong candidate for whatever you suspect? Then someone else has a clear field, and you're left guarding a mouse hole with a false exit."

"I gave Sierra the same damn argument, but she insists I do this her way. When I catch him, I'm supposed to drag him back to her." Hesitance entered his voice. "And make him tell her everything she wants to know. Whoever *he* is."

Fascinated, Fitz asked, "And then what will you do with him? Bury him in an anthill?"

Caleb's eyes glittered in the thinning darkness. He sneezed. "Maybe I'll leave him in a bloody heap on your doorstep. I suppose you have a better suggestion?"

"Go home to bed. Tell Miss Shaw that whoever she's looking for is more dangerous than she realizes. Tell her she's better off enlisting help." He paused. "*My* help."

Shifting position, Caleb grunted his disapproval.

"You can also tell her I said she's being foolhardy, that I'm already in the game. I'll take over."

The Indian's eyes glittered in the darkness. "Don't know what you've done to fire her up so far, but that would blow the roof off the hunting lodge."

Fitz grinned in the darkness. "Got her knickers in a twist, has she?" He leaned closer to the stone divider and whispered, "Tell me, Caleb. Does she take orders from *anyone?*"

"Not unless she wants to."

Fitz gathered his knees beneath him and sighed. Well, he'd tried. "No wonder no one's married her yet. I pity the poor bastard she picks out of this year's crop." He shared a grin with the lad crouched in the stairwell. "You're welcome to sit there till your feet go numb. I'm home to bed."

170

He cast a swift glance around their surroundings and stood, nodding slightly toward another shadowed entryway where one of his men had just settled in place.

Caleb's precise whisper reached him before he'd taken two steps. "Doesn't plan to marry any of them, anyway."

For some reason, the Paiute's verification of what he'd suspected all along warmed Fitz's heart as he made his way home by way of alleys and shortcuts. The cool predawn air swept away his exhaustion, and he paused to relish the sight of the pinkish pre-sunrise brushing the buildings ahead with the color of roses in moonlight.

He visualized the stubborn tilt of Sierra's chin and the way her heavily lashed eyelids lowered when she was challenged. Her expression at such times reminded him of the gunfighter he'd met while on a mission for his father in Texas. What an amazing country America was; the women were apparently as fiercely independent as the men. Yet Sierra had been feminine and yielding when they were sprawled on the floor of his study. His body reacted pleasurably at the memory, and he shook his head, amazed by his own thoughts. He hadn't room in his life for a hard-headed, managing piece of fluff from across the ocean. Certainly not.

Disgusted with himself, he crossed Chancery Lane in the direction of his home. Damn it, he needed sleep. The problem of Sierra Shaw could wait until noon.

At nine that morning, the contents of a telegram arriving at snug, luxurious lodgings in Kensington threw the resident into a black rage.

"Disappeared! How could Finn lose a man with a broken arm? I bloody don't believe it." He balled the message in the palm of his hand and hurled it across the room, where it bounced off an ornate beveled mirror. He sprang to his feet in a rage, kicking two footstools and a papier-mâché japanned table out of his path.

As suddenly as he'd erupted, he threw himself into the chair at his desk and reached for his pen. Since Finn had been so careless, the blighter could approach the Senator's wife himself. To hell with subtlety. Minutes later he jerked the bell rope to summon his valet.

"Take this to the telegraph office immediately," he barked when the mousy little man responded.

Sierra was worried, angry, and just the littlest bit guilt-ridden as she set out for dinner and cards at Lord Southpoole's town house. Caleb's face had been flushed and his eyes feverish when she'd seen him late that afternoon; he'd contracted a cold. Reconciling herself to taking his place that night, she'd ordered him to his bed. She'd known he was feverish when she sent him out, and her conscience pricked.

Caleb's report of his encounter with Fitz infuriated her. Damn the man! She would never allow him to take over. Not with success this close. Someone was sure to make a move soon, and Russ should return from Scotland any day with information which could be crucial.

Meanwhile, she had committed herself to yet another boring evening of pretending interest in the son of another noble family. She turned to her aunt. "If I have to sit through many more dinners where they bring in a baked salmon that stares back at me, I'm going to have hysterics. What's wrong with throwing out the head and skin and frying the thing?"

Dolores chuckled. "That wouldn't look elegant on their ancestral china. Besides, in England, only the lower classes fry fish. These aristocrats are trying to impress you, Sierra. To them, your father's wealth must look like the pot of gold at the end of the rainbow."

"Then they ought to serve my food the way I like it." She pleated the ice-blue silk of her skirt between her kid-gloved fingers, then smoothed the fabric. "When all this is over, I'm going back to Paradise Valley and I'm never leaving." The brief visit to Fitz's bucolic estate had reminded her that city life made her claustrophobic and how much she despised formality. "I thought that fat Marquess at the luncheon today would explode when I slapped him on the back. Did you see how red he got?" she demanded.

Dolores compressed her lips, but laughter danced in her dark eyes. "I thought I was beyond embarrassment, but you surpassed yourself. His wife nearly tripped over her chair to distance herself from you. No inheritance could possibly be large enough to make you acceptable to them."

"That's fine. Their son wasn't acceptable to *me*." Sierra lifted her chin defiantly. "I won't miss this place at all when we return," she lied.

"Are you sure? Many people have been extremely kind."

"Tony Belville for one. You must be the first woman he's ever met who recognizes the Latin names of the plants he talks about. I think he's smitten with you, Aunt Dolores." From the corner of her eye, she glimpsed the heightened color of her aunt's cheek before she turned to peek through the narrow, uncurtained window of the carriage. "Good thing he's invited everywhere we are. Or do you wangle invitations for him?"

"We're almost there," Dolores said evasively.

Sierra smothered a smile. Her aunt might pretend no one noticed Belville's attentions, but the two had been the subject of gossip. Even she had heard speculative comments. The carriage rolled to a stop. "Perhaps I'll only be a tiny bit crude tonight."

What had begun as a harmless masquerade had become an embarrassment. She was conscious of people suppressing their distaste. All but Fitzhugh Kent, who had seen through her. Unfortunately, he seemed more amused than anything else. And suspicious, the despicable snake. He aroused feelings she'd never before experienced. Conscious of warmth rising on her cheeks at the reminder, she turned her thoughts away from him. Once more, she attempted to convince herself she was excited by the prospect of a long night huddled in some miserable doorway.

As the door of the carriage swung open, Dolores murmured, "Thank you for warning me. I prefer to be prepared."

Sierra smoothed her gloves over her fingers and teased, "I never know ahead of time . . . until I discover the lengths to which people will go to snare me for their son." She adjusted her cashmere shawl across her shoulders and stepped from the carriage.

When Dolores joined her, they ascended the stone steps. Sierra looked up at the well-kept building. "The Southpooles aren't hurting for money. I've heard David's a gambler, which would be a very good reason to want to send him to America. Why would someone think I need a husband who'd bet the ranch on the turn of a card? The rumor mill says they're also hunting a husband for their daughter. The Honorable Emma is terribly sweet, but she's older than I am, and clearly desperate. I met her at the Enderbys' ball."

The butler led them up the curving marble staircase to the formal drawing room, where the first person Sierra saw was Fitz Kent, wineglass in hand, in laughing conversation with Emma Southpoole and her brother David. The rather plain young woman clasped Fitz's arm possessively, and looked up at him with hunger in her eyes. Sierra was surprised by how much she wanted to snatch Emma's hand from the fine dark broadcloth of Fitz's jacket.

"How kind of you to join us, Miss Shaw. And Mrs. Shaw," Lady Southpoole gushed. Her husband, standing behind her, huffed something unintelligible.

One look at her hostess revealed where Emma had inherited her looks. Sierra felt a sudden stab of pity for the girl. Possessed of nondescript features and a small dowry, she'd probably been imprisoned on the nursery floor until she was old enough to be launched into society with the expectation that she would miraculously transform into a dazzling flirt. Not for the first time, Sierra gave thanks she'd been born on the other side of the Atlantic. "The pleasure is ours, ma'am," she responded as sincerely as she could manage.

"Ah, Miss Shaw. Mrs. Shaw." The Honorable David Southpoole joined them. "You've time for a glass of sherry before dinner."

Although her entire being focused on Fitz, she couldn't help observing that David had inherited his father's rather florid good looks. In twenty years, the son would probably look like a well-fed squire.

David stopped before a cart holding a cluster of decanters. "We're serving ourselves tonight," he added unnecessarily as he lifted a stemmed glass and deftly poured the pale amber liquid.

Sierra thanked him and looked around the room, recognizing most of the two dozen people awaiting the butler's announcement of dinner. "I'm surprised to see Fitz Kent here this evening. I wasn't aware you knew him," she said casually.

"Fitz? Everyone knows Fitz." David touched his glass to hers before drinking. "Here's to closer friendship between our countries."

Ignoring the hint of desperation in his voice and in his hooded brown eyes, Sierra sipped from her glass and continued, "Your sister and he look as if they know each other rather well."

"Not as well as she'd like," he answered bluntly. "Our Fitz is very quick on his feet when a woman sets her sights on him. The income from his mother's estate puts him well into the eligible category, but he makes rather a thing of being useless, if you get my meaning." David took another sip of his sherry. "My sister's had a liking for him since her come-out, but he don't seem to return it. Pity. He's nice enough."

Relief flooded Sierra. She'd seen the promises in the girl's eyes. Many men would find that sufficient . . . an opportunity to take a wife who was so pathetically grateful she would spend the rest of her life worshiping the man who saved her from spinsterhood. Sierra was well aware that only her father's money prevented people from calling her an old maid. "Perhaps he feels as I do. Being single is preferable to marrying someone you don't love. 'Nice enough' would never be enough, David."

With quick understanding, he smiled ruefully down at her. "I know. But try to pretend it might for a few days, would you? For my parents' sake."

Sierra patted his arm gently. "Why *do* you gamble so much? That is if you don't mind telling me."

"It's the church or the army for younger sons. Since I'm too cowardly for either, I gamble and drink." He shrugged appealingly and his lips twisted in a bitter smile. "If I were the butler's son I could emigrate to America and make my fortune as a . . . cabinetmaker, perhaps. As it is, I'm The Honorable Third Son of a viscount. Forever and ever." He lifted his glass and drained the contents.

Just then, the butler announced dinner. With amusement, Sierra watched Fitz's fruitless efforts to disentangle himself from Emma. *Serves you right, you slimy polecat,* ran through her mind. She took pleasure in the idea that he would spend an uncomfortable evening. Smiling inwardly, she slipped her hand into the crook of David's arm and allowed him to lead her into the dining room. A footman carrying a platter featuring a baked, reconstructed salmon stood to one side. Avoiding her aunt's gaze, she began to count the minutes until she could leave.

Across the ocean, Charlie Finn ordered a bottle of whiskey and settled himself into the corner booth of a Washington, D.C., establishment known for the shadiness of its clientele. He glared fiercely at anyone who approached him, enjoying the way their glances slid away from him. He then proceeded to drink himself into oblivion. As his efforts succeeded, he bolstered his spirits as surely as did the liquor he poured steadily down his throat.

With each refill, his internal dialogue with the fast-emptying bottle grew in venom. "Bloody barstid! Tells *me,* Charlie Finn, hit's my fault the sodding nancy boy give me the slip! 'Ow was I to know the sodding barstid was goin' to do a bunk, eh?" He gulped another swallow and belched so loudly that two furtive-looking men at a nearby table turned and stared.

Finn scowled at them and wiped his mouth on the sleeve of the neat twill jacket he'd donned for his late afternoon call. On receipt of his boss's telegram, he had taken the first train to Washington, arriving barely in time to complete his mission. "Orders me to get the papers from the Senator's mort or not to bother comin' back to bloody England. Din't I try nice and perlite like? Walked right up to that frigging front door big as life and asked fer 'er." He belched again.

" 'Taint my fault they 'opped a bloody boat to England. Must 'a passed the blighters in the middle of the bloody ocean," he told the bottle earnestly before pouring another drink. "Serve him right when they get there an' I ain't tole' 'im to expect 'em."

He raised his glass as if in salute and continued triumphantly, " 'E can do his own dirty work next time. Charlie Finn's goin' ter be a bloody Hamerican."

CHAPTER FOURTEEN

The evening had gone downhill after the fish, Sierra thought as she stepped from an ancient hackney onto High Holburn in a misting rain. She hunched her shoulders and dug her hands into her jacket pockets. Setting out after midnight on her own frightened her more than she cared to admit. Even in her buckskins, her hair securely braided and concealed by her knit cap, she felt conspicuous. She was aware that the few people still on the streets were night people busy stealing, selling what they sold, or preying on the unwary.

This was as close as she dared ride in the cab. At least the streetlights illuminated the walkway and showed her the alley she sought. Under duress, Caleb had given the directions to his snug vantage point behind Child's Bank, his arguments punctuated by gigantic sneezes. "Damn you, Sierra!" he shouted when she'd informed him she would find her own place if he didn't tell her the way. Then he'd fallen back on the pillow in surrender.

Sierra slipped into the narrow, shadowed pathway, telling herself firmly that threatening figures weren't lurking on either side. *I don't want to do this. I don't. But I have to. What if I turn coward and run home . . . and tonight's the night?* Her thoughts ran in circles, terror clawing at her insides. *I'll feel safer, not so exposed, when I find that stairwell,* she reassured herself, looking over her shoulder. Although nothing loomed out of the darkness, she nearly ran toward the misty light at the other end of the alley.

Only one narrow street to cross, and I should be there. To her right lay blackness; to her left a streetlight illuminated the corner. She fought an overwhelming urge to run in the direction of that blessed brightness. Her stomach clenched at the memory of the dark passage behind her, and the knowledge that she would have to retrace her footsteps when she returned home.

As she stared longingly at the light less than forty feet away, a figure appeared, pausing as if waiting for someone. He wore a flat, nondescript cap and a ragged sweater of some sort. Sierra was about to turn away when a man leaped into the swathe of misty light, his arm upraised. The waiting man dodged away, but not quickly enough. The attacker's arm slashed down at an angle, striking the first man on the side of his flat cap, which spun away into the darkness as its owner slumped to the sidewalk.

Light from above burnished the victim's dark red hair to copper.

Fitz's name shrieked in her head as she flew toward him. Arriving just as the attacker raised his arm to deliver a second blow, Sierra seized his free arm, braced her moccasined feet on the cobblestones and jerked his body forward. Instead of falling as he should have, he swung around. She saw the cosh in his hand.

A voice from somewhere behind her warned, "Bugger off! Someone's coming!" Then everything went black.

Voices wakened Sierra. Her jumbled mind selected one that sounded familiar, and she tried to open her eyes to identify the speaker. The effort set her head pounding as if her brain were being crushed, and she abandoned the attempt. Where was she?

Unwilling to risk setting off the sledgehammers at the base of her skull again, she took a mental inventory of her body. Moving her toes didn't seem to hurt; she flexed the muscles in her legs tentatively. She explored the texture of the smooth surface beneath her body with the fingertips of her left hand. Inhaling deeply, she recognized the faint scent of sachet. Definitely linen. Well-cared-for linen.

Her efforts drained what little strength she had, and Sierra focused on deciphering the murmured words she heard from somewhere in the vicinity of her feet.

"That's an impressive bruise behind your ear, Fitz. You should be in bed yourself," a calm bass voice asserted.

"I didn't ask for your medical opinion, you old fussbudget. I've had worse and still danced the night away." Fitz paused, then asked anxiously, "You're sure she'll be all right?"

"She's slightly concussed, but I suspect her head's as hard as yours. She should be coming around any time." The voice sounded closer. Sierra felt a gentle touch on her forehead. She tried to form words, but the effort seemed too much. Cautious fingers raised her left eyelid, and she stared steadily back at the baldest man she'd ever seen.

"I say. She's awake." The doctor smiled at her and said, as if telling her something new, "Bit of a headache, eh what?" He removed his hand from her face and grasped her right wrist, which rested atop the blanket. "Good strong pulse. You were a very lucky young lady tonight. After this you'd be much better off letting the bastard have another go at Fitz. He's tougher than an old boot." He released her hand.

"More wit than brains, if you ask me."

In spite of his sarcasm, she heard profound relief in Fitz's voice. Braving another onslaught of pain, Sierra opened her eyes and said blearily, "Should have . . . guessed . . . your head was full of . . . sawdust."

181

"Knows you well, Fitz. I can see I'm not needed here any longer." The doctor backed away from the bedside. "You'll do well to spend the next day or two in bed, Miss Shaw. After that, take it easy. Let your headache govern your activities. I've left some powders for you to begin taking in the morning."

With that, he stepped into the hall and closed the ivory-painted door behind him. Sierra lowered her eyelids, prepared to savor the blessed silence, then realized she hadn't asked the crucial question. "Where am I?"

"My house. Two of my associates arrived just as you fell, but the bastard got away. They thought it expedient to bring the both of us here."

Fitz's warm hand enveloped hers. "Since you're weak as a cat and can't attack me, I must point out that although brave, your leap to my defense was abysmally foolhardy and unnecessary." He squeezed her fingers. "I found it rather touching, Yank."

Sierra discovered she hadn't the strength to pull loose from his hold, so she settled for, "Go to hell, Brit. Did your friends get a look at the second man?" She forced her eyes open so she could see his face.

"Second man?"

Fitz's arrested expression was so satisfying she felt stronger. "He warned the first one. What were you doing there?" She closed her eyes once more. Her lids felt as if weights hung from her lashes.

"More to the point, what were *you* doing there?"

"Caleb is sick," she whispered, her lips scarcely moving. In spite of the comfort of Fitz's warm hand grasping hers, she wanted to sink back into that cotton wool world where her head didn't ache.

Fitz replied sarcastically, "Didn't Caleb tell you I

dropped in to see him night before last? The boy amazes me. He's as queer in the attic as you are, allowing you to venture out alone on a fool's errand."

Sierra struggled to pull herself up, a thousand arguments jockeying to be first off her tongue. Her head rang as if a full set of timpani and a man with three arms had taken up residence, and she collapsed back on the pillow, helpless.

Fitz lifted her right arm and tucked it beneath the covers. He pulled the sheet up to her chin, smoothed her hair back from her forehead, then bent to kiss her softly. "You never give up, do you. By morning I'm sure you'll have the energy to tell me in more detail which path I'm to take to Hades. Until then, give that head a rest. Paxton will waken you every few hours tonight to check your eyes. He's a bit of an old granny, so don't let him worry you to death. I'll send someone round with a note for your aunt to let her know you'll be here for a few days."

Her brains must be more muddled than she thought. He actually sounded shaken. Sierra had forgotten how worried her aunt would be when she discovered her missing. Guilt snaked through her. "She . . . ah, doesn't know I'm gone. I'll be well enough to return tomorrow."

"Why do neither of those statements surprise me?" He came nearer, his scolding words a teasing caress. "Someone has to keep you out of trouble, dear heart, and it seems fate has turned the matter over to me. What *has* your father been thinking of all these years, to allow you unrestrained freedom?"

Sierra felt his lips against hers once more, and this time she sensed anger, as if he were suppressing deep inner rage. Dear God, she was dizzy and weak in a strange bed in an unknown house, completely in Fitz Kent's power. Beneath his soothing facade he was furious. In spite of this, she felt safe. She knew that as soon as her strength returned she would rebel, but for now it was exceedingly pleasant to lie here, soothed by the fragrance of fine linen and Fitz's quixotic kindness. Tomorrow would take care of itself.

The headache he denied the night before had vanished by the time Fitz awoke shortly after ten the next morning. He could sense, rather than hear, Paxton's presence in the dressing room, and without opening his eyes, he called, "Has she wakened yet?"

"If you refer to Miss Shaw, I'm happy to say she is sleeping soundly." The valet glided into the room carrying a silk dressing gown. "I checked her throughout the night, just as you instructed, and feel sure she will suffer no ill effects other than a slight headache for several days. She will need something to wear." He held out the dressing gown.

Fitz eyed the robe he'd never worn and inquired, "Are we pretending Miss Shaw might somehow walk in here and find me in the buff this morning, Paxton? I thought you said she was still asleep. Before you deliver that, be a good sort and run my bath. While you're about it, invent a reasonable explanation I can give her for how she came to be clothed in one of my best batiste shirts."

Paxton delivered a quelling glance as he eased the door closed behind him.

While he waited for his bath, Fitz lay flat on his back and stared at the blossoms sculpted in bas-relief at the border of the ceiling. If he lived as long as Methuselah, he would never forget his terror at the sight of Sierra's limp figure stretched across the opposite seat of the carriage. Only half-revived himself, he had nearly babbled his fear out loud.

She had looked so little and broken.

By the time they'd reached Queen's Square, he'd recovered sufficiently to supervise her careful transport to the airy bedroom overlooking the park behind the house. Street sounds wouldn't disturb her there.

Because his hands had shaken so badly, it had been Paxton who removed the knit cap and loosened her tight braids so they could examine the growing lump on the back of Sierra's head. After that, tremors or not, he had selfishly performed the task of slipping the supple buckskins and her undergarments from her delicious little body, wishing he were performing the task under more favorable conditions. He'd felt quite righteous as he buttoned one of his finest shirts all the way to her determined chin.

His hands had shaken even more after that exercise in discipline. A vivid memory of the perfection of her exquisite curves was etched into his brain.

"Foolhardy wench," Fitz muttered as he stepped down from his bed. Lowering himself into the welcome warmth of his bath, he called to Paxton, "Have Cook fix a tray for Miss Shaw and one for me. Bring them to her room in half an hour, whether she's awake or not."

The tantalizing fragrance of hot chocolate and fresh-baked muffins teased Sierra's nostrils. Her attempt to sit up triggered a dull ache in the back of her head, but nothing to compare with the thunderous pounding she remembered from the night before. The first sight that met her eyes was Fitz, who had made himself at home at the oval table near her bed, slathering marmalade on a steaming muffin. Her stomach rumbled. "I'm starving," she asserted.

The dripping morsel poised in his hand, Fitz looked at her with bright, mischievous eyes. "Well, you can't have my breakfast. If you prove you can sit up, there may be one or two of these beneath the cover on your tray. I asked Paxton to have Cook send you invalid food, but Paxton said she just snorted. My orders count for very little in this house."

Sierra braced the palms of her hands on the bed to lever herself upward then stopped, her eyes on her chest where the covers had fallen back. "How did I get into this shirt?" she demanded.

"Much the same way anyone does, I imagine. First one arm, then the other," Fitz responded. His attention was focused on dissecting the kipper on his plate.

"*You* undressed me, didn't you!" she accused. Sierra felt the blood rushing to her cheeks. *How could he?* "You . . . you perverted . . ."

"Oh, come now. Perverted would have been monkey business while I had you starkers, and I nobly refrained from that." He tucked the last bit of muffin into his mouth and chewed, his face thoughtful, then added, "Of course, my dreams last night *might* be construed as perverted."

Sierra pulled her legs beneath her, fully intending to leap from the bed and dump the contents of the steaming chocolate pot over his head. The movement caused her head to spin, and she collapsed against the pillows. "You're disgusting, interfering and arrogant, and if my father were here, he'd have you strung up from the nearest tree."

Although her experience was nonexistent, her mind filled with visions of herself and Fitz Kent, unclothed and locked together in various amorous positions. The shudder which shook her wasn't one of fear. Heat spread throughout her body, while her rebellious stomach rumbled once more.

Opening her eyes, she demanded, "My tray, please."

Fitz wiped his fingers fastidiously on an embroidered linen napkin, rose and approached the bed. "Let me plump your pillows behind you first."

When she eyed him suspiciously, he held both hands in

the air. "I promise not to ravish you until after you've had something to eat."

She bit back a grin at his earnest expression. She grumbled with pretended ill will as he positioned the down pillows and helped her sit up. Even though she felt as if she had been dragged backward through a knothole, she reveled in the intimacy of being alone with Fitz in the sunny, simply furnished bedroom. Aware that the sheer batiste of his garment covered her only as far as her knees, Sierra discovered she was unable to meet his impersonal gaze.

"Here's your tray," Fitz announced, settling her breakfast over her lap. "There's even a copy of the *Daily News* if you enjoy reading about the wickedness infecting the world while you fortify yourself for the day ahead."

Sierra recognized his detached briskness as a kindly attempt to ease the awkwardness of the situation in which she found herself. Did his teasing mask anything else? Had he truly found the sight of her unclad body arousing?

Deep down, she was insecure about her own desirability. Her male playmates had seemed like brothers, so it wasn't until she was an adult that she was aware her appearance could have an effect on the opposite sex. She'd credited the attention she'd received in London to the general knowledge that she was the daughter of a wealthy man. Now, through her own impulsive scheme, she was alone and unchaperoned in a man's house. The Victorian hostesses who had welcomed her into their drawing rooms would dine out on this for months if they knew.

Shouldn't she be grateful Fitz was behaving like a gentleman? How silly she would be to return his kindness by reading anything more into this.

During her silence, Fitz had returned to his chair and was dispassionately consuming his own breakfast. She gath-

187

ered her nerve and said, "It just dawned on me that you've been put into a compromising position, Fitz." She pushed scrambled eggs around her plate with her fork. "I'll slip away as soon as I've eaten and dressed."

"You'd look a trifle odd travelling in daylight wearing those buckskins," he drawled. "Besides, they're locked away. The doctor ordered a day or two of rest, and that's what you're going to get."

"No one orders me," Sierra snapped, her softer feelings evaporating. "Least of all you, you . . ."

"Bloody bastard is always a nice way to start," Fitz finished for her, reassured by Sierra's healthy color and the combative light in her eyes, which were very blue this morning. He filled his cup and pushed his chair away from the table, then slouched against the carved back and crossed one ankle over the other, fully prepared to argue with her.

"I prefer black-hearted, interfering son of a . . ."

"Very nice. One can't help but notice that although someone, at some time, tried to effect a softening influence on you, you weren't a very receptive pupil," Fitz said softly.

Gratified that his statement had the desired effect, he sat back, prepared to wait out her anger. Her voice had risen, reminding him he, too, had received a healthy blow to the head within the last day or so, and her apologetic, "I was shouting, wasn't I," assured him she was experiencing the same discomfort.

"You were."

"You're quite right about my needing more rest." She leaned back on the pillows and closed her eyes. "My head's pounding dreadfully."

Sierra's sudden acquiescence aroused Fitz's suspicions.

Casting aside his lazy pose, he stood and walked quietly to the edge of the bed. "This has all been too much for you. Shall I take away your breakfast?"

At her weak nod, he lifted the tray. Her hand reached for his wrist and stayed his movement. "Perhaps that muffin might revive me a little." He heard her stomach rumble.

"Trying to turn me up sweet with the fade-away performance, Sierra?" He settled the tray firmly back in place. "You might as well give in and eat. There isn't a piece of clothing anywhere within reach. Paxton has locked my dressing room, and the servants have been warned to be on the watch for you sneaking down the stairs wrapped in a blanket."

Sierra's full lower lip tightened. She opened her eyes. "You're despicable. I hope Aunt Dolores arrives on your doorstep with her scalping knife."

"That's much better. As to your aunt, she sent a gracious note not half an hour ago. I believe she intends for you to remain here until you've recovered sufficiently to return home." He paused, then added for emphasis, "She mentioned something about being sick and tired of discovering your room empty in the morning. Surely you've not been up to *other* things not quite out of the top drawer?"

Her gaze falling to her plate, Sierra responded, "You would be the best judge of that, since you turn up every time I venture out after dark." She scooped eggs onto her fork and raised it to her mouth with delicate greed.

Suddenly all Fitz wanted was for the fencing between them to stop. "I appreciate your objection to my surveillance, but surely you realize I couldn't let you endanger yourself. Perhaps we should talk about joining forces against a common enemy. But eat your breakfast first." Positive his words would pique her curiosity, he left the room.

CHAPTER FIFTEEN

Sierra's mind worked furiously while she ate. Although the food and hot tea restored her physically, her thoughts raced. The worthless railroad shares. In Suffolk, Fitz's expression had changed, become focused, at mention of them. Why?

She worried at the question throughout the bath a pleasant, elderly maid drew for her in the claw-footed tub in the adjoining bathroom. Never before had she been so grateful for modern amenities. The lingering pain in the back of her head all but disappeared when she gingerly shampooed her hair with the lavender-scented soap, and the tight muscles across her neck and shoulders eased when she lowered herself into the tub's porcelain depths.

After toweling her hair dry and combing her tangled curls, she reached hesitantly for the man's dressing gown the maid had laid out for her. The rich sapphire-colored garment could only belong to Fitz. The thought of it against her skin seemed like an intimacy she could ill afford, considering the way her body, and her emotions, reacted whenever she was near him. Actually, all she had to do was think of him to have the same reactions, she admitted to herself with searing honesty.

No familiar mingling of sandalwood and citrus rose to her nostrils when Sierra buried her face in the robe's silken folds, and she laughed at her own fancies before sliding her arms into the sleeves and turning up the cuffs to free her hands. Fitz had never worn this robe. Slipping the belt from its loops, she lapped the lapels across her chest and carefully hitched up a fold above her waist before knotting the silk length firmly.

Turning to look in the freestanding mirror beside the armoire, she realized to her horror that she'd created still another problem. Her breasts played hide-and-seek from behind the drooping lapels.

A tap at the door made her clutch at the opening. "Don't come in!" she called sharply.

"Shall I return in half an hour?" Fitz's voice inquired.

"I . . . I don't think half an hour will be enough," she squeaked. She tucked the left side further beneath the right and released the sleek satin. The lapels fell into the same sinfully revealing position. "This isn't going to work," she said plaintively.

In the mirror, she saw the door ease open and Fitz's head appear cautiously. "Who are you talking to?" he inquired.

His eyes widened with appreciation, and she snatched the lapels together again. "I want my buckskins back!" she demanded.

"Why should I do anything so idiotic?" Fitz drawled as he closed the door and leaned his shoulders against the panel.

She backed away, clutching the robe in a death grip. "I can't sit around here wearing this. My . . . my arms will fall asleep." His warm gaze told her she was babbling.

Fitz pushed back the left side of his jacket and probed in the flat pocket of his matching vest. He sighed loudly as he pulled something out. "I was afraid you would object to lounging around my house like an houri, so I brought you this."

Sierra eyed his extended hand with suspicion, then edged nearer. The engraving on the heavy gold bar pin gleamed in the sunlight flooding through the simple linen curtains. Eyeing him cautiously, she moved closer, freeing one hand to snatch the pin. "You beast! You could have pinned this to the robe when you sent it to me." Turning from him, she stepped away from the mirror, removing her reflection from his line of sight, and carefully fastened the lapels of the robe together just below her chin.

Pushing away from the door, Fitz crossed the room to a chaise upholstered in violet-printed linen and pulled an ottoman alongside. A wry smile tilted one corner of his mouth. "Yes, but then I wouldn't have had the pleasure of presenting you with the solution. Come over here and sit on the chaise. We need to talk."

She eyed him cautiously, positive the temperature in the room had risen. The tight sash and overlapped lapels were uncomfortable; she felt flushed and overly warm. Damn him! He was as relaxed as if he were enjoying a day in the mountains, and tiny beads of perspiration had broken out along the back of her neck. Refusing to allow him to fluster her further, Sierra eased past him and settled onto the chaise. She kept her feet on the floor, moving her knees to one side as he occupied the ottoman. "What do you want to talk about?"

"Those railroad shares. My father was murdered because he was about to investigate the people behind the venture. Now you're in London looking for more certificates." His hazel eyes were suddenly very gray, very bleak. "Where did you get the ones you have, and what else do you know about them? More importantly, why are you looking?"

She couldn't tell him. Not as long as there was a shred of a possibility that Geoffrey had miraculously survived the paddleboat explosion and could stage a "return from the dead" to threaten Melanie. She decided on a partial version of the truth. "I don't know anything more about them than what you've guessed. As to why I'm searching for them, and who owns them, it's a personal matter which is none of your concern."

A muscle at the side of his lean jaw twitched, then quieted, and Sierra realized he was angry. Further efforts to put him off with flippancy would be futile. Fitz Kent was dead serious. But so was she.

He stood, suddenly tall and menacing, and looked at her. "You must not have heard me, Sierra. I believe, and will shortly have proof, that my father was murdered because of manipulation of the stock in this venture. You know something that could help me unravel who's behind the whole bloody mess, and you're going to tell me."

Sierra rose also, fisting her hands at her hips. She risked tilting her head back to glare up into his stark features. "I'm sorrier than I can say about your father, but I can't help you."

He glared back. "You can, and you will. And until you do, you won't leave my house." He turned on his heel and stalked toward the door.

Remorse flooded Fitz as soon as he turned the key in her door. After he'd delivered his ultimatum, the defiance in her eyes had been overlaid with fear. He desperately needed her trust, trust that would allow her to reveal her reason for tracking the stock. Most of all, he wanted her to trust herself to him emotionally.

If only the enormity of his loss hadn't suddenly struck him, and he hadn't behaved like a heavy-handed clod. He, who prided himself on his detached finesse.

He shoved his hands into his pockets and stared moodily

at the ivory-painted panel. Would she pound on the door demanding release?

He'd never met a more stubborn woman. Her hard-headed response affected him like a lighted match tossed into a barrel of gunpowder. She couldn't be after more of the shares. Her father had all the money in the world, and the report he'd received indicated the Senator thought his daughter walked on a moonbeam. Why was she obsessed with a failed railroad venture in northern Scotland? All she had to do was trust him enough to explain.

Yet she'd stood there, her delectable little body naked beneath a silky robe he'd never worn, its slick fabric sliding over her curving hips and high, curving breasts, and defied him—when all he wanted to do was rip the damn thing from her and sink into her tight warmth.

"Did you require anything, young master?"

Paxton's voice and wry address startled him. For a moment, Fitz stared at his valet with unfocused eyes, still picturing himself curved over Sierra's unclothed form. He was a blazing idiot. He would have her secrets and he would have *her*. The hell with subtlety. "Just woolgathering, Paxton. Miss Shaw has information I desperately need, and she's being a tad stubborn about sharing." He smoothed the hair he'd unconsciously ruffled and buttoned his coat.

"I've locked her in her room. Take a footman with you when you deliver her meals in case she makes a run for it. She'd have few qualms about strolling down the Strand wearing nothing but my robe. I'm lunching with Lady Lockwood in half an hour, and won't be home for dinner." He turned toward the stairway, a sense of something he might have forgotten nagging at his thoughts.

Sierra forced herself to stay calm. The bright noonday

sun flowing through the multipaned windows would keep at bay the panic that attacked when she was unable to come and go freely. When night came, it would be much worse.

An incipient headache still nagged, and she recalled the doctor's recommendation. A day of bed rest. Tonight, or tomorrow at the latest, she would escape. Settling herself on the chaise, she fixed her gaze on the park behind Fitz's house.

She would devote her depleted energy to the problem of figuring out what she knew that could be of the slightest help to Fitz. The shares had been Geoffrey's legacy to Melanie, but someone, perhaps even Geoffrey, if he were somehow still alive, wanted them. Desperately. If she told Fitz the entire story, Melanie and her father could be engulfed in scandal.

Only the close-knit, trusted friends who had accompanied her to England knew of the threat to her father's happiness and career. They loved him as deeply as she did. None would jeopardize one hair of his head; each owed him too much.

Her aunt had been considered one of the family long before she had married Uncle Zephath, and her loyalty was absolute. Her father had rescued Russ from a mine cave-in, paid for his education, then retained him as the ranch's attorney and agent. His salary was equal to what the government paid her father for sitting in the U.S. Senate.

Her father and Zephath had discovered Caleb's parents in an abandoned Indian village. They had been unable to migrate with their tribe because Soroki had been in labor with Caleb—a long, exhausting delivery that nearly killed her. The siblings who followed him had arrived easily and frequently, probably because Soroki had been well-nourished from the moment Theodophilis Shaw settled the little family in the tiny village north of Paradise Valley. They had joined eight other Paiute families who'd been left behind in the flurry of tribal emigrations as white men invaded Indian territory.

Adrian Harding had said she could trust Fitz; her instinct agreed. What held her back was fear. Fear that the attraction she felt would turn her into one of those women who deferred to the supposedly superior intellect of a man whenever a problem arose. Even though his life appeared to be a mass of contradictions, Sierra didn't doubt Fitz's abilities. She just believed she was as capable as he of tracking down and eliminating the threat to her family.

But she had to escape so she could continue her search. Her thoughts jumped from her predicament and the threat to her father's happiness, then back to Fitz Kent. The strain brought a return of her headache. Sierra poured one of the doctor's powders into a glass of water and drank it, then stretched out on the bed, willing a solution to present itself in her dreams.

While Sierra slept, Fitz enjoyed excellent Dover sole and amazing conversation with Heloise Lockwood. He broached the subject boldly. "About this business with Sierra Shaw, Heloise. Are you sure you can't share the particulars of loaning your box at Child's?"

The stiffening of her already rigid posture told him her answer before she spoke. "My dear boy. I impugned my honor by even revealing the arrangement. Considering the number of minions you command, I expected you to have discerned both Miss Shaw's problem and her plan by this time." In spite of her acerbic reply, a twinkle lurked in her dark eyes.

"As you well know, I have to mind the store occasionally. The outcome of the Congress of Vienna is no certainty, and developments in the Transvaal don't offer much peace there for ten or fifteen years, and probably more," he explained. He stared at his plate for a moment before placing his fork carefully at an angle and saying bluntly, "I spoke with Madeleine Dorsey this week."

"After all this time? What has she to say for herself?"

"She reinforced my theory that my father was murdered. Madeleine said that during lunch the day before his death he'd spoken of looking into the railroad scheme. He had an appointment with a man connected to the venture in some way. And he'd sent an operative to Scotland to investigate the accidents that killed the three principals. The operative's report was apparently misfiled. My staff is searching for it." He closed his eyes tightly in an attempt to regain his composure, then continued. "My father was eliminated because he was asking too many questions. But Geoffrey had already left the country by then. Who else was involved?"

Heloise patted his hand. Fitz knew that was the closest she would come to offering comfort. "As I recall, the dead property owner's heirs refused to honor the agreement for the right-of-way. I wondered at the time why people believed that flimsy tale, but then the others died, too. And of course the investors' money was missing," Heloise mused. "Do you still have all those certificates your father bought from Geoffrey Trowbridge?"

Fitz toyed with his crystal goblet as he answered, "I had thought they were the only ones Child's didn't redeem. But Miss Shaw has one, and I gather she has a great many more. Where did she get them? And why is she using them as bait?" The pale blush wine washed back and forth and nearly splashed out onto Heloise's embroidered linen luncheon cloth.

Heloise's eyes were suddenly alight with laughter. "So that is why you were wandering Fleet Street last night. I heard you were struck down and some urchin leaped in at the last minute to save you a worse beating."

"The urchin was Sierra Shaw, Heloise. Caleb had been there the night before, watching the service entrance to the bank, but he contracted a cold. She meant to take his place." Fitz wasn't surprised his hostess knew about the attack, but was grateful the servants hadn't included the identity of his rescuer in the story. How had Sierra earned such protected status?

Heloise patted her lips with her damask napkin and eased her chair away from the table. "I assume Miss Shaw is unharmed. You could both have been seriously injured." She strode to the door and beckoned for him to follow her to her private sitting room. "I fear I must break Miss Shaw's confidence. Your father was murdered because of this railroad venture, and now you and Miss Shaw have been attacked." She ushered him in and closed the door behind her before seating herself at an ornate writing desk, waving him toward a comfortable armchair.

"From what Miss Shaw told me, she suspects Geoffrey Trowbridge may still be alive."

Fitz laughed. One of his own people had already brought back conclusive proof that Geoffrey was dead.

"Or that someone is impersonating him. Although she would not confide the name of her suspect, Miss Shaw is convinced he can access Child's at night, so you're correct in assuming she's setting a trap. She banks elsewhere, so she made quite a thing of secretly borrowing my box, which of course set people talking."

"But that's ridiculous! What if this person retrieves the

stock? She's risking everything on a suspicion with no facts to back it up."

Heloise leaned forward and released a hidden lever at the back of the writing surface. A sizable drawer slid open, and she handed him the contents. Fitz began counting. "My sainted aunt! There are five hundred of these! Are you saying she never put anything in that blasted box at all?"

"Some hot air, perhaps."

Sierra slept through the afternoon, awakening only when Paxton's light rap at the door broke the silence. She pushed her hair back from her face and looked down at the robe, which had lost some of its carefully tied and pinned elegance.

The robe was the key to the plan she had formulated just before she dozed off. "Come in," she called.

Paxton, followed closely by an expressionless footman carrying her dinner tray, entered the room cautiously, blocking the opening with his body. Sierra wondered what he would do if she set off at a dead run and simply bowled him over on her way out. Instead of following through on the idea, she yawned, patting her mouth with polite fingers. "I believe I've caught up on some of the sleep I've lost since I arrived in London." She paused to lap the right side of the robe more snugly over the left and tighten the belt.

"To be sure, miss. Would you like the tray here?" Paxton said repressively, pointing at the table where Fitz had eaten his breakfast.

"That will do nicely," she answered, still fussing with the robe as she rose from the chaise. "Did Mr. Kent say when he would be home this evening?"

"Only that he would return too late to dine with you."

Sierra was amused by the way he watched her from the

corner of his eye as he set her place and whisked the covers off the offerings on the tray. The footman who carried her dinner had all but thrown himself spread-eagle across the doorway. She tugged at the shoulder of the robe once more, then said, "I don't suppose you've anything else around here for me to wear. This is not only too big, it's slippery."

Paxton's eyes narrowed with suspicion as he inspected her garment. "Mr. Fitz mentioned specifically that the robe is the most suitable thing we have."

"You mean he said I wouldn't dare be seen on the streets in this, so there was no chance I'd try to escape. The man has a devious mind, Paxton," Sierra said, fashioning her most winning smile. She lowered herself into the chair he pulled out for her.

"To be sure, miss."

Paxton busied himself straightening the room. His back was to her, but Sierra made a show of tasting her soup, then setting the spoon on the service plate while she fussed with the upper lapel, finally repinning it beneath her chin. She resumed eating, pausing every few bites to tug at one part or another of the robe.

"If I may be so bold, Miss Shaw, I believe the, ah, garment could be better secured if you had a number of safety pins to assist you. The bar pin appears to be insufficient," Paxton pointed out apologetically.

Amazed at the success of her ploy, Sierra wondered if Fitz frequently harbored women in his house. Both he and Paxton had taken the attack the night before very much in their stride. And the doctor, whoever he was, seemed not at all surprised to be summoned in the middle of the night. At the thought, her tongue stumbled over itself as she answered, "Yes, of course. Why didn't I think to ask? Could you find some for me?"

The footman was dispatched, and Sierra continued with her meal.

When the pins arrived, Paxton inquired what else she might need. Assured that she had everything she required, he bid her good night. As soon as the door closed behind him, Sierra abandoned her meal and upended the tiny tin on the pristine bedcovering, counting to see if there were enough pins for her purposes. Then she untied the sash and let the extra length of the robe drop to the floor. Reaching down, she seized the hem at the center of the back and pulled it up between her legs.

By the time she finished pinning and tucking and tying half an hour later, she had fashioned a strange-looking garment which freed her arms and legs for her escape. She had no intention of staying prisoner any longer than necessary.

Feeling more and more hemmed in as the night closed around her, she willed herself not to light any lamps and went to stand flat against the wall by the window to peer down at the garden. No lights reflected outward from the back of the house, although she assumed the foyer and perhaps one of the rooms in the front were kept alight for Fitz's return.

She stood thus for ten more minutes, until the darkness and silence began to weigh on her, then eased the casement upward and looked out. The house was built of stone, with irregular joinings forming a network of rough mortar. Leaning out over the sill, she saw, to the left, a drainpipe attached to the wall. It led to the gutter of the roof over the rear entryway. If she could just reach that . . .

Without hesitation, Sierra climbed through the window and hung by her hands, searching with her bare feet for crevices deep enough to provide a toehold. Cautiously, she reached for the pipe, heaving a sigh when it proved firmly attached. Then she released her left hand from the sill and fumbled for a handhold. Soon she created a rhythm, moving either one hand or foot at a time, then grasping and pressing flat against the stone.

She felt little fear at being suspended so far above the earth. This was no different from the cliff faces she and Caleb had climbed from the time they were quite small. The fresh air, the unconfining garment pinned around her—her relief at being free was almost tangible.

When she and Fitz Kent next met, she surely would have conquered her attraction, the tug that generated these feelings of weakness and yearning. They would meet as equals, not as captor and prisoner.

Her toes brushed the tiles of the narrow, slanted roof, and she shifted her weight until she knelt atop them, relishing the day's heat that radiated from the clay into her flesh. The sun had fully set, and peepers and night insects spun a chorus to the night. The scent of early roses wafted up from the garden, and she inhaled deeply before turning onto her stomach and inching closer to the edge of the roof. In moments, her legs, with the ridiculously pinned brocade pulling against her calves, hung over the edge. She reached for the gutter, tested it for stability, then gripped it with both hands and allowed the rest of her body to follow her legs.

CHAPTER SIXTEEN

The quarter moon provided sufficient light for Fitz to appreciate the shapely legs dangling before him. An hour earlier, while shuffling a mountain of papers at his desk, it had dawned on him Sierra would never submit to imprisonment. Only one escape route was available, one he'd neglected. He had arrived minutes before she crept cautiously over the windowsill.

He wondered if he should be a gentleman and step back, allowing his houseguest to make her way home in the unorthodox garment she'd fashioned. He then recalled that his treatment of Sierra Shaw hadn't been particularly conventional thus far. This was no time to deviate.

He caught her before her feet touched the ground. Her startled shriek pierced the night air before Fitz could press his hand gently over her lips. He shook her gently, cautioning, "Not so much noise, you little twit. You'll have the entire household down on us, and poor Paxton's had enough shocks for the day."

Her left leg curled itself around his ankle and he grinned, bracing himself against the sudden pressure and murmuring in her ear, "What a delightful idea. But surely you'd prefer more privacy." Her subsequent shrug thrust her hips against his lower body, and Fitz realized he was fully aroused even as he shook with laughter.

"Give off, Sierra, or you'll find yourself tumbled behind the rosebushes." Moving his hands to grip her shoulders firmly, he lowered her feet to the ground. "There's a good girl. If you promise not to shriek again, I'll let you walk into the house under your own power." *And then I'll tumble you.*

When she didn't dignify his offer with a response, he clamped one arm around her and guided her in through the domestic region of the house, drowning in the fragrance of her hair and suffering the movement of her rounded buttocks against his thighs. "Turn here," he murmured, guiding her through a doorway to the servants' staircase. "What *have* you done to my new robe?"

"Only a perverted Brit would wear something like this."

Sierra's bare foot missed the top step, and she nearly dragged both of them down before he caught her close with both arms and swung her to the landing. Holding her snugly against him, he negotiated the last step, muttering, "You should be more aware than anyone that what I have in mind isn't perverted in the least. Here, turn right."

Sierra followed his instructions numbly. Heat from his body surrounded her. And the bastard wasn't playing fair when he called attention to the hard presence she'd felt against her back since she'd landed in his arms. His hand against her belly felt wonderful. Strangely, she felt nothing but eagerness at the inevitability of what was to come. The beat of his heart against her back accelerated. As did her own.

He released her briefly. A lock clicked and a door swung open. "In here, my adventuresome Yank." He guided her through the opening, pulling the panel closed softly behind them. He lit a wall sconce, turning the light low. In the dim glow, she recognized the room she'd just escaped. Fitz turned her in his arms, and his voice was dark and seductive as he murmured, "I'm afraid you'll have to be punished for trying to run away wearing my clothing." His lips descended.

Sierra rose on her toes, pressed herself against him and wrapped her arms around his hard torso, knowing in that instant that she was abandoning all pretense of dislike, knowing she would tell him anything he wanted to know, if only he continued to hold her and kiss her like this. Her skin tingled and that unmentionable area at the juncture of her thighs quivered expectantly.

Without volition, her hands roamed his back, the pads of her fingers defining each muscle and sinew, discovering the strength and solidity she'd speculated about and craved. He fit in her embrace as if he'd been fashioned for her alone.

He slanted his lips against hers as their tongues feinted and thrust. She wanted more. Much more. Sliding her hands around, she reached between them to tug at the buttons of his coat and waistcoat. "Help me," she whispered breathlessly.

Fitz obliged, his fingers nearly as clumsy as hers. "Undressing *you* will be more complicated," he said as he jerked his shirt from his trousers and brushed her trembling fingers away from the pearl buttons. The feel of her, naked beneath the satin brocade, the material slipping and sliding across her narrow back and the graceful swell of her hips, had nearly undone him. He paused at his task and cupped her breast, the tip of his thumb circling her thrusting nipple. "I'm not sure I've the patience."

She held his hand against her breast, her lids closing dreamily. "Maybe Paxton can find us a pair of scissors."

Fitz slipped his arm beneath her knees and lifted her slight weight. The silk slithered against his bare chest where his shirt fell open, and he bestowed a hard kiss on her eager lips. "Excellent idea. The experience would leave him speechless." He lowered her to the bed Paxton had turned down and reached into his trousers pocket for the engraved pocketknife his father had given him thirty years earlier. Her eyes widened at the sight of the razor-thin blade. He chuckled. "I'll try to be quick. And to keep my hands from shaking."

The center of the robe's hem was pinned at the waist, its edges angling downward to below her knees. Sierra had pleated excess fabric up each side of the bodice, shortening the sleeves and eliminating the overlap of the right lapel. Pins and clumps of fabric left him no starting place. His fingers shook in spite of his promise. "I'll have to start over," he muttered. Placing the knife on the bedside table, he slid his arms beneath her and turned her onto her stomach.

In the rear, the excess material had been left to its own devices. With exquisite care, Fitz plucked a gleaming fold and slit the silk from her nape to her delectable derriere. Pausing only to fondle one dimpled cheek, he cut away the fabric to both knees, then made even shorter work of the sleeves. Sierra lay still and flat, not even responding to the little touches and caresses he bestowed as each part of her seductive body was exposed.

Shreds of glowing silk littered the linen sheets and outlined her body, the dim light from the sconce turning her into a landscape of flickering shadows. Fitz had never felt such a need to touch, yet he stood motionless, frozen by his own desire.

Without stirring, Sierra asked grumpily, "May I please move now?"

"Not yet," he said, shaken by the visual feast before him. Her pale skin took on a translucent luster in the nest of shredded sapphire silk. Sierra's makeshift braids had long ago unraveled, and pale gold curls tumbled over her cheek. Fitz was seized by a mindless compulsion to explore every inch of her. He stripped off his jacket and shirt and flung them to one side with his waistcoat sandwiched between, grinning at Paxton's probable reaction when he found them. Then only one goal filled his thoughts; he stretched out beside Sierra.

At the press of his lips on her nape, she shuddered. "Fitz, I . . ."

Instead of replying, he touched the tip of his tongue to the shallow indentation at the base of her hairline and brushed his fingertips over her shoulders. Her breathing became ragged.

Sierra moved beneath his hands. "I want to . . ."

Even as Sierra surrendered to his caresses, Fitz forged a meandering trail of kisses across her slender back and down her spine to its dimpled base. She lay quiescent, her muscles quivering beneath his lips. The leisurely savoring drenched Fitz's senses until he felt drawn tight as a bow.

Anchoring her restless thighs with his knee, he clasped her shoulders firmly. He murmured against her skin, "You can't take charge of your own seduction. I've every intention of allowing you to seduce me, but later." He memorized her flesh with his fingertips.

She was silken fire beneath his hands, and when he finally turned her onto her back she reached for him hungrily. "Let me learn all of you," he breathed, anchoring her wrists above her head. Her scent surrounded him, and he was suffering agonies tamping down his urgency.

Nothing the shocking Sierra Shaw had done should have led him to think she was a virgin—her hoydenish travels through the dark streets of London dressed as a boy were only one example.

Yet instinct told him otherwise. And she, who fought

tooth and nail to control every aspect of her life, was giving herself to him. At the realization of such generosity, his mouth went dry with hope. Fitz had nearly abandoned the idea of finding the other half of his soul. Now that he had, he intended to convince her they were meant for each other. He lowered his lips to the valley between her breasts, against the quick heartbeat beneath, closed his eyes, and inhaled wild violets and pure Sierra.

Even as she quivered beneath his touch, everything within her yearning for his touch, she knew she must tell him. "Fitz, you should know something before . . . before we . . ."

His hair gleamed deep copper in the dimly lit room, gaslight creating shadows in the waves that had sprung to life. He lifted his head and met her gaze. "You're a virgin. I already knew."

Involuntary laughter pushed at the back of her throat. "Was that in the report you received?"

He kissed the swell of her left breast. "No. I just knew. Don't be crushed, but that first time I kissed you, I knew."

His assertion relaxed something within her, but she had to finish. "The only reason I tried to leave tonight was that I . . . I can't stand being shut in anyplace alone. Particularly in the dark."

His lips travelled to the hollow at the base of her throat, his words vibrating against her skin. "You should have told me at breakfast."

Flutters of excitement radiated from where his mouth rested. "I . . . this thing between us frightened me. I refused to believe I could trust you. Fitz, I'll tell you everything you want to know."

"Everything?" he asked, his voice vibrating with wicked

amusement. His mouth settled in the sensitive hollow beneath her ear.

Nearly unable to breathe from wanting, Sierra swallowed laughter. "Anything you want to know . . . about the railroad shares." She shuddered as his teeth closed delicately over her earlobe. "And about why I'm here."

He rose above her, his eyes dark with passion. "Later. What's between us has no bearing on any of that. I've wanted you from the moment you told that dreadful whopper about hunting a husband. You looked at me as if daring me not to believe you, then batted your eyelashes like a Covent Garden tart. It took me two seconds to realize you weren't what you appeared to be."

"You've been a pain in the ass ever since," she said lovingly, straining to reach his lips. Their conflicts were behind them; now all that remained was the task of convincing Fitz she wasn't a bossy, managing shrew. At least not all the time.

She began by tugging her wrists from his gentle hold and wrapping her arms around his neck to pull his head down for her kiss. "Please," she begged. Sinking her fingers into the cool softness of his hair, she pleaded against his lips, "Please."

Fitz complied so quickly that she gasped at the wonderful weight of his body and the heat of his flesh against hers. Her legs and hips moved restlessly beneath the sweep of his hands. She wanted more. Tugging on his shoulders, she demanded, "Kiss me, Fitz. Please."

"I didn't know you could beg so prettily," he murmured against her lips. Sierra opened to the greedy invasion of his tongue and her desire escalated almost past bearing.

His hands continued their delicious forays at the sides of her breasts before sliding down and clasping her buttocks to hold her even closer to his pulsing heat. When he broke the kiss and buried his face against her neck, his fingers moved to the juncture of her thighs. Her insides coiled and tightened with exquisite pain.

Fitz stroked her soft folds. She was ready for him. Without pausing, he removed his hand and eased into her. He slanted his lips against hers, thrusting his tongue deeply into her welcoming mouth. Her body tensed as the flimsy inner barrier gave way. Then, her virginity gone, she wrapped her legs around his hips and surged against him, destroying Fitz's noble vow to treat her gently.

She met each thrust with eager intensity, and he raced toward fulfillment as if this were his first time; Sierra was with him, her hands and body urging him on.

When her body convulsed around him, the last vestige of his control fled, and his body arced with the force of his release.

Eons later, Fitz lay atop her, his mouth resting slack in the hollow of her throat, breathing heavily, inhaling their combined scents. He pressed the tip of his tongue against her skin, awed by the feel of her life racing through the vein beneath.

Never had he lost control so completely. From the moment her sleek, silk-covered body slid into his arms, an entire regiment couldn't have stopped him. She was so responsive. And so tiny . . . "I'm crushing you," he mouthed against her skin as he braced himself to roll to one side.

"No, you're not," she whispered, wrapping her arms around him more tightly. "If I say 'please,' will you stay?"

Content to let her have her way, he warned, "Be careful. The word might become a habit."

Her gurgle of laughter vibrated against his chest. "I never knew it could bring such wonderful results."

Sierra's hands stroked down his back, over his hips, and Fitz felt desire stir again. Bringing her with him, he rolled to his side, then to his back, careful to stay within her. "If I give in to your begging again tonight, you'll be uncomfortable tomorrow." He placed his hands on either side of her face, studying her softened features, her glowing eyes, and her mouth, full and pink from his kisses. "Thank you, Sierra. I've never been so honored."

Her eyelids fell, masking her eyes, and a soft blush pinkened her cheeks. Fitz thought her lower lip trembled, just once, before she said softly, "I . . . didn't have any other choice."

The surge of elation he felt left Fitz wondering if his mind had slipped its moorings. Then he remembered the unanswered questions standing between them, and he nearly groaned. A bed drenched with the musky fragrance of lovemaking was no venue for him to demand information.

Sierra saw the confusion in his eyes, saw him mask it as quickly as it appeared. Fitz controlled his social persona ruthlessly; his ability to mask his shrewd intelligence was superb. From their first meeting she had sensed annoying little mysteries floating around him like an aura. Just now she'd seen a flicker of uncertainty in his eyes. And she knew the cause. Their minds were on the same track.

Reluctantly, she rolled from atop him and reached over the side of the bed for Fitz's discarded clothing. Pulling his wrinkled white shirt from the muddle, she slipped her arms into the sleeves and clutched it around her as she sat tailor-fashion on the bed. "This may be the safest time to tell you what you want to know," she said.

As if agreeing to the distance she'd put between them, Fitz pulled the sheet up to his waist and propped himself against the carved headboard. "I don't know if it's exactly flattering that my lovemaking precipitated such soul-baring," he said, grinning ruefully.

"If I can trust you with my body, I can trust you to help me avert a family tragedy. My new stepmother inherited five hundred of those certificates from her first husband, Geoffrey Trowbridge." Sierra pushed her curls back from her face with both hands and embarked on the sordid little tale of blackmail from the grave.

Fitz sat through her recital without moving or changing expression, and by the time she finished, Sierra wondered if she had sufficiently emphasized the delicacy of the matter. Perhaps her narrative had been too emotional . . . His reply astounded her.

"What a pity you didn't approach me with this the first time we met. When Adrian Harding suggested you contact me, he must have been so discreet you misunderstood, but of course he couldn't have known about the blackmail. What *did* he tell you about me?"

"He said you were much more clever than you appeared. Then Chloe giggled. He frowned at her, then he laughed too." She pleated his shirtsleeve with nervous fingers. "When I met you, I couldn't imagine what they had found so amusing. You . . . I noticed too many contradictions in you," she blurted, plucking at the monogrammed shirt cuff.

He stilled her restless fingers with one hand and lifted her chin with the other until his bright, inquisitive gaze met hers. "Fascinating. People who've known me forever accept my public self, yet you look at me with those beautiful eyes and see through it." His eyes darkened and his mouth twisted wryly before he continued, "Darling Sierra. I'm director of an anonymous little bureau that gathers bits of obscure but pertinent information for Her Majesty's government."

"Why didn't Adrian tell me?" she inquired, determined not to show her surprise.

"It's not something one runs about tossing into polite conversation. Besides, he worked for me at one time."

"Spying?" Throughout her time in Washington, Sierra had heard numerous stories of the games governments played with each other and the lengths to which they would go to gain or retain mastery over both friends and enemies. She also knew the harsh punishments meted out to those who were caught. Had Adrian been in her country to spy? She pulled away from Fitz, but his body followed her. He bracketed her face between his palms before answering lightly, as if reading her mind, "You missed the past tense. There was a spot of trouble, and Adrian went through rather a bad patch, which was made worse when he met and fell in love with Chloe smack in the middle of the mess. He retired before they married." His voice darkened as he continued, "There's nothing sinister about my department. 'Information gathering' describes what we do more precisely. I've never asked anyone to jeopardize himself, but sometimes a situation escalates more rapidly than we anticipate. When I know in advance things could get dicey, I go myself or send a career man."

"Then you already know all about the railroad venture. You were left the shares and you'd already investigated the project," she said, feeling deflated and superfluous. She must have looked like a fool in her clumsy attempts to track the blackmailer. Her heart fell. Fitz had been amusing himself at her expense. She attempted once more to pull away, and once again his hold tightened.

His voice was pain-filled. "My father was murdered, remember? The railroad shares were only one of a dozen reasons someone could have wanted him out of the way. Do you know how many leads we followed? How many dead ends we hit? None of us in the department accepted the verdict of natural death, but there were too many directions to look."

Sierra steeled herself against the desolation in his eyes. "Still . . ." She tried to ignore the sudden realization that Fitz's work could put him in danger, too.

"The railroad scheme smelled from beginning to end. I was in South Africa when my father invested. He assured me he'd vetted the project. He even expressed pleasure at Geoffrey's connection with something legitimate for a change. Now I'm beginning to think whoever managed the investigation for him was in on the scheme from the beginning."

"One of your father's own people betrayed him?"

Fitz closed his eyes. "Quite likely. Only now that person may be one of *my* people." He was silent for several heartbeats before he said, "Whoever is behind all this has an uncanny ability to cover his tracks. You must be driving him bonkers. He can't know what you've discovered or what you'll do next."

"But why? What's to be gained?" Goose bumps rose on her forearms.

"In a moment," Fitz said, slipping down from the bed. Unself-consciously naked, he crossed to the window she had used as an exit and lowered the sash. He drew the linen curtains closed, the tabs sliding smoothly over the waxed wooden rod. Returning to the bed, he swept the jumble of silk tatters to the floor before climbing between the sheets and drawing her with him, tucking her close to his side. He said lightly, "I'm just discouraging anyone who might be watching my lighted windows."

She tried to sit up, but his hand, flat against her hip, held her inexorably against his side. "Surely no one could see . . ." She couldn't bring herself to supply a word for what had happened between them. None she could think of were adequate for such a glorious experience. The thought of some stranger spying from one of the centuries-old trees in the park froze her blood.

What happened tonight had been inevitable. Dear God! She'd fallen in love with a man who harbored secrets from all over the world. Surely, once he realized they were pre-destined for each other, he wouldn't keep *that* a secret.

Fitz turned on his side and buried his face against her throat. "Fascinating, don't you think? I've never before worried about anyone watching my house. No one knows what I really do. I'm just a useless booby who happens onto things, so *you'd* be the one they want to see." His voice be-came tender. "By the way, it's impossible to actually see in these second-floor windows. When I was a boy, I climbed each tree out there to spy. The angles are wrong. All anyone can see is whether the lamps are lit." He nuzzled her ear and added, "However, if someone *did* happen to be watching my house, he would have had a clear view of you climbing out the window in that charming outfit. I'd rather they not know you were back inside."

Sierra wanted to hit him, but she was too busy exploring the contours of his chest with inquisitive fingers and arching her neck to give him better access to the sensitive skin beneath her chin. She marveled again at the interplay of the flat muscles beneath her hands, and wondered how his tailor managed to disguise any impression of strength.

Making a purring noise in the back of her throat, she murmured, "I don't feel sore at all, Fitz. In case you should feel inclined to, ah, repeat the experience."

"Oh, God, yes," he replied, his lips browsing the swell of her breast. "Everything in its time. Heads may roll tomorrow, but tonight we make love."

CHAPTER SEVENTEEN

The clock in the downstairs hall struck twice, rousing Fitz. Sierra's breast and taut belly remained still beneath his hands. *By God, I'll have the hammer yanked from the bloody thing before nightfall.* The chimes disturbed him only when he was troubled. Even sexual satisfaction and the contentment of holding Sierra curled against him hadn't prevented worry about her safety from lurking in his subconscious.

Normally, once he relegated a problem to the next morning, he slept soundly. This time the threat involved not his country's future but his own . . . and that of the woman he was determined would never return to America except to visit. No wonder he'd wakened.

Despite his fear, his groin tightened pleasurably as Sierra pressed closer in her sleep. Fitz ran his fingers down her thigh, half hoping she would waken and respond, calling himself a selfish pig.

Just as his conscience quieted she turned, sliding her bent leg between his thighs. Fitz eased the upper half of her body onto his chest, relishing the delicious press of her breasts. He ran his hand down the silky skin of her back to her rounded buttocks, lifting her into the cradle of his hips.

Just as her sleepy response made Fitz drowsily contemplate satisfying her without further damaging her abused tissues, he heard a subdued rap at the door. His mind woke completely and he opened his eyes wide, staring into the darkness until his pupils became accustomed to the night. The rap sounded again.

Moving an inch at a time, Fitz reluctantly eased himself

from beneath Sierra's delightfully accommodating frame. Paxton wouldn't disturb him unless the situation was urgent.

He padded silently across the floor and slipped into the hall. Paxton was a shifting shadow in the faint light from the single lamp to the left of the downward-curving staircase.

"Miss Shaw's friend Caleb is in the kitchen. He demands to see you."

Cursing beneath his breath, Fitz strode to his own room, where he pulled on a pair of trousers and a dark jersey. What could the fool boy want at this time of the night?

Moments later he strode barefoot into the shadowy confines of the kitchen. Paxton had produced the remains of a cobbler and settled Caleb at the scrubbed worktable with a generous serving. Fitz wanted to preserve for posterity the sight of his starchy valet solicitously handing an American Indian a spoon. "I take it the news isn't critical or you wouldn't be here at this ungodly hour eating me out of house and home. Are they out of invalid food at your house?"

"Cold's better. I came for Sierra," Caleb said, his clubbed hair swinging as he turned to look at his host. "I should have time to eat this while she gets dressed."

Fitz didn't miss the calculation in the Indian's glance. "What's the rush?" he queried. He rounded the table and settled himself on a stool, casting a glance at Paxton, who nodded, then left for the library, where Sierra's buckskins were locked in the window seat.

Caleb swallowed and said stolidly, "A telegram from her father arrived last night. He and his wife are in Southampton. They should be here before noon. Mrs. Shaw thought Sierra should be home when they arrive." He coughed, then dug his spoon into his bowl once more.

"Bloody hell," Fitz said disgustedly. "Is there anyone watching her house?"

"One. Clumsy fool's behind the postbox." Caleb snorted. "I didn't kill him." He spooned cobbler into his mouth.

Fitz shifted on the stool. "Don't you tire of impersonating a bloodthirsty savage? There's a similar fellow here."

Swallowing hastily, Caleb's closed features relaxed. "Wondered if you knew about him. He's watching from behind the hedge at the end of your garden wall."

"I needn't ask if either of them saw you."

Caleb threw him a disgusted look and returned to his snack.

Fitz sighed and stood. "Then I suppose you can be trusted to escort Sierra back home without either of our friends noticing. I'll go wake her. When you leave I'll guide you both out a safe exit and then follow from a distance." Ignoring Caleb's narrowed stare, he left.

Fitz's thoughts tumbled furiously over each other as he ascended the stairs and eased into the room where he'd left Sierra. As he approached the bed, she said reproachfully, "You left me. What's happened?"

He remembered the surprising fact that the intrepid Yank was claustrophobic. "Your father and your stepmother are arriving this morning. Your aunt sent Caleb to fetch you."

"Damn! I suppose Melanie's told him everything. My father will shout the house down."

Fitz laughed uproariously. Forgetting his resolve to keep his distance until she was clothed, he threw himself down beside Sierra and said smugly, "Serve you right. If you had half sense, you would have shown him the blackmail note immediately. He could have dispatched the matter through official channels and no one would have been the wiser."

He felt her tension before she spoke. "I wanted to do this one last thing for him."

"What the hell is that supposed to mean?" Fitz demanded.

Sierra didn't answer.

"Damn it, woman, I want an explanation. Do you mean you've come on this fool's errand because of some half-baked notion of owing your father something?"

Silence greeted him. He soothed her stiff shoulders, then rolled to his feet. "I want to see your eyes when you answer me." He left the room and found what he sought in the closet at the head of the stairs. Sierra's clothing was neatly piled beside the top step. Returning to the room, he dropped the buckskins on the bed beside her before lighting a hooded lantern, which he set on the floor with the open mantle facing the door. The faint reflected light cast smudgy shadows across her features. "Explain."

She sighed and said bluntly, "My mother died giving birth to me. My governesses used to speak of it behind their fingers. I worked hard to assume as many of my mother's duties as I could. If my mother had been alive, he wouldn't have had to worry about me."

"How can anyone as sensible as you believe anything so illogical? Does your father drag this out every so often just to keep you in line?"

Sierra stood and reached for her clothing. "Don't be ridiculous. He's the kindest man in the world." She stepped into her lace-trimmed knickers and fastened them at the waist, then pulled on a sheer batiste half-shift. She reached for the leather leggings. "I don't expect you to understand, Fitz. He deserves happiness with Melanie. I just wanted to do one last thing for him, give him one last gift." She turned her back and stepped into the buckskins.

"And then what will you do? Gracefully descend into a decline and fade into the background?"

"Get on with my life, you ass." She reached for the shirt. "You've spent five years trying to find out who killed your father. I spent twenty years trying to atone for something I'm aware wasn't my fault. And now I feel guilty because I'm happy about being free." She pulled the shirt over her head and tied the fastenings.

Fitz wanted to shake her until her head bobbled. Instead, he said, "Once you've dispensed with your guilt, give a thought to marrying me and staying in England."

Sierra was speechless. She snatched her moccasins from the bed and bent to slip them on. She kept her head down, waiting for the blood which had drained from her brain at his words to make its way back. Then she faced him where he stood at the foot of the bed. "You're not under any obligation to me. Tonight was my choice, not yours."

"Now who's being an ass?"

She retreated as he stalked toward her, words stumbling from her lips. "Just because I . . . trust you doesn't mean I . . ."

Fitz cut her off by pulling her into his arms. His deep, bruising kiss left her in no doubt of his feelings, and the tight knot within her unraveled. She melted against him, relishing the hard feel of his body and the sudden tenderness of his lips.

The pressure against her lips dissolved, and his words were slurred with passion as he said against her cheek, "I hope this disabuses you of any notion that I suggested marriage to preserve our respective honors."

Sierra was afraid to hope. They'd insulted and misled each other ever since they met. Tonight she'd discovered the man she'd sensed behind his facade. His work both fascinated and frightened her; the secrets he gathered and guarded were of such enormity she could scarcely imagine the life he lived in that other personality, the one she had only glimpsed. Was someone capable of maintaining such an elaborate deception capable of loving and sharing his true self with her?

"You're trying to decide which is the real Fitz, aren't you?" he said, mirroring her thoughts. "Have I given you any reason to believe my actions tonight are those of yet another character from my repertoire?"

Even in the faint light, Sierra saw the tension on his features. And she heard pain in his voice. Beneath her hands, his body was tight and hard, as if braced for a blow. For the first time, she glimpsed the vulnerability his other personas masked. She smoothed her hands across his chest, up to his face, to cradle his cheeks. "You clumsy Brit! I'd consider such an outrageous proposal for only one reason. That you love me as much as I love you."

The muscles of his face collapsed beneath her fingers. "Oh, God, yes, Yank. I love you." He buried his face against the side of her neck, and to her surprise she felt moisture where his lashes brushed her skin.

Sierra felt as if her breath had been forced from her body. It scarcely mattered that she didn't fully comprehend all the different facets of this man. She loved him and he loved her, and she had the rest of her life to learn the rest. "You'll never really make an Englishwoman of me," she challenged.

"I bloody well hope not," he said, slipping his hands beneath her buckskin shirt. "The thought gives me the shudders."

"You Brits have such a way with words," she said, shuddering against the play of the clever fingers shaping her breasts. Her blood heated and thickened, and she returned the pressure of his lips, wishing the rest of the world to hell. Finally, she pulled back, murmuring, "Fitz, isn't Caleb still waiting downstairs?"

He pulled her against him and groaned. "No wonder you were so indispensable to your father. You've a mind like a ruddy secretary." He set her away and complained, "In another minute I'd have denied the chap even existed. Come with me while I get some boots." He closed the lantern and opened the door wide enough for the two of them to slip through.

"Damn it all, Sierra! What took you so long?" Caleb demanded when they entered the kitchen. His gaze swept over them, and a hard look came into his eyes. "You've a lot to answer for when you meet the Senator, Kent."

"Caleb!" Sierra protested.

"Then let's hope he asks the right questions," Fitz said imperturbably. Still carrying the hooded lantern, he opened the door to the pantry and pressed one of the ceramic tiles outlining a rank of shelves. The unit slid back smoothly, and he opened the grid on the lantern he'd brought with him. Light splashed against a paneled opening. "This leads to the park, beyond where our friend is watching. I don't want him reporting any activity here."

"A secret passage. Now I can go home to America happy," Caleb said sarcastically.

Sierra patted his cheek playfully, then a little more firmly. "You're becoming a pain in my . . ."

"Hip," Fitz furnished. He put his hand on Sierra's shoulder and steered her toward the opening. "We haven't much time. It will be dawn in less than an hour, and I want to return without being discovered."

"I don't need your help to ferry her home safely." The belligerence in Caleb's voice alerted Fitz, and he glanced over his shoulder at the young Indian before stepping into the passage.

"Humor me," he ordered, proceeding swiftly down the shallow steps.

Just before they reached the exit, Fitz doused the lantern and reached for Sierra's arm. "Take Caleb's hand and I'll guide you out," he whispered.

Minutes later, they emerged from behind a mass of shrubs that masked the cleverly designed opening in the hillside. Pulling Sierra close, Fitz murmured, "Don't look back. I'll be behind you. And I'll deal with young Caleb after I call on you tomorrow." He kissed her hard and gave her a little shove.

Sierra's soft laughter was a whisper of sound in the moment before the two shadows faded into the dark landscape. After counting to twelve, Fitz drifted behind them. He sensed, rather than saw, their movement ahead. Half an hour later, sooner than he had hoped, he breathed a quiet sigh of relief as the service door of Sierra's rented house closed behind them.

Slipping soundlessly away, he skirted the opposite side of the street and saw for himself the watcher Caleb had discovered. The postbox obscured only half of his body. Obviously an amateur, as Caleb had pointed out. The young Indian had executed his errand with extraordinary skill. He had used one shortcut even Fitz had never been aware of, and cut the time of the journey between the two houses nearly in half. Too bad the boy was half in love with Sierra himself.

★ ★ ★ ★ ★

"Daddy! I'm so glad to see you," Sierra exclaimed mendaciously later that morning. Under ordinary circumstances, she would have been delighted, but she had a bad feeling about this unexpected arrival. She threw her arms around him and kissed him soundly on the cheek, then turned to her stepmother, forced a bright smile and welcomed her. "Melanie, you're more beautiful than ever."

"Cut the hogwash, Sierra," Senator Theodophilus Shaw snorted. His booming voice filled the room. Extending one powerful arm, he pulled Sierra back to face him. "Melanie's confessed, and I want to know what kind of ruckus you've been kicking up here. Are you in any kind of trouble?"

Although he had turned sixty two months earlier, Shaw was as large and forceful as he had been in the days when he and his brother had ventured into the Nevada mountains to make their fortunes. In spite of his demanding voice, the hand clasping her arm was gentle. She should have known Melanie's yielding nature wouldn't allow her to keep the blackmail attempt from her new husband. Sierra's heart swelled with love for her father . . . and she knew there was no way to avoid answering any question he might ask. *Almost* any question. "Of course I'm not in any trouble. You know I'd never do anything to embarrass you."

The Senator lowered bushy, graying eyebrows and rumbled, "Think it doesn't make me feel like a phony when I hear my little girl's prancing around London offering to buy a trophy husband?"

Sierra grimaced. The plan had seemed logical at the beginning. It was only when Fitz had sardonically offered to assist her in her search that she realized how very shallow she must appear. "Now, Daddy," she said coaxingly, using the tone of voice she employed when she wanted particu-

225

larly to ingratiate herself.

"Don't 'daddy' me." He drew her over to a straight chair and pressed her down onto the needlepoint seat, settled himself on the sofa opposite her, and cast a long-suffering glance at her aunt, who had quietly seated herself on a channel-back chair to his left. He gestured to his wife to join him. "Dolores said you've been roving high, wide and handsome since you got here. Out of control. Sending Russ and some foreign detective all over hell's half acre. I want to know what's going on."

Sierra smoothed the blended blue stripes of her silk over-skirt with her fingers while thinking where to start. "Actually, Russ has uncovered some interesting leads re-garding the shares. And he's discovered some sheep that are perfect for . . ."

"The sheep can wait. The railroad shares."

Sighing, Sierra continued, "I have a friend who investi-gated the scheme for another reason five years ago, and I've . . . I've convinced him to take a second look at everyone in-volved." From the corner of her eye, she saw her aunt staring fixedly at the ceiling.

Her father leaped to his feet and waved one arm dismiss-ively. "I don't want to hear about any of your *friends* helping you. Those limp-wristed Johnnies you've been running with wouldn't know how to find their asses in the dark. Now that I'm here, I'll do what should have been done as soon as that letter arrived." He paused to lean over and pat Melanie's hand lovingly. "It wasn't your fault, darlin', I know you were upset."

Thus softened, he turned to Sierra and said, "You just leave this to me. A pretty girl like you doesn't have to buy a husband. I talked to the head of the state department before I came and got the name of a Johnny they trust. They said this Kent fellow was like a cat at a mouse hole when it came to hunting varmints." He beamed with pride at his pronouncement. "I'll turn the business over to him. And when he turns up the yellow-bellied coward that threatened my wife, I'm goin' to shoot the bastard."

An hour later Caleb delivered a heavy cream envelope to Fitz's house. Surprised to hear from Sierra so early in the day, Fitz opened the missive with eagerness. His desk was littered with papers a messenger had delivered from his office two hours after Sierra's departure. A thick stack of lined sheets covered with his neat script sat on one corner. He swiveled his chair so that the sun shining through the bay window fell on the letter and began to read.

Darling Fitz—
This may already be too late. My father is on his way to engage you to find the bastard who threatened my stepmother so he can shoot him. Someone in Washington told him you were just the Johnny to do the job. I can't imagine how my aunt and I kept our faces straight. If he hasn't found you yet, you may want a stiff shot of whiskey to fortify yourself. I love him, but he believes strongly in taking the bull by the horns.
　　　　　Yours if you survive—and you'd better,
　　　　　Sierra

After checking his pocket watch, Fitz rang for Paxton. "Apparently we can expect Senator Shaw to honor us with a visit. I want to set some things in motion before I talk with him, so I'm going to the office. When he arrives, suggest he come back late this afternoon, say about five-thirty."

Paxton drew himself up to his full height of five feet six

and looked down his nose as if he were already putting the brash American in his place. "Indeed. I am more than capable of dealing with that sort of person. You may rely on me," he said as he stalked to the door.

"Don't treat him like a tradesman, Paxton. The man's going to be my father-in-law," Fitz called after him. Paxton's silence and his rigid back spoke volumes.

Chuckling, Fitz transformed himself into a street person, then gathered his papers into a battered black box, tied it with string, and tucked it beneath his arm. Fifteen minutes later, after carefully checking the nearby shrubbery, he slipped from his private entrance.

CHAPTER EIGHTEEN

Half an hour later Fitz initiated a frenzy of orders and wires that stretched the patience of his small, but efficient staff. "Has anything come in from Freeman yet?" he demanded for the fifth time.

Harrison looked at him as if he were demented. "You only called 'im in an 'our ago. If 'e's gone 'untin' for somethin' 'e ain't going to get yer message till 'e gets 'ome. Could be next week."

The five-year-old report on the deaths of the principals of the MacDonough Railroad Venture littered his desk. Fitz snapped, "If he doesn't reply by tomorrow, send someone after him." Sitting, he read the narrative once more. MacDonough, the elderly landowner, had deeded the crucial right-of-way to the venture, which would build track miles north of the existing lines, offering an alternative route between Edinburgh and Glasgow.

MacDonough's nephew, an engineer, was to have headed the project, and a financier from Glasgow issued and registered the stock. Geoffrey Trowbridge, through a family connection with the financier, had represented the venture in England. Family, friends and even acquaintances, had breathed a sigh of relief that Geoffrey had finally found an honest outlet for his considerable charm and ability.

Very straightforward, Fitz reminded himself for the sixth time. Then came Freeman's report, which his father had ordered. The information would have alerted him at the time, but it had just now surfaced. Even then, it would have been

229

only one of several dozen leads, and he had been numb with grief. Now his nostrils quivered from the stench of the narrative.

In a bizarre twist of fate, MacDonough died in a hunting accident. His nephew and the Glasgow financier had conveniently perished when the carriage in which they were riding had lost a wheel and tumbled off a steep, winding road. The report did not treat the incidents as unusual occurrences, but Matthew Kent's death threw too much weight to one side of the scales for coincidence.

With the principals deceased, the plan had been abandoned. Geoffrey had fled the country, and his family had been about to bankrupt themselves to cover their friends' losses—when Child's, with every appearance of philanthropy, had stepped in to quiet the furor.

Why? And why, after all this time, had the stock suddenly become someone's primary concern?

Having warned Fitz, Sierra whisked her stepmother off for a shopping trip. "You've never seen anything like it," she promised as they settled into the carriage. "Even Aunt Dolores takes jaunts through Harrod's at least once a week to see the newest accessories, and you *know* she despises shopping."

Melanie clutched her arm and repeated the apology she'd been offering since her arrival. "Sierra, I didn't want to tell your father what you were doing. It was only when he began to talk of how much help you had been to him and how much you deserved an extended vacation overseas . . . and the story just . . . I just . . ."

To her embarrassment, Sierra watched tears tumble from Melanie's great brown eyes onto her own gloved fingers. "Melanie . . ."

"No one in the whole world has ever made such an effort to help me. When I realized you could be in danger from the blackmailer if he realized you intended to expose him, I knew your father was the only one who could save you."

Sierra suppressed a grin. Her father wasn't the only guardian she possessed now. Wouldn't he be surprised to discover that the man he counted on to discover the villain was not only fifty paces ahead in the game but had joyfully relieved her of her innocence not twenty-four hours before? "Don't cry anymore, Melanie. You won't look your best."

"Sierra, you don't sound grateful that your father has arrived to protect you." Melanie patted her cheeks carefully with the square of embroidered linen she had removed from her pocket. "I do believe you've been enjoying this."

Harrod's came into view, and Sierra busied herself smoothing her gloves. "Don't be ridiculous, Melanie. At least now I needn't pretend to look for a titled husband, and that makes me happier than you can imagine." The coachman drew to a stop, and Caleb leaped down to open the door for them. She stepped to the sidewalk and delivered a conspiratorial wink to her friend before calling to Melanie, "We're here, darling. You must look at lace first. It's a wonderful bargain just now, what with all the Russian emigrés in London. For many of them, lace-making is their only means of support, so we must be sure to buy a great deal."

"My dear Miss Shaw. What a happy surprise!"

Nigel Brockington's cheerful greeting startled her so completely Sierra nearly dropped her reticule. One topic she and Fitz had not discussed the night before was her arrangement with Lady Lockwood or the reason for it. Nor had she mentioned her suspicions of Francis Lancaster. And Brockington and Lancaster were nearly inseparable.

She looked around for the dour banker, expecting him to appear. "What . . . what a surprise, Mr. Brockington." She gestured to Melanie, who had just stepped from the carriage. "Melanie, may I present Nigel Brockington? This is my stepmother, Mrs. Shaw," she added. "She and my father have just arrived from the United States."

"How do you do, Mrs. Shaw." Nigel brushed the top of Melanie's gloved hand with his lips. "I'm delighted to be one of the first to welcome you to England. Miss Shaw never told me she had acquired such a beautiful stepmamma. Doesn't the Senator worry about two such lovely ladies on their own in the wicked London streets?"

Sierra had heard enough syrupy compliments. "Don't give our safety a thought. Melanie and I each carry derringers in our reticules." She paused to relish his surprise, then continued wickedly, "Besides, there are greater rogues in some drawing rooms than those I might encounter elsewhere."

Brockington's shout of delighted laughter drew the attention of several passersby, and he grinned apologetically. "If I didn't have an appointment, I'd accompany you ladies, just to protect the population. As it stands . . ." He tipped his hat and bade them farewell.

"Sierra, whatever has gotten into you?" Melanie said, her voice quaking. "I never carried a pistol in my life."

"No, but *I* do. And I'm not sure I'd trust Nigel Brockington with a wagonload of corncobs." She took Melanie's arm and led her toward Harrod's imposing entrance, calling over her shoulder, "Pick us up here at five o'clock, Caleb."

"Nice of you to see me on such short notice, Kent." Senator Shaw's smile was wide, his handshake solid. "I heard in

Washington you were a straight shooter. My friend said you might be able to help me with a problem."

Fitz sighed inwardly. Maintaining stuffy British demeanor in the presence of such genuine warmth would take effort. But then he should have known that anyone who had made a fortune by dint of hard physical labor, survived the power-broker atmosphere of Washington, and fathered Sierra would be larger than life. Perhaps bluntness would be his best tack. "I shall be delighted to offer any assistance I can. Please sit down and tell me what you need. That brown chair is the most comfortable." Fitz gestured toward it before seating himself in his swivel chair, childishly delighted that he had just outmaneuvered his guest, who now sat with the afternoon sun in his eyes. He shifted several papers and two files, then ventured, "I believe we have several interests in common, Senator."

Shaw's hand paused above the bottom button of his tweed suitcoat. "I haven't yet told you why I'm here." His eyes, blue and very like Sierra's, narrowed suspiciously.

"You want to enlist my services to discover the blackguard who is blackmailing your wife in an attempt to obtain what you assumed was a worthless legacy inherited from her first husband, who was a scoundrel from start to finish," Fitz responded matter-of-factly.

"Schafley at the State Department told me you were good, but by damn, you're better than that," the older man enthused. Then his eyes narrowed once more. "Of course, you could already have heard all this from my daughter. If she's the other interest we have in common, maybe I should bark up another tree."

Fitz rose and extended his hand. With great solemnity, he replied, "There's no need for that. My actions toward your daughter are quite honorable. I intend to marry her, whether you approve or not." He braced himself for an explosion, hoping he had read his man correctly.

"Damned if I don't like your style, son," the Senator said as he stood. He clasped Fitz's hand rather more firmly than necessary. Fitz sensed a certain reservation, however, and so wasn't unduly surprised when his guest leaped right to the point. "Is there any reason to hurry this along?"

"Not at all, sir. In fact, I would prefer to have the untidy business of the blackmail attempt out of the way first. Sierra seems to feel your marital happiness is the first order of business," Fitz added.

Shaw's gaze wavered, the wrinkles in his weathered skin noticeable in the strong sunlight. "We had this fool governess when Sierra was just a tiny thing learnin' to write. The woman told that poor little girl she'd killed her mother. Had the dickens of a time convincing her differently. Should have known she'd figure it out on her own. Still, she's full of vinegar, and she's worn herself out being useful. Melanie's half sick from trying to live up to her." He sat once more and smoothed his thick white hair. "Just between us, my wife will do fine on her own. I'll purely miss Sierra, but if you're what she wants, by God, she can have you."

He switched subjects immediately, as if they hadn't just covered, man-fashion, a host of family problems. "Now about this damned stock. Do you know the name of the son of a bitch that's causing all the trouble?"

"If I knew for sure, the man would already be dead. I've reason to believe he murdered my father." Fitz struggled to appear detached. The person behind this confidence trick had the patience of Job, the cunning of a master manipulator, and no compunction about shattering innumerable ordinary people's dreams of financial independence. Fitz craved retribution for his father's death. A previously un-known barbaric side of his personality wanted to see the bastard's head on a pike, and even that would not ease his loss.

Clearing his throat, he shifted the papers in the file be-fore him, then spoke. "Sierra apparently has a candidate, but if it's who I think, I'm not at all sure he's devious enough to have contrived such a scheme on his own. I have a report which should have alerted me five years ago, but it must have been misfiled, as I never saw it. Anyway, at the time I might have been . . . too consumed by rage and grief to pick up on the nuances." He set the file aside and opened another.

"Recent rumors say the railway project is about to be resurrected, and those who own the most original shares will be the majority stockholders. Your wife's holdings and those my father refused to redeem are crucial, since we ap-pear to stand in the way of total control."

"I'll be thrice-damned to hell," said the Senator.

The pause was broken by a knock on the study door. Fitz sighed resignedly and called admittance. Paxton ap-peared, frowning. "A disreputable individual has appeared at the servants' entrance demanding your attention, sir." He waggled his eyebrows.

"Did he give a name?" Fitz demanded.

Paxton screwed up his face and answered as if he were speaking through pinched nostrils. "Indeed not. He did, however, make reference to Freeman, and suggested you might want to speak with him immediately." His eyelid twitched.

Fitz leaped to his feet and hurried through the door, abandoning his guest and nearly upending Paxton. The number of upper-level operatives who knew his real identity and the location of his home could be counted on one hand.

His cook, Mrs. Crocker, eased her considerable bulk out of his path and pointed out the ragged mound of clothing perched on a three-legged stool placed as close to the door as possible. During his father's management, and under his own, the work of the department had never intruded on their private lives. His hand-picked domestic staff took perverse pride in his clandestine activities, but from a distance. Now, for the second time in as many days, threads of an investigation had led to his home. Fitz wondered if the advent of Sierra Shaw into his life was the reason his world had begun unraveling around him.

He looked into the eyes of the gamey apparition and said unbelievingly, "Sterling!"

"Right on, Fitz. Have you anyplace I can rid myself of this disgusting disguise and talk privately? The news isn't good."

Sierra threw herself on her bed, exhausted. Melanie was delightful company, compliant and agreeable, easily pleased and entertained, and affectionate. Why, then, was she so tired after a day in her company?

A soft rap on her door was followed by her aunt's entrance. Dolores crossed the room and knelt to unbutton Sierra's smart kid half-boots. She pulled them off and massaged Sierra's feet. "Really, how could you have forgotten how bored you become after an entire afternoon with Melanie? Her constant pleasantness wears you out. I credited you with more intelligence," she said sharply as she pulled her niece upright and unbuttoned the jet buttons that marched down her silk twill bodice. "For heaven's sake, get into something more comfortable."

Sierra pushed her aunt's fingers away, pulled her arms

from the indigo sleeves and cast it aside. Then she stood, obediently presenting her back to her aunt. "Oh, that feels wonderful!" she exclaimed, relieved to feel the waistband of her skirt, and then her corset lacing, loosen. "Daddy took off so abruptly today that I felt obligated to entertain Melanie. After all, she's been through so much. It's not kind to abandon her in a strange country."

"You're not responsible for her happiness." Dolores picked up the skirt and half-hoop Sierra stepped out of and took them to the wardrobe. "Your father should have seen to her welfare before he took off to chase devils. You've already risked your life haring around London on this fool's errand in her behalf. Don't think I can't imagine what else you and Caleb have been up to. And now you're in league with Fitzhugh Kent."

"If I hadn't taken Caleb's place the other night, Fitz could have been killed," Sierra shot at her aunt's back as she stripped to her shift. "Besides, I . . ."

"I don't want to hear anything more. When Fitz's note arrived I washed my hands of any responsibility." Dolores thrust a silk robe into her hand.

As her fingers closed over the soft material, Sierra saw the suspicious moisture in her aunt's dark eyes. The robe fell to the floor as she wrapped her arms around her. "I'm so sorry. It's just that I thought you'd sleep better if you weren't worrying about me. I was sure I could defend myself if I encountered any problems."

Dolores drew her close. Her voice broke as she said, "You've always been fearless, but you weren't born to take on everyone's dragons. You're the closest thing I have to a daughter, Sierra. If anything happened to you . . ."

"Nothing's going to happen to me," Sierra said stoutly as she returned her aunt's fierce hug. "I need only to . . ."

"Do nothing! Do you hear? Nothing." Dolores shook her. "Your father is with Fitz Kent now, and between the two of them they'll put a stop to this plot."

Sierra thought of her blustering, open-handed father working together with Fitz and suppressed a giggle. Even though she loved them both, she couldn't conceive of a more unlikely pair. "I don't imagine Fitz will appreciate Daddy's approach to this problem, and Daddy will think Fitz is either crazy or sneaky, depending on his mood." She pulled away from her aunt and began to pace the room. She realized her father and Fitz would become overprotective and attempt to leave her out of their plans. Well, she wouldn't allow it. "Let them plot and scheme. I'm still the only one who can unravel this mess."

"Sierra, you're to let them handle the problem," her aunt ordered. "Do you understand?"

"Of course I do, darling. It's just that I'm positive I know who's behind this. Don't you think it's my duty to expose the villain to Fitz?"

Fifteen minutes after entering the butler's pantry with Sterling, Fitz paused outside his study to mentally filter the most disturbing elements from Sterling's report. The Senator might think he came to England with some sort of diplomatic protection to ruthlessly search and destroy the threat to his family, but Her Majesty's government would take a very dim view of such proceedings, although a mental picture of Sierra's father confronting Fitz's superiors in Whitehall held a certain music hall fascination for him.

No. Events would progress much more smoothly without his assistance. This decision made, he joined his future father-in-law. The Senator was munching scones and holding a delicate teacup as if he were afraid the porcelain would crack before he emptied it. "I apologize for leaving so abruptly, sir."

"No need. No need," Shaw replied, nesting the cup in the saucer at the edge of the desk. "Your man made sure I was comfortable in your absence. You Johnnies make a real to-do over this tea business, don't you," he declared, waving at the tray laden with elegant pastries and tiny sandwiches.

Fitz ambled to the tea cart and helped himself to a watercress sandwich, then poured his own tea, which he set on his desk before dropping into his chair. "Something about the ritual soothes the nerves, particularly after a busy day. The ladies take the whole process quite seriously. Would you prefer a stronger tipple?"

"I grew up drinking rotgut, and the poison that passed for whiskey in the mining camps put me off the stuff. Never could work up a liking for the fancy stuff from Scotland after that." He grimaced and emptied his cup before continuing, "Besides, drink and business don't mix worth a damn. I've seen too many men sign away fortunes with a jug on the table."

Fitz grinned conspiratorily. "Agreed. In my line of work I also have to keep a clear head." He sipped the strong Earl Grey, then set his cup down while he searched out the suspicuously innocuous report on the Scottish railway scheme. "The gentleman who wanted my ear just now brought disturbing news. It seems Freeman, the individual who filed this peculiar outline of the affair four years ago, has had an unfortunate accident."

The Senator set his empty plate back on the tea cart and eyed him shrewdly. "Accidents happen, Kent. Timing a little too convenient?"

"Wonderfully so, I thought." Death by falling in front of

a speeding train was somehow fitting, and certainly a clear warning, but he kept that information to himself. "That certainly explains why Freeman didn't respond to my request that he return from the field. He must have been dead before I put the word out." The building that housed Freeman's squalid little flat had burnt to the ground last night, but Shaw needn't know that.

"Lose many people like that, Kent?"

"Never when they're under orders. Just the occasional accident when they're on their own time. The few who encounter trouble have stumbled over something biggish by mistake. We turn that over to the fellows with truncheons." Fitz drained his teacup and stood to stare at his guest before saying somberly, "You do understand that my work for the government is unknown and unmentioned. Anywhere."

Shaw's shrewd gaze never wavered. "Does Sierra know what you do?"

"Some of it," Fitz admitted. She hadn't turned a hair when he revealed his activities, although he'd seen a flicker of concern in her eyes that he'd hoped was for his personal safety. On the other hand, Fitz rather thought she might be jealous of the adventures she pictured him having. Surely her experience the other night would dissuade her from pursuing that avenue any further . . .

As if reading his thoughts, Shaw chuckled and said, "She'll probably try to talk you into putting her to work, you know. She'd be damned good. Smart little gal, if I do say so." As he stood his smile faded. "This fellow's death put a crimp in your progress?"

Fitz winced inwardly. It would be necessary to go through back files to trace the partner Freeman worked with five years ago, in addition to setting Scotland Yard to work investigating Freeman's death. "There are always other avenues. I'll let you know as soon as I've anything to report."

Fitz rounded the desk and escorted his guest to the door, stopping only to assure, "As for Sierra, please don't think I'd encourage her to undertake anything that would put her in danger. My nerves couldn't take it."

"She hides hers damn well, but she . . . well, never mind. I'm usually a good judge of a man's worth, so I'll leave it up to you. Don't disappoint me, son," he said with a piercing look.

"I shan't." As they walked toward the entrance hall, Fitz asked, "Will you and your wife be joining Sierra at the Avondale gathering this evening?"

"She said somethin' about a soirée. Damn things are just a bunch of folks standing around talkin', each tryin' to impress as many of the rest as they can. She means well, so I'll do the pretty. Melanie'll enjoy it."

Fitz shook his hand and grinned. "Your description will make it difficult for me to attend similar entertainments in the future without laughing."

CHAPTER NINETEEN

"Oh, Sierra, this house is like a museum!" Melanie said breathlessly, her eyes round as she stared up at the glittering gaslit chandelier in the entrance hall of the Avondale mansion. "Imagine actually living in anything so grand."

Hating herself for the thought, Sierra hoped her stepmother wouldn't ask for a tour of the upper floors. Or the kitchens. In her present brittle mood, she visualized her family being ostracized as American barbarians.

The line awaiting admittance to the connected receiving rooms moved forward several feet.

"Now, honey, you wouldn't feel at home in a house like this," the Senator soothed. His proud gaze travelled from his daughter in her rose-colored Worth creation to his wife, whose amber brocade, American-designed gown held its own amongst the fashionable silks and satins worn by the other women. "Damned if I'm not totin' the two prettiest gals in town tonight. Sure wish Dolores would have come along. Folks would think I was one of them sultans." His brow furrowed. "Can't think why she'd rather attend a lecture on plants."

"Theo, I know I'd hate living in anything this big and grand, but look at those rugs. Can we buy just a few things while we're here? I saw some wonderful carved furniture in a showroom Sierra took me to this afternoon."

Sierra's tension eased. Her father was responding to her stepmother's soft little voice and glowing dark eyes like Ulysses's crew to the siren's song. He had said little about his interview this afternoon, but she could picture Fitz's reaction to a stranger's blunt demand that he locate a villain so frontier justice could be applied.

As if her thoughts had conjured him up, she heard the distinctive timbre of Fitz's voice. He was speaking with the dignified couple behind them as if he'd known them all his life, asking if they'd object to his joining the party in front of them. Her nerves thrumming, she turned in time to see his charming smile as he kissed the softly wrinkled cheek of an elderly woman. "I promise to pop in for tea within the week." He looked up to see Sierra watching him and winked wickedly, then continued, "I warn you, Godmamma, if you persist in looking younger each time I see you, you may need a chaperone on call."

Smiling inwardly, Sierra turned her back and advanced with the crowd, confident he would join her. Seconds later, he murmured close to her ear, "One never knows who one will bump into at one of these intimate little parties."

"Fitz, there must be over a hundred people here!"

"By Jove, I think you're right," he said, craning his neck to look ahead. "Just the sort of party your father will hate." He smiled, as if at a secret joke, then whispered, "But your stepmother will have the time of her life, I'm sure." His warm breath against her cheek raised tiny goose bumps at her nape.

Sierra whisked her feather fan before her face and asked from behind it, "How did you and my father get on this afternoon?"

She watched him survey those present with a bright hazel gaze, as if memorizing each face and cataloguing it for later consideration. His concentration excited her, and she pictured the two of them sprawled naked against satin pillows sipping champagne as he reported his observations of each person. Then she visualized herself cutting off his recital. Heat suffused her cheeks.

"Like two frogs in a pond, as I suspect he might describe the encounter." His lips scarcely moved as he spoke, and she realized he really *was* mentally recording the faces present.

"Really, Fitz, has no one ever called you to task for this habit of yours?"

He grinned unrepentantly. "You're the only person who's ever questioned my habits, so I assume no one has noted my rudeness before now. I shall endeavor to be more discreet." He edged closer. "You're looking extremely ethereal and innocuous this evening. I do hope this means you've decided to give up your quest and let the burden fall on my shoulders. In fact, your father made the same suggestion this afternoon after he accepted me as your suitor."

She was right. They intended to exclude her. If it hadn't been for her efforts, Fitz Kent might never have discovered the connection between the railroad scheme and his father's murder. Her cheeks warmed, this time with anger. Lowering her fan, she turned on him, speaking as precisely as possible. "Neither of you has any say in the matter. In fact, I was under the impression we would proceed as partners."

The Senator's rumbling voice intruded. "Here now. Right good you've turned up, Kent. Melanie, I want you to meet Sierra's friend."

The interruption didn't diffuse Sierra's anger. She tapped her toe impatiently. Her annoyance mounted as Fitz charmed her stepmother. She wanted to tell both Melanie and her father what she thought of the lying snake. How typically male of them to conspire to set her aside while they claimed the exciting part—the triumph.

As the line moved more quickly, so did the conversation.

No one appeared to notice her silence, and she used the interval to review the plan she had conceived while she dressed. Fitz would regret his attempt to exclude her.

Not even this surprisingly faceted man she loved was going to rob her of a share of the excitement. She would unmask the villain herself. Nothing her father or Fitz could do would stop her.

Fitz didn't need to be clairvoyant to notice that Sierra was annoyed. It was evident in the swirl of her short train as she stepped ahead of her father and Melanie to present them to their host and hostess, in the proud arc of her neck above the profusion of blush-pink lace rimming the décolletage of her exquisite tissue silk gown. With her pale hair drawn up in back and arranged with curls clustering down to her nape, she reminded him of an exceedingly angry fairy from one of the Brothers Grimm's tales.

The amenities over, she drew her parents away from him as if he didn't exist. Wryly amused, he greeted Lord and Lady Avondale before locating a spot against the wall from which to watch.

Her introduction of her father to Lord and Lady Satterly as they stood at the punch bowl was well within his hearing. "Y'all have a pile of things in common with my father, Lord Satterly. Aren't you glad you don't have to kiss babies to get into the House of Lords?"

Surprisingly, the amiable lord chuckled and shook the Senator's hand. "Campaigning sounds rather jolly. Your refreshing daughter and, of course, your beautiful wife must be assets to you."

"Don't know about that. All the ranchers' wives and daughters are jealous 'cause these two are so damn pretty. I'm always nervous in case the wives force their husbands to vote for my opponent out of spite," Shaw replied expansively.

Fitz watched Sierra's back stiffen even more. He wouldn't be surprised to learn she planned her father's campaigns and coordinated his appearances. He rested his shoulders on the silk-covered wall, content to be a spectator. If Satterly and her father didn't watch out, she would erupt like a spitting cat. Instead, Sierra's laughter rang out, a musical, full-bodied sound that hardened Fitz's body. He observed the little group closely. She might make light of the heavy flattery, but she was angry. Her posture proclaimed the fact.

And he was the primary object of that fine rage. Fitz wondered how he had managed to wend his way through London society all his adult life with scarcely a ripple, then behave so maladroitly with this forthright American woman who'd taken possession of his mind and heart. She should be relieved to put the blasted mess into the hands of professionals. Had she forgotten that crack on the head two nights ago? His blood ran cold at the memory, and he repressed an urge to carry her off and lock her up until the affair was concluded.

"Woolgathering, Fitz?" Devon Carrington's voice interrupted his musings. "Or just admiring our luscious foreign import?"

Startled, Fitz replied honestly, "Both." He stepped into an alcove, drawing his friend with him.

Devon laughed appreciatively, then ventured, "What could drive someone of Miss Shaw's obvious intelligence to perform such a hoax on so many unsuspecting people? Have your superior powers of detection and analysis twigged the reason yet?"

Amazed at his friend's astuteness, and aware his friend's

green eyes were observing him closely, Fitz refused to acknowledge that he'd been taken in for even a minute, so he shrugged and admitted, "The matter is well in hand. I've hopes she'll abandon the role now that I've joined the game."

"Not that one," Devon said flatly.

Fitz turned to stare at him. "You sound very sure."

The skin at the corners of Devon's eyes crinkled with laughter. "She's a competitor. A fierce one. I'm surprised you haven't already figured that out. Miss Shaw's probably never backed away from anything, even after she's been ordered off the playing field. Gets the bit in her teeth, so to speak."

Fitz wanted to beat his head against the wall. He'd sensed Sierra Shaw's stubbornness within five minutes of meeting her. But he'd become complacent, assuming love would distract her from her purpose. Any sensible woman would step gratefully into the shadows and leave everything in the capable hands of her lover and her recently arrived father. Sierra most definitely wasn't like any other woman.

"You're really much brighter than I thought, Carrington. Your mother must be relieved," Fitz said sarcastically. It was well-known that Devon's mother despaired of his ever acknowledging the responsibilities he'd inherited. He much preferred a gadfly existence, interrupted occasionally by tasks for Fitz. Tasks Devon performed with uniform brilliance.

"You know, old man, I'm tempted to plant a facer on you for that." Devon drank from the champagne flute he'd been carrying, and his eyes were speculative as he watched Sierra progress through the room. "However, I believe I'll leave your punishment to Miss Shaw. You really must cease watching her when you're not in her company, you know.

People are beginning to notice." He patted Fitz's shoulder consolingly and wandered off, chuckling.

"Lady Lockwood! It's right nice to see you," Sierra said, knowing the American colloquialism would test the elderly lady's composure. "My father and stepmother are around here someplace. You must meet them." Sierra tucked her arm beneath that of her partner in deception and drew her to one side. Lowering her voice, she said, "I'm so glad to see you. Will you help one more time?"

Ignoring her appeal, Heloise surveyed the room through her lorgnette. "What a mixed bag this is. If you had not inveigled me further in this ridiculous scheme of yours, I should have returned home and welcomed the quiet." She lowered the tasteful chased silver instrument and turned her shrewd dark gaze toward Sierra. "What mad scheme are you up to now?"

Sierra relaxed for the first time that evening. Now that she was actually executing her plan, her anger had abated. "I simply need you to give credence to what I say. No one in the world would suspect you of being involved with anything questionable. And of course my shares are supposedly in your lockbox."

"If you will pardon my saying so, I never thought that little ploy would come to anything." Satisfaction with her judgment filled Heloise's voice.

"Actually, my bait drew response," Sierra confessed. "But a dreadful mix-up occurred, and the blackmailer's henchmen got away," she said ruefully. "I have a plan to draw him out again, and this time I'll make sure he doesn't escape."

By the time she finished speaking, they had entered the next room, an over-decorated salon in which the owners had used plant stands and fringed table covers with a heavy hand. Even the piano, currently being played by a pudgy girl Sierra rather thought was the Avondales's oldest daughter, was draped with a colorful silk paisley shawl edged with black silk fringe. "Deplorable," announced her companion, looking around her.

Ignoring the comment, Sierra stopped short and murmured, "My suspects are next to the piano talking with that funny little man with the straggly muttonchop whiskers. Why don't you sit here?" She pointed to a heavily carved settee upholstered in a dense pattern of embroidered leaves. "I'm quite sure they'll gravitate to us when they see me."

"My dear, your confidence is worthy of one of the royals," Heloise commented as she settled her black moire skirts around her. "I do hope this charade will not take a great deal of time. This room is appalling. I shall become despondent if we linger."

For the first time, Sierra looked at their surroundings. Grimacing in agreement, she seated herself carefully on a fringed ottoman. Her modified bustle and the fashionable drape of her skirt left her unsure whether she had lowered her body or just her garments. She couldn't feel the horsehair-stuffed cushion beneath her. Settled at last, she looked up and smiled beckoningly toward the group at the piano. "This won't take long at all. In fact, I believe . . . Mr. Lancaster! And Mr. Brockington! I reckon just about all the folks I know are here tonight," she gushed, holding out her pink-gloved hand to each man in turn.

Lancaster looked gloomier and more saturnine than ever as he bent over her fingers. She was struck by the deep contrast between the two friends, and wondered once more what possible pleasure they found in each other's company. Then she plunged ahead. "You gentlemen are just the people I want to see. I was about to discuss my little problem with Lady Lockwood. She's been as much help as if she was kin, but I need advice from people on the inside." Sierra beamed, directing her pleasure around the little group.

"Any expertise I possess is yours," Brockington enthused, drawing up a chair. "I'm ever available to damsels in distress." Lancaster hovered above the little group as if it were beneath his dignity to sit.

"Please join Lady Lockwood on the settee," Sierra urged. "I'd like our conversation to be private." She glanced around the room, glad the gloomy atmosphere and expressionless piano playing drove most people to the other salons. She waited until he had seated himself before leaning forward and beginning her carefully rehearsed tale.

"My father and stepmother arrived in London this morning. They're here with me tonight, but I think Daddy's upset with me," she confided, trying to appear guilty. "The certificates I put in Lady Lockwood's lockbox for safekeeping belong to my stepmother. I came to England to discover for her if they were of any value," Sierra murmured.

"Surely that is a task more suited to your father, Miss Shaw," Francis Lancaster said accusingly.

Sierra lowered her lashes and bowed her head as if in agreement, then spoke. "Before she married my father, my stepmother was a widow in very poor straits, and she's afraid people think she married Daddy for his money, when in fact they're very much in love. When he died, her first husband left her these worthless railroad shares. Then she heard something that made her think the opposite. She was afraid to mention the possibility to him until she knew for sure." She smiled confidingly, encouraged when Nigel Brockington nodded. "We women have our pride, you know. I felt sorry for her, so I promised to help her."

"I have always felt it a grave injustice for a woman's property to become her husband's at the time of their marriage," Heloise interjected.

"After I arrived, I began to worry about them," Sierra went on. "Someone broke into my library shortly after we arrived, I'm sure of it. Fortunately, I had hidden the certificates in a safe place, but I didn't want anyone to know I'd rented a lockbox in my own bank, so Lady Lockwood generously allowed me to put them in her box at Child's for safekeeping."

Brockington nodded his enthusiastic approval. "Perfectly good sense, Miss Shaw."

Sierra rewarded him with a smile, then lowered her voice and continued, "Well, at any rate, I've located a man who knows everything about this particular venture. I'm to meet with him tomorrow afternoon. But he insists I bring the certificates so he can see them." She saw Lady Lockwood roll her eyes upward, and switched her attention to the faces of the two men to gauge their reactions. They both looked properly horrified.

"I'm not sure this will be safe, particularly since I don't know the city well, but Melanie insists I meet with him. She isn't brave enough to go herself, and I hate to break her confidence by asking my father for advice. You're all much cleverer than either of us. What do you think I should do?"

Nigel Brockington's genial expression disappeared, replaced by a frown. "Obviously this person is a confidence trickster. Rumors are flying everywhere. Is this stock from the MacDonough venture that fell apart some years back? Worthless pieces of paper."

"That's the name on the shares! Do you mean I've gone to all this trouble and gotten Melanie's hopes up over nothing?"

"He is quite correct, Miss Shaw. If your stepmother's certificates are from that particular project, they are worthless. As I recall, Child's redeemed a number of them at the time. I was not with the bank then, but Nigel's father was on the board of the venture, and he felt responsible. So when it defaulted due to the untimely deaths of the principals involved, he redeemed the stock with his own funds." He shook his head to emphasize the foolishness of such an action. "I've no idea what finally became of them. Or if there were any heirs to the original corporation papers of the venture."

Sierra sprang to her feet and clenched her fists tightly. "Then I nearly fell into some kind of a trap! Well, this makes me just so furious I could . . ."

"There's no need to become overwrought, Miss Shaw," Lancaster reassured her. "Although I highly disapprove of your undertaking such a quest without proper parental guidance, I must applaud your efforts on your stepmother's behalf. You have shown true generosity of spirit."

A worshipful expression graced Nigel Brockington's features as he said, "If you hadn't taken the chance, I might never have met you, Miss Shaw. I didn't know Americans were so beautiful or so charming."

Sierra didn't have to force the moisture gathering in her eyes. She was so relieved they'd bought her story she wanted to cry. "How kind you are. Lady Lockwood, I'll remove those certificates from your box first thing tomorrow and take them back to the house. Melanie and I will burn every last one. My father knows her worth, and money has nothing to do with it. He'll never have to know about this foolishness." She fumbled in her reticule for a handkerchief, finally locating an embroidered square of lace to dab at her cheeks and hide her grin of satisfaction.

CHAPTER TWENTY

Fitz damned the animated group of young women clustered just outside the wide opening into the room where Sierra held court. Peering over their shoulders for long would attract attention, and their conversation and laughter prevented him from overhearing a single word. He stepped to one side and was rewarded with a brief view of Sierra. Without sound, her performance reminded him of a Drury Lane performance. Her hands moved gracefully and pleadingly, and her face was lifted beseechingly toward those seated around the low ottoman where she was perched. He doubted the seating arrangement was coincidental.

If he didn't know better, he would have suspected her of attempting to convert her audience to a new evangelistic enterprise. When she groped for a handkerchief and patted her cheeks delicately, he swore both gentlemen leaned forward as if to comfort her. Heloise appeared to be having difficulty maintaining a neutral expression.

Without doubt, he would have to visit that redoubtable lady tonight before he retired to his office in Cambridge Circus.

"My little girl's puttin' on quite a performance in there, ain't she?"

Theo Shaw's voice was a proud purr, indistinguishable to any of the people near them. Fitz nearly jumped out of his skin. How long had the man been standing behind him? "Quite right, sir. I can't decide whether she's selling snake oil or recruiting souls for one of the more extreme religious sects."

"Most likely snake oil," the Senator replied, his expression long-suffering. "Been suspicious of her ever since she huffed away from you on our way in. You didn't make the mistake of tellin' her to stay home with her knittin', did you, son?"

Fitz wondered if everyone in the world read Sierra's character more accurately than he did. "Not in so many words. Actually, I implied I had the situation in hand. I don't want her to take any more risks."

The Senator's bark of laughter caused the giggling women to eye them curiously. His amusement abated, he wiped his cheeks with his hands and threw his arm around Fitz's shoulders. "The thing is, she don't like to be left out. You just shot yourself in the foot, son."

Annoyed at being reminded that he'd been blinded by his emotions, Fitz retorted sharply, "Your daughter was struck on the head two nights ago, Senator. If my men hadn't been there, God only knows what would have happened to her." He had the painful satisfaction of feeling Theo Shaw's arm tighten before it fell from his shoulders.

"The hell you say."

Fitz turned to face him. Keeping his voice low, he said, "She was travelling the streets of London dressed like a bloody boy and came across me awaiting an appointment with an informant. Someone else arrived first. When I was attacked, she leaped to the rescue." Fitz glanced over his shoulder to be sure no one could hear, then continued, "My men were close by, but didn't arrive in time to prevent her from receiving the same treatment."

With the color drained from his face, Shaw looked every one of his sixty years. "I guess I didn't pay close enough attention this afternoon. Your father was murdered, you said. And those bastards struck my daughter! Why aren't you out with the dogs and a shotgun looking for 'em?"

"Because I have the matter in hand. Unfortunately, I had some asinine notion I could convince your daughter not to expose herself to any more danger. But I muffed it. She's in there setting up some cockamamie scheme to bring the rats out of their hole. With snake oil."

Fitz's frustration was almost too much to be borne. Suddenly he was aware several people had moved closer, drawn by the intensity of their conversation. As if in corroboration, Devon's voice sounded in his ear. "Unless you gentlemen intend to provide the main entertainment this evening, I'd recommend you adjourn to that anteroom over there to the left."

He nudged Fitz's shoulder in the proper direction and smiled broadly, as if he'd just been let in on some joke. Fitz bared his teeth in return, and the three made their way to the discreet paneled door. Devon stepped aside, murmuring, "I'll stick around to make sure you're not interrupted."

"How come Dolores didn't tell me about Sierra bein' hurt?" Shaw demanded as soon as the door closed behind them.

Fitz realized the interruption had given the man time to think, and answered honestly, "I don't know. Sierra and I were taken to my home, where my doctor diagnosed a slight concussion. She remained there until Dolores sent Caleb early this morning to warn us you were to arrive. Mrs. Shaw probably assumed Sierra would tell you." The small room, lit only by a low-burning gas sconce, was furnished with two comfortable chairs and a small table. Fitz sank into one of them, anticipating the next question.

"When I asked if there was any reason to hustle along a wedding between you two, you said no. Any reason for me not to think you lied about that?" The Senator's voice had hardened, and there was challenge in his blue gaze.

Fitz hadn't felt this intimidated since he'd been called in front of the Harrow headmaster when he was in sixth form. "Perhaps I was being optimistic."

"Wahl, for starters, let's expect the worst. Ah'm a man of quick decisions, and for once Sierra is goin' to do as I say. I expect a weddin' within the week, if you've enough pull with the license people." He paused, then added, "Unless you want me to meander into Whitehall and jerk diplomatic strings."

For one fleeting moment, Fitz felt resentment. Who did this American think he was, ordering him around. Then he remembered. The white-haired man was the father of the woman he loved. "I'll apply for a special license in the morning," Fitz replied, hoping his relief wasn't written across his forehead. He watched as the older man, apparently satisfied, lowered himself into the other chair. "By then I should have the report I need, and I'll also know what kind of scheme Sierra's hatched."

"Good. The girl's smarter than a monkey," her father said fondly, even though worry creased his forehead. "How you goin' to find out what she's up to so quick?"

Fitz stood, his confidence restored. Smiling at his future father-in-law, he couldn't resist a jaunty wink. "Your daughter just wasted a performance worthy of a Dame of the Empire on one of the most successful operatives my father ever employed."

Sierra rose early the next morning, garbed herself in a garnet twill walking dress, then hurried downstairs. Bypassing the breakfast room, she hurried to the stables. She stuck her head in the open door, calling, "Caleb!" When no response was forthcoming, she stepped inside and called once more.

The thud of heavy boots, a far cry from the soft padding sound of Caleb's moccasins, sounded from the tack room. A burly, neatly dressed individual appeared. "Caleb bain't here, miss. 'E be sick again. Missus Shaw sent around to the liv'ry early and asked 'em to send someone ter fill in. Me name's Gurley, ma'am."

Sierra berated herself for not checking on Caleb yesterday. He'd coughed heavily several times during the trip from Fitz's, but her mind had still been enchanted by the night just past. Even now, the memory of Fitz's tender love-making engendered a tingling feeling beneath her skin, and her cheeks warmed. Then she recalled his perfidy. How could he be so gothic as to expect her to sit calmly by while he pursued the blackmailer in his own way? She sternly returned her thoughts to Caleb.

He should never have been out wandering the streets. He'd been feverish and ill that night she took his place, and the very next night he'd braved the early morning air to bring her home. No wonder he was sick again. "I shall require the carriage at ten, Gurley."

On the way back to the house, she ignored her doubts about the morning's expedition. She'd counted on Caleb driving her to Child's, but the errand itself was harmless. Lady Lockwood was to meet her. They would pretend to retrieve the certificates from the lockbox and she would return straight home. Surely she would be safe travelling in daylight. Her pistol nestled in her purse and her knife strapped to her ankle would provide adequate protection. Still, she wished Caleb weren't ill. She'd tell him what she had done as soon as she returned, but for now, he needed sleep more than anything.

She hurried toward the breakfast room, rehearsing her plans. Almost as an afterthought, she made a mental note to fetch the leather portfolio Russ had left in the library.

Once home, she'd send a message to Fitz suggesting he station people on Adelphi Terrace this evening. He'd learn then that he'd underestimated her. Sierra visualized her triumph when her suspect or one of his people appeared to whisk the certificates from her possession. Smiling at the pleasant scenario, she filled a small plate with sliced oranges and fresh strawberries.

A rustle of crisp cotton announced her aunt. "You're up very early, my dear."

Sierra spun around, demanding, "Why didn't you tell me Caleb was so ill he couldn't work? I feel like a pig because he was out in the damp night air chasing me down."

Dolores selected a slice of toast and filled a thin flowered cup with coffee before answering. "He wouldn't have caught cold in the first place if you hadn't sent him to sit out all night on a fool's errand." In spite of the tart words, her aunt's face had a soft glow about it that Sierra had never seen before.

Guilt, an unfamiliar emotion, washed through Sierra. Her fingers shook as she set her own cup on a saucer. Afraid to lift the fragile porcelain, she set her fruit plate beside the saucer on the sideboard and slipped into a chair at her aunt's right. "Have I been that selfish since we've been here? Caleb's my dearest friend, and now he's sick because he's been helping me."

"He would have refused if he hadn't wanted to do as you asked. You know that, Sierra," her aunt said bluntly. "Even though he's convinced you're foolhardy, he supports you."

"I'm not being foolish," Sierra replied stubbornly. She stood and retrieved her coffee and fruit, then sat once more.

"You've never understood why it's necessary for me to help my father."

"You know my feelings on that, Sierra. He's a grown man. Although he blusters unfortunately at times, he's most capable of taking care of himself."

Sierra changed the subject, fearing the discussion might lead to questions about her recent activities. "I wish Daddy and Melanie would have been able to stay here with us."

"They'll be much more comfortable at the Savoy. This house isn't big enough, and we haven't sufficient staff. A hotel with seventy bathrooms will give your father something to rave about when he returns to Washington." Dolores sounded distracted.

"You'll be able to tell your friends the same things," Sierra said, pretending absorption with the task of cutting an orange slice into bite-size pieces. Sierra saw lines crease Dolores's smooth forehead.

"I've been meaning to discuss that with you, Sierra. There's . . . there's a strong possibility I won't be returning with you."

Feigning surprise, Sierra dropped her knife on the embroidered linen tablecloth. "Whatever are you talking about?"

Dolores's cup landed in its saucer with a distinct snap, and she retorted, "What do you suppose I've been doing while you flitted about at all hours with Caleb and slept all afternoon so you could keep up with the social whirl? I certainly couldn't be expected to sit in the parlor and drink tea." Her hands moved agitatedly, and Sierra watched, fascinated, waiting for her to continue.

"I wanted to see the sights of London . . . attend lectures . . . visit museums. And I certainly couldn't do those things alone."

"Of course not, Aunt Dolores. I hadn't realized I was be-having shabbily to you, too." Sierra put her hand over her eyes as if stricken. "I truly am a greedy, spoiled creature."

"Buffalo feathers!" her aunt spat.

"We can stay a month or so after Daddy and Melanie go back to America. I'll take you everywhere . . ."

"I intend to marry and remain in England," Dolores an-nounced stoutly. "You're not the only one who's met an at-tractive Englishman." Her eyes glittered between the slits formed by her narrowed lids.

"Tony Belville!" Sierra shouted. Her suspicion con-firmed, she jumped from her chair and threw her arms around her aunt, hugging her warmly. "I'm so happy for you, I truly am." She kissed Dolores's cheek, which had turned rosy beneath her bronze coloring. "You two are per-fect for each other. I can see you marching at his side on his 'plant hunts.' "

"Life's too short to waste on the proprieties. We decided two nights ago that at our age we would be foolish to carry on a long courtship by mail simply to satisfy convention. I confess that's why I didn't send Caleb for you sooner. I didn't see your father's telegram until nearly two in the morning," Dolores confessed. She avoided Sierra's gaze for a moment, then said almost defiantly, "Tony's already ar-ranging a trip to America this fall to record plant life along the glacier line in the Midwest. He plans to bring back seeds and cuttings."

"He's a dear man, and you're well-suited. Will you come to us for Christmas?"

Dolores cupped Sierra's face between her hands, staring into her eyes with great tenderness. "Do you mean here or at your father's?"

Sierra wrenched away from her probing glance to scoop

scrambled eggs from the copper chafing dish onto a plate. In the face of Dolores's happiness, she saw her resentment of Fitz's protective attitude the night before for what it was. Childish. Still, the wheels had been put in motion. Adding toast from the rack, she settled into her chair with great ceremony.

"Nothing has been decided. I'm extremely put out with Fitz right now." She spread marmalade on her toast and bit daintily into the golden slice. "He told me last night not to worry about Melanie's blackmailer anymore. In so many words, I was to tend my knitting while a strong, intelligent man took over and found the bastard."

"And of course you have no intention of doing so."

Relief at being able to speak of her hurt flooded Sierra. "I was sure you would understand. When I've flushed that rat out of his hole, Fitz may have the honor of capturing him. But I want to be the one who finds him." The more she thought of the idea, the more pleased she became. It would serve Fitz right to be left with only loose ends to tie together. "Oh, and by the way, you might wish to stay out late this evening. Daddy's meeting with people from the English Board of Trade, and the house could be dangerous when the blackmailer comes to call."

Two operatives, their attention focused on Fitz, stood before his desk. "The streets will be full, so I don't anticipate any attempts until Miss Shaw returns to Adelphi Terrace. They'd be foolish to risk attracting attention while she's on her way home from Child's, but you'd better track her from there, just in case." Fitz felt as scruffy as they looked; the bristles at his jawline itched. He wanted a bath and a shave, and saw no chance of either for at least another hour. "Don't let her carriage out of your sight. The fellow's a greedy sod who'll stop at nothing."

"Right ho, Guv'ner," the shorter man said. "Yer be wantin' us to report when the lady harrives 'ome?"

"One of you is to come straight back here as soon as the front door closes behind her. At least Caleb is on the premises. His cold has laid him low, but I've sent him a message outlining her plans." Fitz pushed his chair back. "He and Miss Shaw are capable of holding off any possible attempts before reinforcements arrive. I don't want anyone to venture into the neighborhood until she's safe in that house."

He watched the two men file out, then opened the cabinet containing the reports pertaining to his father's murder. From behind the files he drew out a flat tin box, which he set before him on the desk. Lifting the lid, he addressed the thick stack of certificates his father had bought in good faith, hoping to assist in the rehabilitation of a young man who had fallen short of the promise of his birth. "Geoffrey, you were a bloody rotter. I wonder what my father would say if he were alive to see these miserable pieces of paper worth something."

He was tired, desperately so, but everything was in place. God willing, he could steal three or four hours of sleep before it was necessary to take up vigil on Adelphi Terrace. Damn Sierra's bullheadedness anyway. When Heloise had revealed her plan, the simplicity of it struck him as ridiculous. As the night progressed, he had realized that very simplicity might be as effective as any of his own convoluted schemes.

Still, he wanted to shake her senseless for putting herself at risk. Laughing bitterly, he closed the box, then restored it to the sturdy file. "Your cunning friend would jump out of his knickers if he knew where these were. I can hardly wait to tell the bastard to his face." With that he picked up his disreputable cap and jerked it down over his ears. On his way down the stairs he rucked the collar of his jacket up around his neck and automatically assumed the slouching, discouraged walk he utilized during his trips through the London streets.

His thoughts occupied him so completely that when he reached the park he passed the entrance to the secret passage without thinking. A quick glance ahead showed the short alley behind his stable deserted. Too weary to backtrack to the safety of the hidden opening, he slipped through the hedge to the alley and looked up at the window of the room he and Sierra had occupied two nights earlier. The memory of what had happened there nearly overwhelmed him. A sudden movement to his left alerted him too late, and the last thing he saw was Paxton's face at the upper window, his mouth open as if he were shouting.

Promptly at ten, Sierra descended the stone steps to the waiting carriage. Instructing Gurley to take her to Child's Bank, she stepped inside and settled against the squabs. She was strangely nervous, but attributed the feeling to excitement and her annoyance with Fitz.

What if the Fitz who'd clumsily told her to stay out of the way was the real Fitz? Throwing caution to the winds, she had fallen in love with a stranger, and now it was too late. She was so deeply in love that she contemplated spending the rest of her life in a country other than that of her birth.

Sierra looked out at the buildings lining the streets. They conveyed a sense of permanence and history she had never felt in the United States. Even in Washington. Normally she disliked crowds, but the bustling streets of London had gradually ceased to bother her, and they endeared themselves to her with their endlessly interesting denizens. And there was always Kent House.

The carriage slowed as they travelled down Fleet Street, and she saw Child's marigold sign ahead. As she alighted, she told Gurley, "Please wait. When I finish here I wish to return directly home."

Heloise met her in the lobby, and their spurious errand at the lockbox took less than twenty minutes. "May I drop you anywhere, Lady Lockwood?" Sierra inquired for the benefit of the clerks rushing to offer service to their illustrious depositor. A portly gentleman entered the lobby; rain dripped from his Burberry. "I believe it's begun to rain."

"No, my dear. Like you, I have a carriage awaiting me." She gestured toward a waiting footman carrying a furled umbrella. "I feared this would happen, and have come prepared. May we escort you to your carriage?"

Glad for the shelter, Sierra welcomed the beat of the heavy summer shower against the umbrella as she crossed the sidewalk to her carriage. Now that she had set her plan in motion, she didn't care if it snowed. When the steps were let down, she turned to Lady Lockwood. "Thank you for your help."

"You're most welcome, my dear. Although I feel you would have been wiser to leave this in Fitz's capable hands, I quite understand your reasons for insisting on completing your . . . mission on your own terms. I would have done the same."

As soon as the door closed behind her, Sierra set the empty leather case on the seat beside her and smiled with satisfaction. Now all that remained was to send Fitz a message. She hoped Caleb had recovered sufficiently to run the errand, but if the rain continued, she had no intention of asking him to set out. Perhaps Gurley would do it.

The curtains were drawn tight over the windows, and the rumble of the carriage wheels over the pavement and the rain pounding against the roof were soporific. Soothed, Sierra settled into the corner of the seat and attempted to review the day ahead, but she'd had little sleep the night before. Content that the most difficult part of her plan was behind her, she dozed off.

She awoke when her side of the carriage rose as if the wheels had gone over a rock in the roadway. It stopped abruptly, tipping her off the seat to the floor. Before she could gather her senses, the door swung open, bouncing back against the side of the carriage. Gurley's square figure filled the opening.

"What's happened?" she demanded, groping for her reticule and the reassuring weight of the pistol within.

He seized her shoulder roughly with one hand and snagged the leather case off the seat with the other. "Yer'll not be needin' this no more," he growled.

Her fingers found the reticule as he hovered above her, and she swung it recklessly at his head. "You yellow-bellied thief! Get your hands off me!"

"Bloody little bitch!" He scarcely wavered from the blow, moving only to release her shoulder and strike her chin with his meaty fist. The reticule fell from her fingers. He wrenched her from the carriage, dragged her down the steps, and flung her to the ground.

Dizzy from the blow, Sierra blinked to clear her vision. The taste of blood from a cut inside her mouth revived her. As she opened her lips to scream, Gurley pulled a filthy handkerchief from his pocket and crammed it into her mouth, securing it with the ribbons he tore from her fallen bonnet.

Raindrops spat cold against her heated skin. Sierra watched dazedly from the cobbles as he unsnapped the latch of the portfolio. His enraged roar when he found it empty sent a spurt of adrenaline through her, and she gathered her legs beneath her to run. She cursed the snug lines of her walking skirt. She'd have to . . .

Flinging the empty case back into the carriage, Gurley grunted, "Now you're for it! 'E'll be at yer fer this trick." She was scarcely to her feet when he seized her from behind, one hand closing over her breast. "I 'ates pushy wimmen wot meddle."

CHAPTER TWENTY-ONE

Sierra pulled from his grip. Turning toward him, she punched his face and kicked at his lower body. Turning sideways to shield his vulnerable groin and belly, Gurley reached through her attack and seized her with both arms. He flipped her over his shoulder with ridiculous ease, sending air whooshing out of her lungs.

Seconds later, Sierra got a second wind and began to pound furiously on his back.

"Yer hits me again, yer bloody mort, an' I'll break yer leg." To emphasize his threat, he twisted her left leg painfully at the knee until she let her arms fall limp. "We'll have ter put yer away till yer tells me where they are."

With that, he pivoted and trotted down an alley. Sierra could make out little but the lower wall and the filthy cobblestones beneath his feet, and before she could raise her head to look around, he had entered a narrow door.

The dimly lit hall was cold, as if they'd entered an ice house. Sierra inhaled the pungency of damp and rot. Her captor moved so swiftly she couldn't focus on their surroundings. He stumbled, and her upper body slammed against his back. She swallowed the bile her abused stomach sent into her throat.

Dread gripped her when she realized no one but Heloise knew of their appointment at Child's. Since then she had been in the duplicitous care of Gurley, who was obviously not a coachman.

Her head bobbed helplessly against his back as they passed through a narrow passage, down a flight of stairs and through a dimly lit room. The tenor of Gurley's footprints changed, and she thought his boots were striking a stone floor, travelling so quickly the surface was a blur to her up-side-down vision. They descended yet another staircase, definitely stone, and definitely dark.

Cold. The temperature seemed to drop with each downward step. The air smelled as if it had been confined in this cellar for a thousand years. She lifted her head to gain reassurance from the diffused light far behind them.

" 'Ere's yer room, bitch. Lunnon swells bin waitin' in line ter git in, so yer'll 'ave ter share till yer empty yer budget." He chuckled rustily as he swung her off his shoulder. Her spirits plummeted even further when he pulled her arms behind her back, tying them snugly with rope he pulled seemingly out of nowhere. Shoving her down onto the floor, he bound her ankles so tightly she moaned. "Me 'eart's bleedin' fer yer," he said coldly before walking away.

His heavy footsteps retreated, the sound fading, and Sierra's stomach knotted. She was alone. In the dark. And she was cold. The terror began to edge into her mind. Even though her hands were bound behind her, she knew in a detached way that they were shaking, just as she knew her throat was closing and cold sweat forming on her brow. She wanted to call Gurley back. *Any* presence would be better than this void.

Sobs formed in her chest, and her throat convulsed as she fought to keep from choking on internal tears. She struggled and contorted her body in an effort to free herself. Only the pain of the rope sawing at her wrists through the thin covering of her kid gloves stopped her. Her body tensed until her muscles ached, while her mind slowly shut down.

★ ★ ★ ★ ★

"Sierra." Fitz mouthed her name softly, afraid to move his head for fear of loosing the pain that shot through him at the slightest movement. Roused by the sound of her captor's voice, he had been afraid to move or make a sound until he was sure they were alone. He had no idea how long he'd lain there, unconscious, his hands and feet bound, before the rough cockney voice and the thud of another body landing beside him had brought him round.

Her scent, wild violets and Sierra, penetrating the ancient dust and mold of their surroundings, had identified her. He raised his voice slightly. "Sierra, it's me, Fitz." Ignoring the pounding in his head, he inched toward her scent, his boot heels scraping on the gritty surface of the floor. His shoulder touched her body, and he felt her startled awareness of him plus something frightening. Shudders racked her slender frame.

"Sierra, if you're not seriously injured, push back against me." He rocked until his arm touched her hip.

After what seemed like a lifetime, she rolled slightly toward him. "Bloody hell. You're gagged, and you're probably bound as snugly as I am." Remembering her horror of being shut up in the dark, he kept his voice soothing. "I imagine our captors are royally miffed because you came away empty-handed from Child's. They wanted those certificates, and they thought you'd be an easy mark," he said lightly, determined to help her relax.

He inched upward along her body, the muscles in his calves screaming with the effort. Hoping the sound of his voice would calm her claustrophobia, he continued, "Come to think of it, they must think I'll tell them the whereabouts of my own shares. That poses a tricky problem. The certificates are in my government office, which is guarded like the

Royal Mint. I do hope yours are a trifle more accessible."
Now wasn't the time to tell her he knew exactly where they
were.

Her arm moved slightly against him, and he ventured,
"Well hidden, eh? Then we've a sticky wicket ahead of us.
Don't suppose you've a knife on you?"

This time her shoulder seemed to move up and down,
and Fitz felt a spurt of satisfaction. Certainly she would
have armed herself for the expedition, even though it had
taken place in daylight. "By Jove, you are a helpful little
thing," he said in an attempt at lightheartness. "Too bad
you can't tell me where you're carrying it today. I have a
slight handicap. My hands are tied behind me."

Her body made several convulsive movements against
him, as if she were attempting to push away from him. Puzzled, he said, "No need to get in a snit just because I can't
do anything about using the knife to set us free. I rather like
lying here against you. Brings back memories."

He felt her stiffen as if in anger. Then he remembered
the day he'd met her riding in the park.

Miraculously, just as her mind had teetered on the brink
of shutdown, seconds before she would have retreated into
inner caverns so deep nothing could reach her, Fitz's voice
had come out of the darkness.

Even though she cringed inwardly at the darkness and
their helplessness, his presence had brought her back from
the brink of the bottomless pit she'd feared since she was a
child. She wanted to sob with gratitude, but her throat was
already raw from her attempts to scream around the filthy
gag.

Her wits were returning, however, and if she could, she
would hug him for defusing her panic. Somehow she must

show him where she carried her knife. In her frustration, she formed a mental picture of her calf. Inching her body upward, she concentrated once again.

Still speaking softly, as if someone might overhear, Fitz said, "That day in the park. Your riding habit skirt slid back and your knife was in a sheath at the top of your boot."

She nodded her head violently enough that he was bound to feel the motion in the dark. The sheath was fastened to her leg, just above her buttoned half-boot.

As if reading her mind, he observed casually, "I'd be surprised at someone as fashionable as you wearing riding boots with a gown, so the knife must be fastened to your leg." He inched further downward. "Definitely not a standard debutante accessory."

This time she was able to inch upward several more inches. His boots scraped against the gritty floor.

"By the way, last night your father tricked the truth out of me about our impetuous encounter," he said between efforts. The side of his head rubbed against her hip. "Ordered me to obtain a special license, but I haven't had time to take care of that this morning. I would have anyway, mind you. It just goes against the grain to be handed an order like that. Good thing he isn't here to see me dive beneath your skirts. He might pull out a six-gun." He rolled onto his side, his back to her, and his bound hands tugged her skirt upward. "Left or right leg?"

She struggled to tilt her body onto her left side, knocking his hands away with her right knee. The foul cloth in her mouth shifted. Sierra choked and gagged. She heard a strangled laugh.

"You Yanks are so direct. I take it the sheath is on the outside of your right leg."

As if he could see her, she nodded violently, her ear

scraping across the rough floor. Tendrils of hair hung over her face, tickling her nose, and she fought the urge to sneeze, positive the act would be the death of her.

After what seemed a lifetime of shifting and grunting, Fitz's bound hands brushed her calf and fumbled with the handle of her knife. "While I'm here, I'll take a stab at freeing your ankles." He laughed giddily. "Sorry for the bad pun. I promise to be careful. Lie still."

In spite of working behind his back in the dark, Fitz only nicked her once. Even as she winced, Sierra realized his skill. Had he done this sort of thing before? The pressure of her bonds disappeared and she wiggled her feet gratefully.

"I'm going to edge away from you. Can you turn onto your other side?"

The task was easier with her legs free. By the time she rolled onto her side, he had repositioned his body higher.

"Now try to wiggle closer," he said patiently, as if they had all the time in the world.

His calm, methodical approach sent fear hurtling through her. What if their captors returned before they were free? Her heart thumped wildly, and she dragged in a deep breath of the stale, musty air in an effort to calm herself. Then she obeyed.

At the first tentative movements of his hands against hers, he said, "I promise to be much more entertaining the next time we're on our backs in the dark."

I'm going to kill him for making jokes at a time like this! Even as she cursed him, Sierra thanked God for his ability to divert her thoughts from the terror of their situation.

The pressure on her wrists disappeared. She wriggled her hands to restore circulation and she brought them to her mouth to rip away the noisome gag. Her numbed fingers refused to grip the ribbon at first, but she persisted until the knot gave. She spat out the disgusting cloth. Her mouth and lips felt like a dusty road, but she didn't care.

"You probably aren't able to talk yet, but would you mind terribly getting on with the business of freeing me?"

Fitz's plaintive voice reminded her of their need to hurry. She rolled over and ran her hand down his sleeve to where he gripped the knife. In moments she freed his hands, then crawled to his ankles and slashed the rope binding them.

Afraid of misplacing the knife in the dark, she returned the blade to its sheath with a trembling hand. Then, uttering a desperate sob, she rolled into Fitz's arms. His heart beat madly against hers as he held her close. "When we get out of this, I'm going to beat you, Sierra. I must have aged twenty years when they dumped you beside me."

Recognizing the familiar male response to a near escape, she tried to remind him they weren't "out of this" yet, but her tongue felt glued to the roof of her mouth, so she simply clung more tightly. As long as he was with her, she could manage the darkness and the panic threatening to engulf her.

As if aware her fear went even deeper than their danger, Fitz held her close. "Whoever he is, he's obsessed with possessing every damn one of those certificates. Someone will be back. Soon, if I'm any judge. We have to make plans," he said firmly, "but first . . ."

His devastating kiss set Sierra's whole body to vibrating. The gargoyles hovering at the edges of her mind retreated further, and she knew only the heat of his lips and the passionate thrust of his tongue. As suddenly as he had kissed her, Fitz pulled back, laughing. "Did that make your mouth feel any better?"

Sierra had never loved him more. "I'll show you how

much better when we're out of here," she whispered huskily before pulling away. Her hands clung to his. As long as she could touch him and he continued to speak, she would survive.

"We may not have time to escape before someone comes. You wanted to bring the blackmailer into the open, and he could show up anytime now. Do you feel strong enough to employ some of your less feminine skills?"

"I feel like hitting someone!" she croaked. Neither mentioned her earlier paralyzed state, but his understanding seemed to flow through her fingertips. Physical activity would dissipate the last of her fear.

"Good girl. Stand up."

Puzzled, she obeyed, stumbling a little. She felt his hands go beneath her skirts. "This is no time to . . ."

"I just want the knife."

She felt a tug, heard the sound of ripping cloth. "You're cutting my skirt."

"The damn thing hobbles you. While I'm at this, you might want to work at getting out of your corset from the top if you can," Fitz commanded. "Our jailer will assume we're both still helpless, and you'll be no help in this getup."

Laughter bubbled up in Sierra's throat and she began working the jet buttons of her bodice loose. "For the first time, I'm glad it's dark down here."

"I rather think you do. Now, here's how we'll . . ."

Booted footsteps thudded down the stairs less than twenty minutes later. Fitz held his breath, concern for Sierra clutching at his nerve endings. Once freed, she had been frenetically enthusiastic about his plan. Her tension had been palpable, her skin clammy when she launched herself into his arms. Her . . . collectedness was missing.

He mentally shelved his worries. Too much hinged on their success, and he couldn't allow himself any doubts. He reviewed their preparations. The derringer he habitually wore holstered at his ankle was tucked in his waistband. He grinned in the darkness. His captors' search had been cursory. Amateurs. The tiny one-shot pistol and the element of surprise might work for them, particularly with Sierra's help.

He smiled as the sounds of an argument reached him. "Bloody bitch were lyin'! I swear, the case were empty!"

"If I find you've double-crossed me, you'll end up floating in the Thames." The new voice was muted, but his precise syllables and sneering tone of voice travelled through the thick, stale air with startling clarity. "You'll float right beside the Shaw woman and Kent, if I discover you're holding out on me."

Footsteps on the gritty floor told Fitz they were close. He crouched lower at the base of the wall, peering toward the other side of the room to where he knew Sierra knelt, ready to spring.

Neither of the approaching men spoke again, but their outlines were visible in the glow from a partially shuttered lantern in the grip of a square figure which scuttled on bowlegs, like a sailor just off his ship. The other loomed tall and trim, with a smooth, graceful stride.

A whooping screech echoed throughout the chamber. Sierra's promised war cry. He leaped toward the taller figure, jerking the man's left arm up behind his shoulders with one hand while slashing at the base of his neck with the other hand, cutting off his captive's shout of surprise. His target fell like a stone.

Fitz turned in time to see the shorter man claw at Sierra,

who rode his back, holding onto his ears and twisting his head sideways. Fitz snatched the lantern from the struggling man's hand and set it aside. Keeping sight of his own victim from the corner of his eye, he watched while his wild Yankee woman brought the man to the ground.

From her seat in the middle of Gurley's back, Sierra held her knife at his neck and asked huskily, "Shall I kill him?" The figure beneath her heaved and cried out.

Fitz spoke around his laughter. His headache had miraculously become a thing of the past. "Right ruddy little savage, aren't you?" Lifting the lantern, he sought out the pile of discarded ropes and retrieved the only two pieces of any length. "These should do until we get this pair to the light of day. As soon as I figure out where we are, I'll send for help." He held out one piece to Sierra. "Here. Tie his hands behind him." The tall figure stirred, and Fitz set his foot in the middle of his back.

"Wait. This is my chance for revenge," she spat, jerking her erstwhile coachman's hands tightly behind him. "I hope his fingers rot."

"This bastard's masked," Fitz said, kneeling to draw the rope around his captive's wrists. "I suppose we can wait until we're out of here to make his acquaintance."

"It's Nigel Brockington," Sierra said flatly. She hauled Gurley to his feet.

Fitz's captive sagged at her easy identification. "How do you know?"

"By his walk. Hadn't you ever noticed? He walks too pretty for a man," she said absently.

"I thought you had your mind fixed on Lancaster," Fitz said, hauling Nigel to his feet.

"I did, until last night. Nigel was too eager to help me. Francis was merely condescending and disapproving, as always. Bored, actually. Nigel's eyes gave him away . . . he knew the name of the railroad venture."

As they turned their captives toward the stairs, Fitz laughed. "Heloise said the same thing when I asked her what you were up to. You're two of a kind," he managed between chuckles.

"Why, thank you very much," Sierra said jauntily. She prodded Gurley up the first step with the tip of her knife blade. "That's quite the nicest thing anyone's said to me since I came to England."

Sierra stepped through the recessed door and looked up gratefully at the slanting afternoon sun. "Isn't that the Tower over there?" She inhaled deeply the sour smells of the ancient alley. After the moldering air in the cellar, London's amalgam of damp odors was ambrosia.

"Spoken like a true tourist," Fitz said. His bright gaze swept their surroundings. Recognition lit his face. "We were in the undercroft of All Hallows Barking by the Tower. If we hadn't been able to get loose, and they'd not come back, we wouldn't have been found until we were bones. I don't think anyone ever goes into those cellars."

"Damn your eyes, this isn't finished yet," Brockington cried. "Danvers!"

Footsteps sounded behind them. Fitz shoved his captive into Sierra's, knocking both of them to the ground in a heap. Rough arms seized Sierra from behind. She shifted her weight and grabbed for her attacker's arm, flipping him to the cobbles headfirst. A swift survey of the darkening alley revealed a shadow clutching a cudgel behind Fitz, who had just fended off the attack of a small, wiry man. "Fitz, behind you!" she screamed hoarsely.

At the sound of her voice, he pivoted, bringing his left

foot up to send the roughly clad figure to the ground. Watching with approval, Sierra never heard the attacker behind her. Arms wrapped around her bare calves, pulling her down. Instinctively, she grabbed for his head, jerking his left ear so hard he screamed and loosened his hold. She twisted a second time, then slipped her knife from its sheath and held it against his throat. Her heart raced and her breath escaped through her dry lips in short pants.

"Are you all right?" Fitz called. He knelt beside each of their felled attackers in turn, removing knives and pistols from their persons. Brockington cursed as he attempted to rise without the assistance of his arms. "Looks as if that's the lot. Now we've only to transport them to custody."

Footsteps sounded, bringing Fitz around in a crouch. "Dear me. I'd so hoped we would be in time!" Disappointment filled Paxton's voice, which thinned as he said, "But I see you have the matter in hand."

Both men Fitz had commissioned to watch Sierra earlier were close on his heels. Three policemen trailed behind them as if uncertain of their authority. "When your men told me where Miss Shaw had been taken, I thought it best to bring the law with us, sir. You were unavailable to consult."

"Quite right, Paxton," Fitz retorted. Pushing his prisoner roughly back to the ground, he snatched the silk mask from the prone man's face. "Brockington it is. Not that I had any doubt. Miss Shaw is amazingly observant." His voice held an edge Sierra had never heard before, and his eyes glittered with golden hatred. A muscle in his cheek twitched, then smoothed.

"Go to hell," Nigel snarled, his pleasant features contorted with rage. "If your father hadn't been so bloody-minded, he'd have parted with those shares. That would have left only Miss Shaw's stupid cow of a stepmother." His attention turned to Sierra, and he snarled, "If you'd kept your bloody nose out, I'd have pulled it off."

Before Sierra could react, Fitz twisted Brockington's bound hands upward, and he shrieked with pain. "Count yourself lucky I'm civilized. I'd prefer to shoot you where you stand. You killed my father, you son of a bitch." His voice was thick with rage.

A firm hand came between him and Brockington. "Here now, Mr. Fitz. As much as I'd like a turn at the scoundrel myself, the law will punish him." Paxton pulled the bound man to his feet and pushed him ungently toward the policemen. "Indeed, he's fortunate Miss Shaw and her Indian friend didn't capture him earlier. The two quite frighten me."

He and Fitz's men efficiently bound the other fallen men. "Botts at Scotland Yard kindly furnished a vehicle, sir. Rather a small one, but we've little interest in their comfort."

Sierra wrapped her arms around Fitz, who stood stiffly, his face contorted. "It's over, darling. We can't change what happened to your father, but you've captured his murderer. He'll be punished. It's over."

He remained rigid beneath her touch as he addressed Nigel. "You drugged him before you suffocated him, didn't you?"

Defiance filled Nigel's voice. "Your father threatened me with exposure. He discovered I'd manipulated my father into underwriting the certificate buyback, and he accused me of being behind the accidents that killed MacDonough and the others. An investigation would have given me away. The fool offered to stand by me while I confessed." He laughed humorlessly. "I couldn't let him do that. Not after

279

all my planning. That rail line would have made me a wealthy man. My *future* depended on this, and no one was going to stand in my way!"

Silence fell as his listeners absorbed the horrifying meaning of his bitter words. He was dressed in black, wearing a clerical collar. Sierra realized why her early leads called him The Parson. What a horrible disguise for a twisted soul.

"You killed your own father, didn't you?" Fitz accused.

"You got *your* inheritance," Brockington shouted. "All I wanted was to make mine worth something, too." He was still babbling as he was led away.

Sierra clung to Fitz, attempting to reach the cold, accusing stranger he had become. She nearly cried with relief when his arms crept around her and his body softened within her grasp. She heard Paxton dispatch Fitz's men with the police.

Minutes later Paxton cleared his throat discreetly. "Sir, Miss Shaw. I've a hansom waiting around the corner." When there was no response, Paxton said in strangled tones, "Miss Shaw, your . . . er . . . limbs are quite exposed."

Fitz drew back, his gaze dropping to her knees, then further down. "And very nice limbs they are, don't you agree, Paxton?"

CHAPTER TWENTY-TWO

Thirty minutes later they drew up in front of the house on Adelphi Terrace. Paxton alighted to assist both of them from the cab, his ostentatious efforts to avert his face from Sierra's ruined gown distracting her from her concern for Fitz. During the ride home she had held him close while he told her of the hatred he'd carried since his father died.

"Stupid bastard. Money," he'd murmured. "Just money. I can let go now. Somewhere, my father's rubbing his hands together and chuckling." The bleak satisfaction in his voice had chilled her.

In an effort to dispel his pain, she said, "Poor Paxton. First my buckskins and now this. I could promise to display more propriety in the future . . ."

Her father's voice bellowed from the entrance, interrupting her. "Sierra Shaw, what in tarnation are you doing paradin' around London with your legs sticking out for all these Johnnies to ogle! Get in here right now. There's no time to waste."

Sierra sighed and took Fitz's arm. "No one ever need seek my father's opinion on any subject. He offers it before they ask."

To her surprise, Fitz didn't smile. "We'd better not keep him waiting. He's had all night to work himself into a real snit." He led her up the steps.

"Skedaddle up to your room right now, Sierra," the Senator ordered. "Rig yourself up in one of them Paris outfits and get back downstairs. I've had this fellow waiting for two hours, and he's got to get back to his work." He frowned at her butchered gown as she hurried toward the stairs, then scowled at Fitz. "Don't suppose you'd like to explain why my daughter looks like the dogs dragged her under the house, would you, Kent?"

Fitz checked the tender place at the base of his skull with tentative fingers. When the Senator repeated his question in stentorian tones, he responded, "It's rather a long story, sir."

Fitz followed Shaw into the little waiting room. At his host's instruction, he sat in the same hard chair he had occupied weeks earlier. Unaccustomed to being treated so cavalierly, Fitz eyed his companion with suspicion. He liked Sierra's father; the American's directness appealed to him. But right now he wanted nothing more than to return to his home and retreat to the solitude of his study. He was heartsore, and his headache had returned. "Sir, I . . ."

"You can tell me about it after the ceremony. I forgot to ask you before. You got enough money to support my girl, Kent?"

The question was so far from his train of thought that Fitz surprised himself by answering honestly. "Aside from my London home, I own Kent House and about a thousand acres in Suffolk where I breed sheep. The house and land are from my mother's side, but she insisted on changing the name when she and my father married."

"Land is good, but by what I hear, you don't spend much time there. I hear you're in London eatin' and dancin' an awful lot. What about money?"

The key word in this bizarre interrogation registered in Fitz's mind. Ceremony. The man spoke of a ceremony. Leaning back into the dreadful little chair, he drawled, "Really, old man. Aren't you becoming rather personal?"

Fitz struggled to maintain his calm. Voices and footsteps

in the entry hall intruded but didn't register. He swallowed his growing irritation and concentrated on preserving a polite facade for the blustering man who had fathered the woman he loved—concentrated so intently he didn't notice the sound of the door opening.

"Don't give me any of that upper-crust crap, boy." The Senator reached into the inside pocket of his tweed coat and pulled out a paper. "This here's a special wedding license. I finagled for it myself. A minister's waiting in the drawing room to marry you and my daughter."

He tucked the license back into his pocket and glared menacingly. "Back home we don't hold with this dowry and settlement crap you folks set such store by, but I'm bound to find out how my little girl's goin' to live before I marry her off to some Johnny who took advantage of her innocence."

Towering over Fitz's chair, he announced, "I ain't handing over any of my money for you to squander on parties and fancy clothes."

Refusing to cower beneath the older man's stiff glare, Fitz stood and glared back. He sensed another presence in the room, but refused to turn from the steely blue gaze boring into him. "Sir, I want nothing more than to marry Sierra. Wherever and whenever she's ready. But that's our decision. I suspect she'll balk if you order her downstairs for her wedding without preliminary discussion."

Shaw lowered his brows and backed away, his forehead creased in a worried frown. "She might kick up a fuss, but she knows I have her welfare at heart," he said as if attempting to convince himself. After a moment's thought, he sighed and admitted, "You're right, son. The only way out is for you to bring her around. If I like your answer to my question."

Fitz felt as if a noose were tightening around his neck. He responded stiffly, "Because of the nature of my work for the government, I find it useful to be seen socially. My salary isn't spectacular, but my investments bring in nearly ten thousand pounds a year. And of course, there's income from my land." He added aggressively, "I have no intention of applying to you for funds."

A ripple of laughter sounded from the doorway. For the first time, he looked beyond Theo Shaw's shoulder. How could he have missed Adrian and Chloe Harding's arrival? Adrian's eyes were alight with sardonic amusement; Chloe, shoulders shaking, had buried her face against her husband's chest to stifle the sounds of her laughter. Fitz wanted to kill them both.

Still unaware of their audience, the Senator lowered his brows and stared fiercely at Fitz. "More to you than I thought. Figured you were some kind of dabbler." His laughter rumbled from his big chest. "Well, you are, aren't you? By damn, I think I like you. Yes, sir, even Sierra's brothers will approve. Have to get them over here to visit." He reached for Fitz's hand. "Yes, sir. This will be first-rate. Now you just go up there and sweet-talk my little girl. The minister's gettin' antsy in there, and Dolores is actin' strange."

"For heaven's sake, Edwina, you've been fussing with my hair for ten minutes," Sierra ordered. "My father will be pounding on the door any minute now." A hot bath hadn't relaxed her; she felt keyed up.

A curved silver comb dropped from the maid's fingers, and Sierra saw her averted eyes in the mirror. The girl was in worse shape than she was. "What's making you so nervous, Edwina?"

284

"It's yer pa, Miss Sierra." The girl's fingers made one last, futile attempt to curb the activities of a recalcitrant curl which persisted in escaping. She failed. "He's got the vicar downstairs."

Oh, God. He's going to make Fitz marry me! Sierra had never wanted anything so much in her life. Fitz's offhand mention of Theo Shaw's discovery of their intimacy had been part of the flow of words he'd used to divert the deep hold of her phobia. She'd neglected to warn him about her father's high-handedness. But Fitz was also accustomed to assuming command. What would happen when those two clever, stubborn wills collided?

At the prospect of an immediate wedding, her mouth went dry and her limbs felt as if the circulation had died. Sure as she was of her love for Fitz, a part of her shriveled with fear when she thought of the side of him she didn't know. The side he'd cleverly kept hidden from her. The side that belonged to the Crown.

He *liked* danger and intrigue. This afternoon in the alley he had been lightning and fire, tossing his attackers aside like feather pillows. *She* had been the one quaking inside as she fought alongside him. Even so, the thought of marrying a man who pursued danger appealed to her. Life with Fitz could be a dangerous adventure. Living without him would be a hundred times more difficult.

Sierra studied Edwina's anxious face in the mirror. "Perhaps he's finally concerned about the state of his soul," she said lightly, aware that the small staff she employed was connected to servants' halls all over London. "My hair looks fine. Is my rose silk afternoon dress pressed?"

A knock sounded at the door. Her father's shouted, "Sierra!" preceded him as he pushed the door open without waiting for her permission. He waved Edwina out the door impatiently, nearly catching her dark muslin skirt between it and the jamb when he pushed the panel shut behind her.

"Some Johnny you found yourself. He refused to marry you!" Theo Shaw ran his fingers roughly through his hair, standing it on end. "What if you're pregnant? Did you ever think of that?"

Sierra wondered if a court would acquit her of murdering her father. "You ordered him to marry me? Now? Today? After everything that's happened?" She stood and hurried to the window, her dressing gown billowing around her and hampering each step. By the time she parted the heavy draperies and densely gathered sheers to peer out, the street was empty. The hansom they'd arrived in had disappeared. She whirled on her father. "Did you bother to ask Fitz where we'd been? Why we arrived here looking as if we'd been on the wrong end of a posse?"

Her father's gaze narrowed as he said belligerently, "That don't have anything to do with this. I couldn't sleep all night for thinking about him taking advantage of you." His eyes glistened with sudden moisture. "My little girl and that slick Johnny Bull polecat. He sweet-talked me last night. Tried it again this morning. Then I told him how things was going to be. Even suggested he smooth the whole fandango over with you, so's I wouldn't have to get ugly. He up and walked out."

Sierra's heart contracted. Her father's roughshod approach had pushed Fitz past the breaking point. Since breakfast this morning they'd both been kidnapped, abandoned in an unspeakable dark cellar, threatened with death, struggled to escape, and fought their way to freedom together. They'd apprehended the blackmailer, who turned out to be the murderer of Fitz's father. She doubted she would ever forget the anguish in Fitz's eyes.

His inner pain must be immense, and before he'd been given time to deal with his emotions, her father had ordered him to take a leading role in a western-style shotgun wedding. How could she ever face Fitz again? Yet how could she not? Sierra's thoughts tumbled this way and that, and she shook her head to clear it before speaking. "Daddy, I love you."

She placed her hands on his shoulders and looked him straight in the eye. "I've always admired the way you head straight for your objective. When you're in the right, you ride roughshod over any obstacle. Never have I questioned one of your decisions or actions. Until today."

Hardening her heart at the confusion on his features, she shook him as hard as she could. "And I want to tell you this is the most unfeeling, arrogant . . . blockheaded thing you've ever done."

Theo Shaw tried to step away, blustering, "That Johnny told me to go to hell."

"Good for him! You're an interfering, blustering, insensitive jackass!" She fisted her hands at her sides. "Fitz and I are adults! We make our own decisions. When we stepped out of that carriage it was obvious we hadn't been to the Queen's garden party. We were nearly killed. And we captured the blackmailer." She felt her voice break, drew a deep breath, then continued, "Daddy, he murdered Fitz's father! Did you even ask what had happened? No. Instead, you barged right ahead, the perfect picture of an outraged father."

Sierra released his shoulders and kissed his cheek softly. "Daddy, what if Grandpa had ordered you to marry Mama? Within the next hour."

Her father said stoutly, "I'd have told him to go to hell. I make my own decisions."

"Exactly. I love Fitz so much I'll even apologize to him for my oaf of a father." Sierra laid her hand on his arm and cautioned, "I'm going after him. And you're going to stay out of it."

A twinkle appeared in the Senator's eye. "That's my girl. He's a good man," he said gruffly. Then he grinned. "By the way, those Johnnies who visited us in Washington . . . the Harding fellow and his wife . . . arrived while we were arguin'. Their yacht must have arrived about the same time the steamship Melanie and I were sailing on did. Can't figure out for the life of me why they thought that ruckus Kent and I were having was so consarned funny."

Fitz left Adelphi Terrace in a funk. He walked past the waiting carriage and trudged determinedly through puddles. Rain still fell fitfully. His sodden boots squished with each step, and he wallowed in his discomfort.

Theo Shaw had ordered him to marry Sierra within the hour. *Ordered him!* Then Adrian and Chloe Harding had appeared and *laughed!*

Damn it, a man has the right to court a woman the way she deserves.

Fitz's orderly, if unorthodox, existence had been in shreds ever since Sierra Shaw's wide blue gaze had drawn him into her mad masquerade. At the thought of her, the fragrance of wild violets filled his nostrils. He wanted her so desperately his hands shook.

He needed to get away, to regain his balance. Oddly enough, apprehending his father's murderer now seemed an anticlimax. His love for Sierra meant life, and Matthew Kent had been a great believer in living life as fully as possible. He would have approved of Sierra.

Fitz stopped and looked at his surroundings. The rain

had settled into a thick, polluted mist that penetrated not only clothing and buildings but souls. While he had walked the streets of London, consumed by his thoughts, some inner beacon had guided him to the alley outside his office.

Trudging up the stairs, he entered the outer door and greeted Harrison absently, adding, "I'm not here."

"You'd best be. Chap's coming over from t' Foreign Office to see you. Stepped on any toes lately?"

"Tell him you haven't seen me since yesterday," he responded irritatedly. "I just came in to pick up something."

Closing the door to his office behind him, he cursed solemnly. If the emissary had questions about his dealings with their distinguished visitor from the United States, Fitz would have the devil of a time explaining. It was time to shake the dust of London from his heels. Life in Suffolk would help him find his bearings. Then, after he had sorted out his life, he would begin all over again to woo Sierra.

Suddenly obsessed with the need for solitude, he unlocked the cabinet that held his father's papers and stuffed them into a nondescript cloth bundle. Given the state of his clothing, even the least astute thief would ignore him.

Stepping back into the outer office, he told Harrison, "If whoever arrives is here on Old Firm business, send a message to Queen's Square. Otherwise, you haven't seen me and don't expect to for a fortnight."

Harrison eyed him curiously, but nodded. " 'Avin' a bad patch?"

"Nothing I can't handle. I just need to get away," Fitz replied. "Paxton can reach me if any balloons go up." He hurried toward the stairs and the damp trip home.

This time he didn't make the mistake of approaching the service entrance. He entered through the wild tangle of bushes disguising the entrance to the secret tunnel.

Emerging in the kitchen, he headed directly to his room and commenced ripping off his clothing. "Paxton!"

The little man seemed to materialize from the woodwork. "Your bath is drawn, Mr. Fitz. Shall I dispose of those rags you're wearing?"

"Thank you and yes." Fitz pulled the jersey over his head. "Did you encounter any difficulty handing over our prisoners to the authorities?"

Paxton accepted the snagged garment with the tips of his thumb and forefinger. "None whatsoever, sir, although Superintendent Travers did ask that you send him the particulars before morning, so they could be properly charged."

"You might see to some food. I'll write out a report while I eat." Fitz kicked off his disreputable shoes and unbuttoned his trousers. "Then I'm leaving for Kent House. Harrison will contact you in case of anything dire. Otherwise, you don't know where I am." He dropped the torn corduroys to the floor.

Paxton, his nostrils pinched together as if scenting bad drains, gathered up the discarded apparel before inquiring, "And if I should hear from Miss Shaw?"

"You won't," Fitz replied, heading for the bathroom. "Her father and stepmother are in London. They should be able to keep her out of trouble." The space where his heart normally resided was empty. He could still cave in to Senator Shaw's orders and marry Sierra immediately. But what if she refused? If only he'd seized the opportunity to talk to Sierra. Alone, without her father's bluster impinging on every word.

Senator Shaw's spoiled, headstrong daughter had trusted Fitz with her innocence . . . and he had consigned her father to hell. For the first time in his adult life, Fitz was uncertain. Unquestionably, he needed time to plan his strategy.

★ ★ ★ ★ ★

"If I'd known how interesting the Season would be with you in attendance, I'd have insisted Adrian cut our honeymoon short!" Chloe Harding declared that evening after dinner. Her brown eyes were almost golden with laughter. "You've no idea how amazed I was to find the Senator and Fitz in that little anteroom. I wouldn't have missed being there for anything. Your father was the very picture of an outraged papa, and Fitz looked like death." She leaned forward in her tapestry-covered chair and demanded, "Whatever have you been up to?"

Chloe's tall, blond husband bent to whisper in his wife's ear before pressing her back in the seat. The irrepressible brunette immediately responded, "Nonsense, Adrian. Just last week I read a book that said laughter is good for babies."

Sierra quelled a spasm of envy. She understood Fitz's reaction to her father's interference; she might have reacted in the same manner. But he couldn't have realized how desolate she would feel at his desertion. Sierra realized there was nothing she would rather do than have his children. And he'd walked away. She wanted to complain to anyone who would listen. Instead she said brightly, "I'm so happy for you both. You'll be wonderful parents."

"Before you two become teary-eyed, tell me what's been going on." Adrian propped his shoulders against the mantel and plunged his hands into his trouser pockets. "If I were to describe that little scene between Fitz and your father to any number of my acquaintances, they'd have me put in restraints."

Sierra hesitated, unsure how much to reveal about her mother-in-law's problem. Adrian, as if guessing her dilemma, said, "Did Fitz tell you I used to work for him?"

"He mentioned something of the sort."

"Then he also told you we're friends. I don't gossip about my friends . . . or about their wives' families."

"He refused to marry me. You heard him."

Chloe's laughter filled the room. "No, he refused to be *commanded* to marry you. Actually, at one point, I thought Fitz might knock your father down so he could steal you away and elope. Fitz Kent does exactly as he pleases."

Reassured, Sierra revealed everything, from the blackmail attempt to the present. She skimmed over the night she had spent in Fitz's house; her listeners politely ignored the lapse. "Today was horrendous. Fitz had borne more than any man should have to. And my father's like a . . ."

"An avalanche," Adrian supplied cheerfully. "I can't think when I've enjoyed anything more." He pushed away from the mantel and threw himself on the settee, which shook beneath his laughter. "Poor Fitz. Dressed like a beggar and taking orders from a Yank. No wonder he blew up like a champagne cork."

When Chloe subsided in a fit of giggles, Sierra wasn't sure whether to join the hilarity or to hit them with the pottery pug sitting beside the hearth. "But you're his friends!" she protested.

"It was divine retribution, and I feel blessed to have been present," Chloe said, wiping tears from her cheeks. "There was a time when I could have cheerfully tied a cannonball to his ankles and dropped him off London Bridge." Her laughter dwindled and she gazed at Adrian with her heart in her eyes. "That was before he gave me the gun that saved our lives."

Sierra leaped to her feet and confronted them. "But what will he do now? I want him." Realizing how her words must sound, she clapped her hands over her mouth.

"He'll be back," Adrian said confidently. "I saw his face just before he wished your father to perdition. He was a man standing between a cavalry charge and a cliff, and he simply removed himself from the action. If he doesn't come round, you'll have to go after him. But before you do, you should know what else he told the Senator."

CHAPTER TWENTY-THREE

Twilight was falling when Sierra guided the rented buggy along the tree-shaded drive leading to Kent House. Her hands were sweating within her snug, five-button gloves, but beneath the flowing crepe of her widow's weeds, the rest of her alternated between cold fear and feverish excitement. She hated the confining layers, but once again they had enabled her to travel unchaperoned.

Caleb, although he was reconciled to her decision, had insisted on accompanying her. She had waited until he was out of the house, driving her aunt to visit the small chapel she and Tony were to use for their wedding the following week, then slipped away. If Fitz rejected her, she preferred there not be a witness.

Following the curving drive around the house, she pulled to a stop in front of the stable. When a young lad of perhaps twelve ran out to take the horse's head, she stepped down and said authoritatively, "Mr. Kent is expecting me. Where shall I find him?"

Surprise at the appearance of an unknown widow must have struck him dumb, for he simply gestured to his right, toward a break in the row of arborvitae bordering the stableyard. "Thank you. My horse would appreciate a drink of water, if you could manage it." She threw back her confining veil and favored him with a grateful smile, then set out along the path he indicated.

Two hedges and a meadow later she emerged at the edge of a narrow, fenced pasture where a dozen or more sheep grazed. On the other side was a long, windowless stone shed. A low white door was set in the center, at the end of the worn path. Careful to refasten the gate behind her, she picked her way past the disinterested sheep to the door and lifted the latch.

She stepped into an aisle flanked by bales of hay and straw stacked higher than her head. Breathing deeply of the sunshiny fragrance, she was startled to hear the haunting notes of a plaintive lullaby crooned in a familiar baritone. Her pulse quickened; she hurried toward the sound.

The back of the shed opened on a patchwork of fenced pastures dotted with black-faced Suffolks, the breed Russ planned to purchase for the Indian village. Fitz perched on a hay bale, the slanting sun rays lighting a flaming nimbus around his head. He needed a haircut; his hair curled against the collar of his coarse workshirt. Soft russet stubble covered his chin. In one hand he held a nippled bottle to the mouth of a lamb, which was enthusiastically draining the contents, its tail twitching with each swallow.

The lullaby stopped, and Fitz said gently, "Your mother's a sad story, little one. When her first mating didn't take, she refused to wait till next year. Instead she found a way to seduce the poor ram months later." He tilted the bottle higher. "Then she refused you. Just as I refused what I wanted most."

Sierra's apprehensions melted. Repressing the urge to step forward, she waited.

"Your mother watches you, you know. I saw her. But it's too late for her to change her mind." He scratched the little animal's woolly head. "You'll learn to survive on your own. I'm not sure I could. But I'm luckier than your mother. I can try again."

The lamb ignored him, but the bright-eyed black and white dog watching the pair thumped its tail on the ground and appeared to agree, showing its white teeth in a dog-smile.

Fitz tugged, removing the nipple of the empty bottle from the lamb's mouth and rubbing his knuckles against the fuzzy wool of its head. "No more hand-feeding for you after tomorrow, little one. You'll be fine with the others. Maybe you'll even find a friend." He whistled to the dog, who leaped to his feet, barked sharply, and feinted at the lamb's hind feet. The little animal tripped over its hooves in its haste to stay ahead of the dog on its way back to the pen at the end of the low barn.

Sierra nearly jumped out of her buttoned boots when Fitz said without turning, "Come sit beside me."

She couldn't move. "How did you know I was here?"

"You smell immeasurably better than sheep."

The wistful note in his voice lured her to the other end of the bale, where she sat cautiously, leaving space between them. When all she wanted was to throw herself in his arms.

He made no move toward her, but said, "Have you come to shout at me? I wouldn't blame you if you did."

"No. I came to thank you."

Fitz turned his head to stare at her, his expression guarded. "For what?"

"For keeping the Shaw name out of the charges against Nigel. My . . . my father is very grateful." Mentioning her father might not have been wise, but then again . . . Sierra sighed. "I'm sorry, Fitz."

With one lithe movement, he shifted on the bale until he faced her, his knee touching her skirts. "Whatever for?" he demanded.

Sierra stared at the gloved hands she'd clenched in her lap. "Sometimes I forget the effect my father can have on people who don't know him well. He . . . he tends to take over."

"I noticed."

"He also believes his viewpoint is the only one."

The skin around Fitz's mouth was tight with frustration; his eyes were troubled pools. "Sierra, I've spent nearly two weeks trying to think of a way to apologize to your father for the way I spoke to him. I'm nearly to the sticking point." He managed an embarrassed smile. "Apologies aren't easy for me, but this is the most important one I've ever uttered. I want him to accept me. That is, if you still want to marry me."

Sierra had never before believed people who claimed their hearts leaped for joy. "Fitz, that day was horrible. Hearing Nigel speak so coldly about murdering your father must have broken your heart. And then, before you'd had time to make peace with the idea, to have my father inform you your wedding would take place within the hour . . ."

"We know each other much better than many engaged couples," he said. Teasing laughter filled his voice; his eyes glowed with tenderness.

Sierra felt her cheeks warm with embarrassment. Why now, of all times? Annoyed with herself, she burst out, "You know I don't hold you responsible for that night. For what we did. After all, we're adults."

"We made love, Sierra. Nothing that's happened since changes my feelings." He cupped her cheek with his palm. "Are you having regrets?"

Her sigh of relief started at the tips of her toes. "Oh, Fitz, I was sure you still felt the same way about me. But you disappeared, and I . . ." She turned her face to press her lips against his callused palm, which smelled faintly of the sweetened milk he'd been feeding the lamb. His tenderness with the little animal nestled in her heart; he'd be a wonderful father. "I want to explain about my daddy. He despises anyone he can intimidate. He admired you for telling him to go to hell."

A grunt of disbelief shook Fitz's frame. He raised his other hand, bracketing her face, then leaned forward to kiss the tip of her nose. "Good. Dare I hope he believed me when I told him what he could do with his money?"

Sierra giggled. "He didn't mention that part. Adrian and Chloe told me about it."

"Word for word, I'm sure." He tugged at her bonnet ribbon. When the bow dissolved, he sailed the black straw, veils and all, over his shoulder. "Chloe wouldn't have any qualms about quoting me. She has the vocabulary of a stevedore when she wants to use it. Adrian said she spent too much time in the stables as a child."

Sierra nuzzled his cheek. "She's reforming. For the baby."

"Chloe's increasing?"

She pressed her forehead against his and looked deep into his eyes. "Yes, and I'm incredibly jealous." Sierra snaked her arms around his neck and kissed him so vigorously that they tumbled off the bale onto the straw-covered ground.

"How did you know where to find me?" Fitz asked when he recovered his breath.

Sierra lay sprawled across his chest. "Something told me this was where you were, but I checked with Lady Lockwood. She said this is where you go to ground when you've a problem."

He smiled. "I think Heloise knows everything in the world." Sobering, he reached for Sierra's left hand. Concentrating intently, he loosed the buttons at her wrist, then inched the glove from her fingers, one by one. "I'm not proud of walking away like that. I'd had too much piled on my plate at one time. To me, marrying you under the gun would have cheapened what we feel for each other."

Pressing a kiss on the inside of her wrist, he laid her hand on his chest and proceeded to her right hand, performing the same tender task. "Sierra, I couldn't marry you under those circumstances. You deserve so much more." He pressed her wrist to his lips, feeling her life pulse beneath her fair skin. Looking up, he met her melting gaze and smiled. Her eyes had darkened to cobalt, and there was a glitter of moisture beneath the shadow of her extravagant lashes.

She leaned toward him until her mouth was so close he could feel her soft breath on his lips. "Even if you'd caved in to my father, I wouldn't have agreed to a wedding that day. Deep down, Daddy knew I wouldn't. He was counting on you to bring me around, but even you couldn't have cajoled me into it. Too much had happened, and I needed time to gather myself. I've terrible news for you, Fitz. I'm as stubborn as my father."

"I've already noticed. Even so, I was afraid I'd just cut off my nose to spite my face," he said, grinning. The knot of apprehension which had nested in the vicinity of his stomach for days disappeared.

He released her hand and pulled her into his arms, unable to wait any longer to feel the press of her breasts against him, to hold her warm, strong body. A gurgle of laughter escaped Sierra's lips as she fit herself to him as naturally as if they'd been together like this a thousand times.

Fitz closed his eyes and absorbed the feel of her. For the first time in his life, he knew contentment, happiness. "I love you, Sierra," he murmured huskily. She moved against him as if seeking even greater closeness. "You know, the idea of a hurried wedding has a certain appeal. Might as well let all those poor fortune hunters know you're no longer available." He thrust against her suggestively. "Then, of course, there's this . . ."

"I love you, Fitz. Forever." She covered his face and neck with kisses. "And I was never available. That really *was* a ruse to convince people I was witless. I wanted the blackmailer to think of me as harmless. You were the only one to see through it. You have no idea how nervous I felt when you looked at me as if you could read my mind."

Recalling the risks she had taken and the way his body had been responding since the day of the attaché's tea, he pressed her more snugly into the cradle of his hips. "That's only fair. I've been rather more than nervous myself."

"Daddy promised he'd never push you so hard again."

Somehow, Fitz doubted that, but he whispered, "Hush." Then he cupped her head with his hands and held her still for his kiss, shaping her lips with his and pouring his soul into hers with all the tenderness welling up from his heart. At her response, his knees nearly collapsed beneath him. He slid his hands down her back, relearning each soft curve and thanking God for the way she nestled closer as dusk gathered around them.

Sierra wished time could stop. She'd never imagined anything as wonderful as the sheer bliss washing through her at the feel of Fitz's body beneath hers. Moments later, the heat generated by his kiss and the eager caress of his fingers convinced her bliss wasn't enough, and she wriggled her hands beneath the edge of his sweater. Inching it upward, she pressed her palms against his hard, warm stomach and teased his tongue with the tip of her own. Fitz groaned.

Lifting her head, she whispered seductively, "I can do much more interesting things if you take off your sweater . . . and your trousers."

Fitz reached between them to stay her wandering fingers. "You'll get straw in your hair and in your . . ." The remnants of daylight revealed the suggestive waggle of his eyebrows. "How will I explain to my sheep about the widow who seduced me in full view of half the flock?" He released her fingers and attacked her bodice buttons. "Where *did* you acquire this getup, anyway?"

"I bought it so I could travel without a companion." She freed her hands and fumbled with his trouser buttons. "You have no idea how helpful people are to a woman in deep mourning." Reaching her goal, she slipped her hand through the opening and wrapped her fingers around him. "Besides, I can put this on without help." She slipped her other hand between them. His response exceeded her expectations. Within moments, he had removed her bodice and skirt and was fumbling with her corset.

"Keep still. I'm making a mull of these laces," Fitz told her after she interrupted his efforts the third time.

Sierra kissed him lingeringly, smoothing her tongue against the edge of his teeth. "Now, Fitz. I'm not sure I can wait." Her body felt hot and swollen, as if she might burst.

Shaken laughter lay beneath his reply. "You seem to have forgotten what happens when someone orders me to perform."

"Hand me my hat. My hair's a mess, and the veil will cover it." Sierra tugged at her bodice. A sprinkling of early stars dotted the dark sky, and they dressed by the dim light of the lantern hanging from the barn support.

Fitz brushed straw from her hair, which tumbled about

her shoulders, then picked another piece from the sleeve of her dress. "I threw the thing over there. With any luck, the sheep will find it in the morning and eat it, veil and all." He pushed a lock of her pale hair behind one ear and nibbled delicately on the lobe.

"Your servants will never respect me after the way I look tonight."

"They won't give a bloody damn, not when they see how happy I am. In fact, I've been such a bastard these past two weeks they'll probably fall at your feet and worship you. They've hovered until I threatened to fire the whole lot."

Giving her skirts a pat, Sierra retrieved her reticule and stood on tiptoe to kiss his chin. "Oh, well, then I shan't worry." She held out her hand to him and smiled, allowing all the love she felt to shine from her eyes. "Do you think they've kept dinner warm? I'm starving, and we need to replenish our strength."

A month later, Sierra smiled blissfully up at Fitz as they stood at the rail of the channel steamer embarking for Calais. "My father really does like you, even though you're a 'Johnny.' He's certainly not as fond of you as *I* am, but I think he's reconciled to having English grandchildren." She had been touching him, delivering caressing little pats, resting a hand on his arm, tucking her fingers within his, ever since the ceremony. Now she hugged him impulsively.

"Speaking of which, we really must get back to working on that," Fitz said, returning the embrace. He saw the indulgent smiles on the faces of the other passengers gathered at the rail.

"Darling, I've been meaning to tell you. I've a strong suspicion we accomplished that task the night we sacrificed your dressing gown."

Warmth gathered around Fitz's heart and then spread to the tips of his toes. He knew his grin was fatuous, but when he saw the happiness on Sierra's face he didn't care. He was on his honeymoon, and he had no image to maintain but that of a besotted bridegroom.

Sierra buried her face against his tweed jacket and inhaled. He'd become attached to the habit. "Well, then, I guess we needn't waste any more time on *that* project."

She released her hold on his waist and reached for his arm, which she twisted behind his back. "I'm afraid I didn't quite hear what you said."

Fitz smiled down into her upturned face and murmured, "I said the pleasure was mine, and that I would be delighted to continue to practice so we don't lose our touch." He pulled his arm free of her clinging fingers and lifted her into his kiss. "I adore you, Sierra. I always will."

About the Author

Justine Wittich is a journalism grad who prefers writing romantic fiction (with suspense thrown in) to working with cold, hard facts. She has five previous books in print, including *Chloe and the Spy* from Five Star, and draws heavily on her imagination when writing, also sprinkling in bits of personalities and experiences she has encountered in a varied background that includes teaching and editing.

Gardening, handcrafts, volunteer activities and family absorb the time not earmarked for writing. Justine lives in south-central Ohio with her husband Pete and two cats whose personalities represent both ends of the spectrum.